WATCHMAN'S STONE

"MYSTERIOUS AND ROMANTIC!"
Publishers Weekly

**"A COMPELLING STORY OF
ROMANTIC SUSPENSE."**
Booklist

**"FIRST-RATE AND FAST-PACED
... KEEPS THE READER GUESSING
TO THE SURPRISING END!"**
Library Journal

RONA RANDALL

WATCHMAN'S STONE

By Rona Randall

BALLANTINE BOOKS • NEW YORK

Library of Congress Catalog Card Number: 75-7693

ISBN 0-345-28512-3

This edition published by arrangement with Simon & Schuster

Manufactured in the United States of America

First Ballantine Books Edition: August 1976
Second Printing: December 1979

First Canadian Printing: September 1976

DEDICATION

*To my maternal grandmother, Jane Mackintosh,
whose ancient family Bible, lost for many
years, was unexpectedly found and presented
to me in 1972—leading me to Clachnaharry
and the watchman's stone.*

WATCHMAN'S
STONE

One

IT CAME like a whisper across Drummossie Moor and down toward the Great Glen: a subtle awareness, a feeling that something momentous had happened, or was about to.

I felt it sharply as I sat on the hilltop above Clachnaharry: a flash of that inner knowledge which I had experienced occasionally throughout my life. Sometimes it alarmed me, but not at this moment because I knew instinctively that the event, whatever it proved to be, was exciting and long awaited.

They called it the sight, this gift of mine, but because of Highland superstition I had learned to keep its manifestations to myself as I grew up. But people remembered me as a fey child, and some still regarded me as different. Even so, I never had any difficulty in making friends, for Highlanders were a race of individuals and respected one's right to be an individual too.

But to my Lowland mother this undesirable branding of the elder daughter at Clachnaharry Hall was an acute embarrassment. She desired, above all things, that I should conform to conventional standards, hold conventional beliefs, and behave in a conventional fashion. We were, after all, a family of rising importance, a fact of which she was very much aware, and the elder daughter of such a family should not run wild across the countryside and be known to every remote crofter on the moors—or, as now, sit on a lonely hilltop trying to catch something indefinable in the atmosphere, something which, like as not, other people could neither sense nor feel.

That was taking individuality a bit too far. Worse, it was being imaginative, a deplorable characteristic which I had revealed since early childhood and which she had done her best to discourage. Imagination was an undesirable trait which led to undesirable dreaming, and no man would ever want a woman given to dreaming, even less a woman who claimed the right to be an individual. No wonder I was still unmarried at twenty-three. I would be in the same regrettable state at thirty-three if I continued in my deplorable ways. Why could I not be like Sheena, who wasted no time on dreams and ridiculous imaginary premonitions?

But I sat quite still after the feeling had come to me, staring down at the fishermen's cottages and the boatyard at Muirton Lock. Even from this height I could see the strong figure of Angus Fraser supervising the construction of another fishing vessel, and although I was not close enough to see, I knew that the sinews of his arms were like whipcord and that the muscles of his back rippled beneath his shirt.

Angus Fraser, with his shock of fiery hair and a temper to match it, was a man people noticed and remembered. Especially women. And particularly Sheena who, despite any denials she might make, was falling in love with him. Gladly would I dance at their wedding, if Mother ever allowed it to take place. She had greater ambitions for my young sister than marrying her to a boat-builder who had responsibilities toward two orphaned brothers, even though his business promised to be highly successful. It had not yet reached such heights.

I gathered my cloak around me, knowing I should return home, but held by a strange reluctance. The awareness that something was in the air had me in its grip so strongly that I wanted to remain alone in this quiet and isolated place, gazing down on the village in which I had been born and which, no doubt, I would never leave.

For centuries it had been here: Clachnaharry, "the watchman's stone," taking its name from the very boulder on which I sat. In days gone by, this hilltop perch had been used as a lookout against marauders approaching Inverness, which lay nearly two miles distant. During my lifetime it had always been a refuge, a place where I could be sure of solitude, for in a subtle way it seemed to have an influence on my life. No one else ever climbed up here and I could gaze across the Beauly Firth to the Black Isle, or to the Murray Firth curving away to the west, and even across Inverness to the valley of the Nairn and the heights of Drummossie Moor beyond. For the most part, I turned my eyes away from the moor, with its ghosts of Culloden and its blood-soaked earth, even though the year was now 1822 and the tragedy of Culloden was long past.

But something compelled me to look toward that distant battlefield now, as if the vibrations in the atmosphere actually emanated from it. Drummossie, now more often referred to as Culloden Moor, was the immovable grief of the Highlands, a black and permanent stain on the memory. And yet I gazed toward it, the thickening woods surrounding the graves of the clans, and the bare field where the English were buried.

But Butcher Cumberland's troops had consisted of more than wretched English soldiers, dirty, depraved, and despised, with only bread and water to fill aching stomachs and the fear of flogging and brutality to keep them crawling at two and a half miles an hour through stubble and rough heather. The illustrious duke was also served by regiments of Scots militia, Highlanders who did not support the Stuart cause, disillusioned Jacobite deserters, and the offspring of many clansmen who were wily enough to send sons to fight on both Royalist and Jacobite sides for expediency's sake.

I closed my eyes. I could see colors, vivid tartans in a medley of setts, no clan distinguishable by any particular one because hose, kilts, plaids, and bonnets all flaunted a multitude of patterns woven and designed by the womenfolk of varied districts throughout the Highlands, depending on whatever vegetable dyes they could obtain. St. John's Wort, for yellow; the root of common Dock for black; Dearcan Gorma, or Blaeberry with alum, for blue; Bealaidh, the common Broom, for green; Seileasdar, the yellow water-flag or Iris, for gray; and a multitude of others for a multitude of shades. All were woven into the breacon, which was eventually called tartan from the French *tartaine,* thanks to James V who ordered "three ells of Heland Tartane" for his French wife to wear. Thus he established Royal patronage of the national fabric for succeeding generations until, after Culloden, the Hanoverian government banned its wearing, along with the use of our beloved bagpipes which were classed as weapons of war.

All this I knew, and more besides, of my ancient Highland history, culled from my father's extensive library which Mother considered so boring, so dull, and not for feminine study. Poor Mother—I was her despair.

But at this moment I had no thought of her. My vision was filled with this medley of color and patterns, overlaid upon rows of fighting clansmen who screamed to God beneath bayonet thrust and grapeshot and blazing cannon, their proud blood staining the heather. The checks, the tartans, the plaids—all seemed to hold a significance, as if they had a message for me which I failed to grasp.

A sound nearby jerked me round; the snapping of twigs, a heavy footfall, and through rock and scrub a man emerged, a stranger, unknown to me. Since everyone in and around Clachnaharry was familiar, I stared at him, wondering who he was and what brought him to this isolated spot. My thoughts must have been self-evident, for he removed his wide-brimmed beaver, smiled slightly, and said, "Since this is a public place, I am not trespassing and therefore owe no apology."

"I expect none, sir. I was merely surprised. No one ever comes up here but myself."

4

"The witch of the watchman's stone?" he murmured.

"I have never been called that."

"You have now. And that is how I shall think of you, with your long black hair and your long black cloak. And now you are offended. That is why you have jerked to your feet and are frowning."

I resented his perception, but because I would not acknowledge it, I shrugged slightly and turned away. I was all too conscious of my black hair and pale skin, and averse to both.

"And green eyes," the man said. "Do you dislike them, too?"

I looked back at him, opening my mouth on a swift retort which somehow lost itself, so that I remained silent and disconcerted. He smiled.

"That was not guesswork. It was obvious that you disliked being called a witch, also the reference to your black hair. Since you also have green eyes, traditionally associated with both, the conclusion was logical. But you should be proud of your eyes. They are beautiful."

"My father calls them hazel," I answered distantly.

"Then your father either loves you very much, or knows that Highland women frequently insist on calling green eyes by that name, a remnant of superstition that I should have expected an intelligent young woman to disregard." He put his head to one side and studied me. "I admit, however, that in certain lights they might well pass for true hazel, but I prefer the color they are now, reflecting the green about you."

I knew I should end this discussion, for conversation with strangers was one of the many things about which my mother frequently reprimanded me. I could never convince her that nine times out of ten it was other people who spoke to me first, not I to them. Men and women, young and old—it made no difference. They talked and I listened—and enjoyed it. On my way to the mills (and how she hated my going there!) or walking the one and three-quarter miles from our house to Inverness, folks would always pass the time of day with Elizabeth MacArthur.

"The girl has a way with her," my father would say, "and what is wrong with that? Better to attract people with warmth than repel them with coldness."

But my mother failed to share his view. Talking to all and sundry was hobnobbing with one's inferiors, and therefore unladylike, undesirable, and unsafe. Undignified, too, for the daughter of a man whose name was becoming known in Inverness as a progressive cloth manufacturer.

As for my interest in the family industry, that was to be discouraged. Highland women in days long past, before the tartan was outlawed, had woven and spun and dyed, but the daughters of Aindreas MacArthur were not on a level with clanswomen of old, no matter if his mother and grandmother before her had worked at the traditional cottage craft. That was something that his Edinburgh wife preferred to forget.

A question scattered these thoughts from my head. I asked the stranger impulsively, "How did you know this was the watchman's stone?"

"No one can be sure—not even you." He glanced around. "There are sufficient boulders up here to serve the purpose, but yours is the most dominant—"

"Why call it mine?" I interrupted swiftly.

"Because you are sitting on it with a familiar air, as if adopted as your own long ago. Do you come here often?"

I admitted that I had come here frequently throughout my life, giving as my excuse that the view was unsurpassed.

"Which is probably why the lookouts of old chose it," he agreed. "There is a logical answer to everything."

"As there is for your appearance here? You are a stranger in these parts."

He refused to be drawn, merely acknowledging the remark with a slight inclination of the head. It left me feeling embarrassed, as if I had probed unduly.

I rose abruptly and began the descent. Below me, the straggling path led downward through a tangle of nettles and briar and bushes to the winding road skirting the foot of the hill. Scarcely had I taken a couple of steps before I heard my name called.

"Elizabeth! *Elizabeth!* I know you are up there—come down, for mercy's sake. Mamma wants you home at once."

Well, she most certainly did not send *you,* I thought, with inner amusement. It was the task of old Ann Ross to plod through the village in search of me, or Iain, the coachman, would come puffing up the hill, grumbling because Ann was busy in the kitchen and so the task of fetching me home fell to him. The fact that Sheena's voice now called told me a lot. No doubt she had bribed old Ann or crotchety Iain, getting round them with her wheedling ways, so that she could walk through the village and past the boatyard in order to catch a glimpse of Angus. I was glad, for I wanted her to see the man of whom Mother disapproved so strongly, and I favored every possible meeting between them, particularly since Sheena had returned from Edinburgh so highly polished that she seemed no more than a bright, empty shell.

Provided he did not indulge her too much, Angus Fraser was the man to bring her down to earth, and the right man would be important in Sheena's life. For though I loved her, I knew full well that she needed careful handling.

I called in answer, and from behind me the stranger said, "So that is your name—Elizabeth. I prefer Ealasaid."

I looked back at him, startled. I had heard only one other person use the Gaelic version of my name—my father, Andrew MacArthur, whom I always thought of as Aindreas, just as I frequently thought of Angus as Aongas, having a love of the Gaelic myself.

In glancing back, I saw the man's dark face half

smiling, and thought immediately that there was something different about him, something slightly alien. And yet his voice had a Scots intonation, and the native accent was even stronger as he said, "Beannachd leat, Ealasaid."

Not the usual Scottish "Haste ye back," but "Farewell." Anything more would have been presumptuous—but my reaction was mixed. I was curious about the man, and not because he was good-looking or attractive—he possessed neither attribute, being square-jawed and blunt-featured, with a hint of aggressiveness about him—but simply because it was unprecedented to meet a stranger beside the watchman's stone. At the same time, some instinct told me that it would be better not to know him too well, a totally illogical feeling which I dismissed as one of my flights of fancy. And to prove to myself that it was ridiculous to be disturbed just because an unknown man had suddenly appeared out of nowhere, I asked outright where he came from and why he had chosen to visit this particular spot.

My curiosity appeared to amuse the man. A broad smile spread across his face, subtly transforming it, producing unexpected angles and a sort of cragginess which somehow emphasized the cleft in his chin and deepened the lines running from nose to mouth—premature lines that would become embedded in middle age, adding interest to his looks. But his eyes were his most arresting feature, not merely because they were surprising and somewhat piercing blue, but because they studied me too intently, making me feel that they were capable of seeing a great deal too much. It would be difficult to keep any secrets from a man like this.

He answered, "I came to find out if the view was unchanged."

"You have been here before?"

"Not for a very long time. You are being called again—can't you hear? And even more impatiently."

But I refused to be diverted.

8

"Who are you?" I demanded. "Where do you come from, and why are you here?"

"I come from a long way off. As to why I am here, my reasons are my own. My motives, too."

I resented his tone of dismissal, but my curiosity was aroused. Mistrust, also. I had an unaccountable urge to escape, so without another word I turned and ran down the hill, not because my privacy had been invaded, but because of a disturbing premonition that this man's arrival presaged disturbing events. All too often premonitions I had experienced when visiting the watchman's stone had come true.

Two

SHEENA SAID IMPATIENTLY, "Hurry! Mamma is in a fret because you are not home. Have you forgotten that we are visiting Castle Faillie this evening?"

I had indeed forgotten, an oversight which indicated how little this signal honor meant to me. But to my mother it meant a great deal. The new owner of Castle Faillie was reputed to be not only rich but, being a widower, eligible. Widowers, having normally reached the age of being well established and therefore financially sound, represented good potential husbands, but for my part I had little inclination to sup with an elderly gentleman, and even less to consider him as a possible suitor for either myself or my sister. Not that Mother would seriously consider him for Sheena, who was pretty enough and young enough to wait awhile and take her pick, but I was five years older and still unwed. . . .

I jumped the last two feet from the hillside to the

rough road, landing right in the middle of a lingering pool of rain and splashing my sister's gown so that she drew aside in annoyance. But when I stooped to wipe her skirt she swept it aside indifferently, urging me yet again to hurry.

"They say that Faillie is a beautiful place. It once belonged to the Mackintoshes."

"This being Clan Chattan country, that could well be. Many had minor castles and hunting lodges, but a great many more had humble crofts and mere hovels."

"No history lesson, please. Who cares about the past?"

"I do, because it is out of our past that our future will emerge."

Sheena sighed and walked ahead, tossing over her shoulder, "Another of your predictions, I suppose?"

"No—plain fact. We Highlanders have still to work hard to regain all we have lost. Look at Father, what *he* has built out of nothing! But for his industry, you would never have gone to Edinburgh to be turned into a grand young lady."

"Oh yes I would. Mamma was always determined that one of us, at least, should follow her example. She was born and bred there, not in the Highlands."

Which is why you call her "Mamma" in that affected fashion, I thought, with faint irritation. Edinburgh society aped southern ways.

But my irritation with Sheena could never be anything but short-lived. She was disarming and affectionate and pretty, and not to be blamed because Mother had sought to turn her into a fine lady, having failed with her elder daughter. As I caught up with her, I put my arm through my sister's and hurried along beside her, listening to her eager chatter but watching, as we approached Muirton Lock, to see if she glanced across the road to Angus Fraser's boatyard. Sure enough, she did: fleetingly, but eagerly nonetheless. And sure enough, there he was, hard at work with his men, producing yet another vessel to enhance his growing reputation.

I don't know what made me suddenly ask my sister if she had seen a stranger here in Clachnaharry. "A broad, thickset man, dark-skinned, as if weathered by an outdoor life."

And with eyes so penetrating that they seemed to look right into your mind. . . .

To my surprise, Sheena made no answer. I looked at her, then followed her glance. Angus Fraser had put on his jacket and was striding across the boatyard. By the time we reached the entrance, he would be there.

I put the question again, and this time my sister answered absently that the only stranger to come to these parts for a long time was the widower, Calum Huntly.

"And after tonight he will be a stranger no longer," she prattled, now staring straight ahead and pretending to be unaware of Angus. "I hope Mr. Huntly isn't too old and dull, or I shall be infernally bored. Still, it will be nice to see inside his castle. Mamma says he inherited it from his wife. It was she who was a Mackintosh. He himself comes from Gordon country. Mamma knows everything about him."

My laughter was irrepressible. It was characteristic of Mother to find out all she wanted to know in the shortest possible time. The widower Huntly had arrived only two weeks ago, and already she had gained an *entrée* into his home. I found it difficult to believe that the invitation had come out of the blue, as she declared.

Suddenly my sister gave a little skip of pure joy. "Well, at least tonight gives us an opportunity to wear our finest gowns and look beautiful! I have scarcely had an opportunity to dress up since I came home."

"Come now, Sheena—You returned with a vast wardrobe from your stay in Edinburgh. What did you do at that academy for young ladies, apart from learning the niceties of social behavior? Spend your time changing into different dresses, and ordering more?"

"Why not? It made up for the boredom of polishing our French and studying deportment and elocution. . . ."

"Which is why you now talk in that affected way." It was Angus Fraser who spoke, blocking our path. "But maybe you'll get back a good Scots' accent when you've had your sister's company for a while."

Sheena looked up at him—a solid, immovable figure staring down upon her from his great height. Her eyes flickered momentarily.

"If you please, Mr. Fraser, we wish to pass."

"Pardon *me,* Miss MacArthur."

He bowed and stood aside, but his eyes sparked angrily. He would have to watch that temper of his, a characteristic which had wrecked many a good Scot. I glanced at him in warning as Sheena freed her arm from mine and swept on. For a moment I thought he was going to catch hold of her, but apparently he thought better of it, for he remained where he was, not even glancing after her as she broke into a run and called over her shoulder for me to hurry.

I said impulsively, "You must master her, Angus. Assert yourself, and marry her."

"You are more eager for me to be bedded with her than she is," he retorted, and strode off.

I sighed and went on my way. At the gates of our home Sheena waited, her color high. I walked past her and on up the graveled drive.

Above the solid front door were the MacArthur arms, a cross argent between three crowns, and the motto in a scroll above. *Fide et opera.* By faith and work. Well, at least that characterized my father, who had pulled himself up from the destitution left by the Highland clearances. But only the Aire, or chieftain of a Clan, was entitled to display armorial bearings, so that crest had no right to be above our front door.

Nevertheless it was there, my mother's latest whim, carved indelibly and irremovably. It matched the same desire that made my mother change the name of our home from Clachnaharry House to Clachnaharry Hall.

"My dear Catriona, I fear you are becoming a snob," my father had said.

"Is it snobbish to be proud of one's name, proud of one's home? And Catherine, if you please. No one uses that old Gaelic version nowadays."

"Except myself, who shall continue to use it," my father had answered in that calm, decisive way of his. "You were Catriona when I met you, Catriona when I wed you, and Catriona you will remain to me until I die."

Why did some women fail to realize when men really loved them? I wondered as I entered the house. Mother, with her vain pretensions, could not see beneath my father's bluntness, and Sheena, encased in her newly polished shell, was full of silly, romantic dreams. What did she want—a knight-errant on a white charger? What was wrong with a well-set-up, intelligent, rising young boat-builder?

Irritation touched me. I cared very much for both my mother and my sister, but that didn't prevent me from sometimes wanting to shake them.

As the best family carriage proceeded on its long haul up the hill leading from Inverness to Daviot, my eye caught the turning leading to Drummossie Moor. It was clearly marked. Rich English travelers could help to bring prosperity back to the Highlands, and despite a lingering bitterness, the commercially minded considered it a good idea to turn Culloden Moor into a public attraction.

So the sign pointing to Nairn also bore one saying "To Culloden Battlefield," and another, nearing the approach to the hamlet of Daviot, pointed along a rough track with a hastily erected board on which someone had painted "To Culloden and the Clava Stones."

It would be a skilled horseman who tackled that winding moorland route where Charles Stuart, skulking in the heather after leading his army of unwilling clansmen into a hopeless battle, had survived on wild game and the brandy bottle which, even at twenty-five, he had carried in his pouch and from which he refused ever to be parted.

Arrogant but princely despite his "lisping Italian voice," Charles Edward Louis Philip Sylvester Casimir Maria had needed all his Stuart charm to aid his escape to France after the star of his royal house had been extinguished forever on that fatal 16th April 1746, but it had been more than a cruel day for the clansmen as the sun set upon scenes of savagery and rose again to usher in an epoch of butchery and terror, only equaled later by the bloody orgies of the French Revolution. I never came this way without feeling deep emotion, and I was moved now as I gazed from the coach into the clear Highland evening light and saw the rolling hills, now dark brown with unopened heather which would later dye them a deep purple.

A touch on my hand, and I turned to see my father's kindly eyes looking into mine.

"You were far away, Ealasaid . . ."

"She is always dreaming," my mother said impatiently. "She reads too many books."

"No one can read too many books, my dear. And talking of books, I should mention that I have invited Aongas Fraser to use my library whenever he may wish, so don't be surprised if you find him there, which I imagine will be often. He is a great reader."

"My dear Andrew, have you taken leave of your senses? He will bring his young brothers along with him! I hear he encourages them to read as much as he." She ruffled indignantly. "I think you might have consulted me before giving him free run of the house!"

"Only of the library, my dear, and of the door leading into it from the garden," my father added mildly, but I sensed hidden amusement in his voice. He knew full well that my mother's real concern was based on the fact that Sheena would now be able to see Angus more often, and without even stepping outdoors.

I glanced at my sister, looking as pretty as a picture in a gown of green silk and gazing negligently through the window, pretending indifference to the conversation.

"Stuffy old books!" she declared, her delicate nose in the air. "I can't think what anyone sees in them! I had enough of books in Edinburgh. Papa's library is the last room in the house to interest me."

Her words and tone might deceive my mother, who looked relieved, but not myself. I decided that it was time to change the conversation, so I asked at random what Mr. Huntly was like.

"Mr. Huntly," my mother replied, "is a most distinguished and handsome man. Tall, and of definite refinement."

So he was not the stranger of the watchman's stone, who had been little taller than myself, far from distinguished, and by no means handsome. I felt relieved, for in an inexplicable way I had no desire to meet that disturbing man again.

I saw my mother's eyes skim past myself, primly dressed in black taffeta, and settle on Sheena, and suddenly I realized it was my sister, not I, who was to make the impression tonight.

A silent protest rose in me. Surely not even Mother could want to match off young and lovely Sheena with an elderly widower living in some isolated castle?

My father said suddenly, "What made this man invite us? How did he come to hear of us, or know where we live?"

"My dear Andrew, everyone in Inverness has heard of you. You are a prominent person."

"A weaver, a cloth manufacturer—not a laird, not socially important."

"You are a prominent citizen of Inverness," my mother contradicted firmly. "No doubt Mr. Huntly is entertaining many leading local people. He would make it his business to become acquainted with them, having come here to settle."

15

"And how do you know he has? And doesn't it strike you as odd that a man who never even visited the place during his wife's lifetime should choose to live in it after her death? His wife always came here alone. I understand that not even the servants had ever met him." When my mother shrugged and made no answer, Father glanced through the coach windows and added, "I see no other carriages traveling this way. Surely we cannot be the only guests?"

We had passed the horseshoe bend leading down from Daviot Church and were now climbing up to Craggie. The entrance to Castle Faillie would soon be reached, although the castle itself was invisible from this road which snaked endlessly to Perth.

The castle's setting was unusual for the Highlands, for it stood on no rocky promontory from which it could survey the surrounding countryside, nor upon an island in the middle of a loch where, in days of old, a Chief's constables kept watch, ready to repel invaders approaching by water. Castle Faillie, concealed in a deep valley, its walls hemmed in by the slopes of Cawdor country, was isolated and hidden.

I felt an unexpected quickening of curiosity, sparked perhaps by the fact that what my father said was true—there were indeed no other carriages on the road, and it was logical to assume that if Mr. Huntly was entertaining other citizens of Inverness this evening, they should be heading this way at about this time.

My mother said complacently, "If we are really the only guests, it is gratifying. It will mean that we have been singled out especially."

"Then I would like to know why," my father replied, as Iain, the coachman, took a slow turn left and halted before vast oaken doors set beneath a stone arch. These were the castle gates, and after Iain had pulled a heavy iron handle suspended from a chain, they were slowly opened, heaved apart by a lodge-keeper who needed all his strength for the task.

After we had driven through, I realized that we were traversing a causeway of the kind once constructed to bridge a moat, but now spanning nothing more than an unpleasant bog.

I heard a heavy thud as the gates closed behind us, and promptly had a feeling of being cut off from the world—especially when, having crossed the causeway and entered a courtyard before the main entrance, I realized there was not another carriage in sight. It did indeed seem that we were the only guests.

"It's magnificent!" my mother breathed, as old Iain threw the reins to a waiting stable boy, then climbed down from the box, opened the door, and let down the steps. Something of her awe and excitement was evidently shared by my sister, who descended behind her. I saw them gazing at the castle in delighted anticipation, but I hung back, held by a strange reluctance.

"What is it, Ealasaid?" my father said quietly.

"Nothing. At least, nothing important. . . ."

"Tell me."

"Earlier today I had a feeling that something momentous was about to happen, but I thought it was to be something good."

"And now?" he prompted.

"I am afraid. This place has given me a feeling of terror."

"Tell me."

"I cannot. That is the strange thing. Before, it was no more than a sensation, all mixed up with colors, checks, and tartans. It was exciting at the time, yet now I feel menaced."

He answered lightly, "You must have been thinking of that new pattern we are producing at the mills, my dear." But despite his attempt at reassurance, I was not deceived. My father was the only person who never dismissed my premonitions.

He alighted from the carriage and turned to help me down. I followed reluctantly, halted with one foot poised, and looked up at the thick stone walls. Above me, impressively carved, were the Mackintosh crest and arms. The arms were quartered, the first displaying a lion rampant, inherited from MacDuff; the second, a hand brandishing a man's heart; the third, a ferocious boar's head; and the fourth, a longfhada— a single-masted galley with oars erect, which was a feature of all Clan Chattan arms. The whole was crested with a wildcat above, and two more wildcats on either side, their teeth bared and faces snarling, crowned with the Mackintosh motto: *"Touch not the catt bott a glove."*

Touch not the cat without a glove ...

The faint shiver I experienced was illogical, for I was familiar with the brave reputation of Clan Chattan, the clan of the cats, an ancient confederation of many tribes holding land east of Loch Ness, predominantly Mackintoshes in this area. At Culloden, Mackintoshes had fought for the Royalists, but some had rallied to the side of the legendary Colonel Anne of Moy Hall, the beautiful twenty-year-old Lady Mackintosh, whose husband had departed to command a company of militia for King George. No sooner had he gone than she called up men from the glens, charming them out of their unwillingness and riding at their head to the side of Prince Charles, and bitter defeat.

At some time, I thought, she might well have lived in this very castle, for the arms above me were those of the Aire, and could not be so displayed unless he or his immediate kin had resided here—even briefly. To be touched by apprehension when entering a place which had housed the brave and the spirited was therefore inexplicable, but apprehensive I was.

As if from a distance, I heard my father's voice saying, "Come, my dear. Come, Ealasaid."

I obeyed unwillingly, wanting nothing so much as to beg that Iain should take me home.

Had I had any sense, I would have done so, pleading a headache, sickness, anything. Had I really possessed the sight, I would have realized that the feeling I experienced as I sat on the watchman's stone and the feeling I experienced now were separate and apart—and that what I felt now concerned only myself, and should be heeded.

But for myself I had never had either wisdom or foresight.

Three

THE BRILLIANCE within the castle dispelled my ridiculous fancies. From the courtyard we climbed to a Billeting Room by way of a stone spiral staircase, too well lit to be gloomy, but the walls were chill to my touch when I put one hand against them whilst negotiating the curve. These walls were centuries old, many feet thick, hewn out of rock slabs in which the coldness of time seemed to be trapped.

My family walked ahead, and as I entered the room I heard my mother say, "And this is my other daughter, Elizabeth. . . ." A cough, and then a touch of sharpness, "My dear, Mr. Huntly is waiting to greet you."

The reprimand, coupled with a hint of apology because I was impolitely allowing my attention to wander, did not appear to be noticed by the man whose symmetrical features arrested me as I turned around.

At first I thought his hair was silver, then realized it was of such a pale color that in certain lights it merely appeared so. That first impression of silver hair with a young face was striking. If this was our host, he was by no means elderly.

He bowed over my hand, lace falling from his wrists as he lifted my fingers. I saw then that he was wearing Highland dress.

Apparently noting my surprise, Calum Huntly said, "Do not misjudge me, Miss MacArthur. I have a motive for wearing my clan tartan, with which I shall acquaint your father before the evening is out." When I looked at him in surprise, his mouth curved in a slight smile. "You have an expressive face," he murmured. "Very expressive indeed."

The others were out of earshot, and I was glad of that. As I watched them walking the length of the room with a quiet, unassuming woman wearing a quiet, unassuming gown, I recovered my composure and said, "The authenticity of clan tartans has always been debatable, Mr. Huntly. Prior to the outlawing of Highland dress, only district tartans were largely identifiable."

"That, too, is a matter for debate—in which I should be delighted to engage you." His mouth curved in a smile which was now challenging. I found my attention focused on the movement of his lips, fascinated by it, stirred in a pleasurable way. Then Sheena's laughter caught his attention, and he forgot about me. I saw his eyes turn to her and linger there. My disappointment was illogical, for I was well accustomed to being passed over in favor of my sister. But now I felt shut out, as if I had found myself with one foot about to step through a door which was suddenly slammed in my face.

Calum Huntly said briskly, "Come, Miss MacArthur, let us join the others. You have yet to meet my cousin, Morag Crombie; Morag acts as my housekeeper."

As we crossed the room I asked, "And do you claim the tartan you are wearing to be that of the Gordons, Mr. Huntly?"

"No, indeed. It is exclusive to the Huntly branch, which is precisely why I am wearing it tonight. As a cloth manufacturer, your father should be interested."

"As a cloth manufacturer, he is interested only in a new weave or a new design. My father is a very astute businessman."

"So I am given to understand, Miss MacArthur."

"By whom?"

"By all and sundry. One has only to be in Inverness for a few days to hear of Andrew MacArthur and his progressive industry."

I felt uncommonly pleased, and my resentment evaporated. "You do understand, though, that it would be impossible for him to weave a special bolt of tartan for you. The looms cannot handle personal orders, only bulk—"

I broke off, for Calum Huntly had come to a halt and now stood looking at me with slightly raised eyebrows.

"For a woman, you seem remarkably well informed about business affairs, Miss MacArthur."

"Should I not be? I take a vast interest in the mills. It is in my blood, you see. My grandmother and great-grandmother before her, and generations of female forebears, spun and wove by hand in their living rooms—"

I broke off again, aware that this time my voice was echoing in the vaulted room and that my mother was pink with embarrassment because I had revealed the roots of our ancestry.

Calum Huntly only said pleasantly to my parents, "Your daughter seems an unusual young woman."

"Ealasaid is indeed unusual for this day and age," my father replied.

"Ealasaid? That is unusual, too?"

"You are unfamiliar with the name? I am surprised. It is good honest Gaelic for Elizabeth."

"You shame me, but I have to confess to spending much of my life abroad, and to possessing no knowledge of the Gaelic."

"But you married a Mackintosh from these parts, a clan well known for their pride in Scots' tradition. Your wife, I am sure, would have been well acquainted with our native tongue."

"There you are right, sir. I learned much about Highland ways and customs from my poor Una, but even as a child on Deeside I could never get my

21

tongue round the Gaelic. Nevertheless, as far as Scots'
traditions go, my allegiance was as passionate as my
wife's, and still is—hence my wearing of the tartan
tonight. It is due for a big revival, in which I want
you to help."

A hovering manservant was holding a tray bearing
wine glasses. The Laird of Faillie paused to see that
his guests were served, and as he did so the man-
servant's expression caught my eye. Morose, surly,
unfriendly: a man doing his job only because he
was paid for it, not because he wished to.

Then my father's voice caught my attention. He
was saying, with typical bluntness, "So that is your
reason for inviting us tonight. I thought there must
be one, in view of the fact that there are no other
guests. You have a business proposition to make, or
else you want to pick my brains. Which?"

"Andrew!" Poor Mother was aghast. Her family
was letting her down badly tonight, but I was too
interested in this sudden turn in the conversation to
steer it into other channels.

The Laird of Faillie laughed, unoffended.

"I admire your frankness, and will be equally frank.
Yes, I had a reason for inviting you. I want to enlist
your help in reviving the tartan. You are a Scot, sir,
and a Highlander at that. It must mean as much to
you as to all Highlanders that your national garb
should be restored, and this could benefit you as a
cloth manufacturer."

"I am doing well enough without it, sir."

"But is Scotland? That is the important thing. I can
assure you that my interest in reviving the tartan has
no ulterior or mercenary motive. I have profitable
estates of my own on Deeside. I need no more
wealth. I am anxious only that the people shall wear
the tartan again with pride and dignity, as they once
did."

My father finished his wine and laid aside the glass.
His attitude toward our host had subtly changed.
Suspicion was replaced by interest.

"Alas, Mr. Huntly, when proscription was withdrawn in 1782, many weavers tried to revive the tartan—without success. The old attachment to Highland dress had died within a generation. The clans had lost their identities and the ordinary man felt self-conscious in the kilt."

"We will give the clans back their identities, and the ordinary man his pride!"

My father shook his head sadly.

"Another unfortunate fact is that many of the old patterns have long been forgotten. There were certain traditional patterns, I agree, but who can attribute them to any particular clans?"

"I can. I have proof and, when we have eaten, I will show it to you. I see my cousin waiting. That means supper is served."

For the first time I really looked at Morag Crombie, compelled by something about her that demanded my attention. Quiet she might appear on the surface, but beneath it I felt a smoldering willpower.

I glanced at the others to see if they, like me, sensed her impatience as she waited for us to go up to the Banqueting Hall, but apparently they saw only a quiet woman with her hands clasped serenely before her, back erect. She was the personification of the self-effacing housekeeper. But not to me. All my sensitivity was at work again. Those heavy-lidded eyes, opaque as a cat's, hid much.

As I passed, she turned and looked at me. Our glances struck and held. One of us had to yield, but neither would, and a slow, knowledgeable smile spread across her plain features.

"Miss MacArthur realizes how I hate a good meal to be wasted," she said, in a clear, bell-like voice. "Forgive my desire to hurry you all."

The Banqueting Hall was above the Billeting Room, a long chamber with a magnificent timbered ceiling from which hung vast circular chandeliers handwrought in iron, adorned with emblems of thistle and heather. Candlelight gleamed on polished oak, and within the immense stone fireplace blazed a log fire, its leaping flames casting a warm glow into the room. It caught the delicate sheen of my sister's gown and the copper tones of her auburn hair. I wasn't surprised to see our host's eyes upon her, nor was I stupid enough to deny that I was envious.

I turned my attention to the rest of the room. Emblazoned on the massive chimney breast was the Mackintosh coat of arms and the motto that had made me shiver as I stood outside. Now I read it again, but without the same reaction, for this man was a Huntly, not a Mackintosh, and the hint of savagery in the arms and motto of this ancient house did not apply to him.

I wasted no time in puzzling over why I should be glad of that, for I knew the answer. The Laird of Faillie could be capable of stirring me physically, and from that it could be but a short step to love, for—contrary to all my dear mother would have me believe—I knew that these two processes did not necessarily start in reverse or even go together. But something told me that he was not the man for me, and after tonight I could only hope this attraction would pass.

At the moment, Calum Huntly's face was turned away from me, so I was able to study him in profile: a finely bridged nose, high brow, a clean line of jaw —and a mouth so well molded that I could almost imagine the feel of it against my own. That was dangerous thinking, and I shied away from it. As I did so, I met the opaque eyes of Morag Crombie from across the table and had the uncomfortable feeling that as I studied her cousin she, in turn, had been studying me.

She met my glance without embarrassment, but I felt again the uncanny perception of those pale eyes. Surely no woman could really be so self-effacing as this one appeared to be?

One thing was plain: she was something more than an ordinary housekeeper here, for she occupied the chair that the laird's wife would normally occupy, acting as hostess in her place. Was this because, as a widower, he needed someone for that role, or was she really more than that to him? I doubted it, for I was as sensitive to personal relationships as I was to atmosphere, and felt no rapport between these two.

As she turned to say something to my mother, I studied the woman more closely. She would have been good-looking if dressed more strikingly and with a more becoming hair style. I observed that the quality of her gown was poor. She wore a plain gold band on the third finger of her left hand—an impoverished widow, perhaps, glad of a roof over her head?

My father was admiring the finely carved screen in front of the Piper's Gallery. The screen was about three feet high, concealing only the lower part of the deep, arched recess in the stone wall, close beside a mullioned window.

"It is fine work indeed," our host acknowledged, "but it saddens me to see the Piper's Gallery empty. Can you imagine what it must have been like, in days gone by, when my wife's ancestors sat here with their guests, the skirl of the pipes filling the room?"

"And guards looking down from those unseen slits in the walls above, observing the actions of those in the hall without being detected themselves?"

"Thank God those days are past, sir, and guests need no longer be spied on. I presume you have visited Faillie before, otherwise you would be unaware that the slits are there. They are cunningly planted for concealment."

Aindreas pointed out, with a touch of surprise, that such a feature was traditional in Highland castles originally designed as strongholds. "Surely, as a Scot, you knew that? Or didn't you need such safeguards in the Lowlands?"

"History can prove otherwise, I think."

My father agreed with a smile, adding that even so the Highlands had ever been the cradle of warriors.

"Which is why the Hanoverian parliament banned your Highland dress, as a symbol of warlike apparel, but now that proscription has been removed you should be proud to revive it."

"And how do you propose to reintroduce the tartan when so many manufacturers have failed?"

"They have not failed entirely, sir. The plaid is being worn more and more in Edinburgh, and the sash by ladies. The kilt is only one step ahead, and by the time George IV has paid his State Visit to Edinburgh, no true Scot will be without one. All Chiefs have been commanded to appear at Court wearing their clan tartans."

"Which most of them don't possess, the designs being forgotten."

"Which means the time is ripe for their resurrection."

"By whom, pray?"

"By us. You and me."

"But I have already told you that the traditional patterns have been lost. If the tartan is to be revived, patterns must be invented . . ."

"They are already being invented in the Lowlands."

"Lowlanders designing *tartans?*" my father exploded. "They who once regarded Highlanders as savages?"

"Their ancestors may have done, but today the Lowlander has a healthy respect for Highland traditions, and particularly for Highland dress. He is avidly adopting it. I guarantee that after the King's visit every Highlander will be following suit."

My father was silent, tugging his lip the way he always did when preoccupied or thoughtful. Then he said, "You made an extraordinary claim a few minutes ago. You said you could establish the authenticity of clan tartans which, to the best of my knowledge, no one has ever been able to do."

"The Scottish kings and many leaders had patterns designed especially for them. Did you know that records were kept, not only for the Royal tartans, but also of those designed for clan chiefs?"

"I did not."

26

"Yet that is my source, Mr. MacArthur, direct from the Royal House of Stuart."

"I don't believe it!"

"Nor did I, until I saw the manuscript."

"What manuscript?"

"An ancient Latin one, dating back to the sixteenth century, in the possession of Prince Charlie's grandsons."

"He had no grandsons. No legitimate ones, at least. It is a well-confirmed fact that Princess Louise of Stolberg gave him no children."

"But according to John and Charles Sobieski Stuart, their grandfather did have a legitimate son, their own father. Therefore he was the Stuart heir and, for this very reason, had to be protected in those days of political danger. Consequently, the birth was kept secret."

"Sobieski! That was the name of Prince Charlie's mother."

"Precisely, Princess Maria Clementina Sobieska. I met the brothers in Austria and heard the story of how, many years after the disaster of Culloden and the flight of Prince Charles, a British warship called at Genoa, under the admiralship of an Englishman called Allen. To him was delivered a bundle containing a male infant. It was explained to him that this was the son of Prince Charles, who wanted the child to be taken away from Italy, where Hanoverian plots endangered his life. The Admiral adopted the child, calling him Thomas Allen, and this Thomas Allen became the father of the two brothers, naming them John Stewart and Charles Stolberg."

"And you believe this tale?"

"It hardly matters whether it is believed or not. I doubt if there is enough evidence to support or disprove their story. What matters is the information I gleaned from them. They needed money. I provided it by purchasing some pages of the manuscript delineating the long-forgotten and only true patterns of certain clan tartans. Could anything be more valuable at such a time as this? I have this material in my hands, and it is yours if you agree to reproduce the designs. You would be the first in the field with them . . ."

"I'd have no wish to be, unless convinced that your information has a grain of truth in it."

"I am not gullible, sir. I reason logically. Two young men who had never set foot in Britain would not have any knowledge of Scots tartans, nor how to invent them. I translated from the Latin myself and, since their knowledge of Latin was limited, they could not have written it, either. I tested them pretty thoroughly."

Behind my father's impassive countenance I detected doubt mixed with curiosity.

"I find this story hard to believe," he said. "How do you feel about it, Ealasaid?"

The story seemed credible to me because Calum Huntly's personality was compelling. I also judged him to be honest. But the tale of the two unknown Royal offspring was certainly surprising. History had established the fact that Bonnie Prince Charlie begat no legitimate children, therefore any claims to be his legitimate grandsons were difficult to accept. Nevertheless, history also abounded with unlikely stories which had later proved to be true, so why not this one? And why should the ancient Latin manuscript not be genuine even if its owners were not? Calum Huntly had seen it, translated some of it, and been satisfied. He would scarcely have paid handsomely for the information unless convinced of its authenticity, nor would he have sought out a reputable weaver with whom to entrust it.

"I would like to see these tartan delineations," I said.

My father nodded. "I too. If we go ahead, it is Ealasaid who will create them from your transcriptions. She has an eye for design."

Calum looked pleased.

"Come," he said eagerly. "The information is in my library."

Although I was fascinated during the next hour, I knew my mother and sister did not share my enthusiasm. They were, if anything, relieved when Morag Crombie finally led the way up yet another spiral stone staircase. The castle was small and compact at this point, each long room built directly above the one below and connected by a series of spiraling stairs, but I knew, from my exterior glimpses of it, that somewhere an adjoining wing housed an ancient Keep.

My mother was fussing over Sheena, adjusting the hood of her cloak protectively, for our Highland nights turned cold even in summer. "One cannot be too careful of night air, my precious." Morag Crombie agreed with her; she was being amiable, polite and gentle, but I had the strange feeling that she was viewing us all like pawns on a chessboard. There was something about this woman that made me uneasy, and because I had no desire to converse with her, or listen to my mother's chatter, I flung my cloak about my shoulders and slipped away, heading back the way we had come.

This took me along the narrow corridor above the Banqueting Hall. If I hurried, I would find the master of Faillie where we had left him, alone beside the fireplace of that spacious room, for my father had gone below in the wake of Hamish, the surly man-servant, to see that the coach horses were well blanketed for night driving.

I tried not to walk too swiftly, afraid of betraying my eagerness, but my caution was unnecessary for no sound from up here could be heard below, which was why guards of old could watch unheard and unseen. The spy slits were skillfully slanted, and I pulled up sharply as I reached the first one, arrested by a voice which came up to me as clearly as if I had been in the room itself.

"I want to know," it demanded, "exactly how my sister died."

I had heard that voice before, beside the watchman's stone, and now I looked down through the angled slit and saw the stranger's features, far from handsome in comparison with Calum Huntly's, his figure broad and stocky against the taller and more elegant one.

Something else caught my eye—the sight of the manservant, Hamish, standing to one side, as if he had moved there after ushering the visitor upstairs but had neither the desire nor the intention to depart. Even from this distance I could detect an under-current of surprise and excitement about him, but my attention was distracted by Calum Huntly's voice saying quietly, "My wife died in childbirth. Poor Una, I blame myself. She was too frail for mother-hood."

The controlled grief behind his words did not escape me. I hesitated, wondering whether to go forward or return to the bedroom where my mother and sister were still chattering.

Then I suddenly realized that Morag Crombie was beside me. She had followed me from the room, soft-footed. I hoped my face revealed only surprise and not the distaste I felt at this suggestion of furtiveness.

"Are you lost, Miss MacArthur? The way downstairs lies straight ahead. Come, I will show you. These old places can be confusing, can they not?"

I felt her hand beneath my elbow, impelling me along the passage so that each spy slit passed too quickly for me to glance down. Even so, sentences flashed upward through each aperture.

"She was not frail as a girl."

"Alas, she declined with age."

"Age! She was younger than I by three years. She would be no more than twenty-eight now. . . ."

"Nevertheless, her health was poor. You will be comforted to know that she is interred here with her ancestors. Her casket can be seen in the family tomb."

"So you had her body brought from Deeside? I know she settled there with you after the runaway marriage."

"Of which your family solicitor disapproved. That

man regarded himself as her unofficial guardian in your absence, even though she had already inherited Faillie. I was all too aware that I was not the man people expected her to marry. There was another suitor, I recall. Son and heir of the wealthy Aberdonian family she was visiting when we met."

"How did you meet? I never actually heard. I was overseas by that time and though Una and I always kept in touch, we were neither of us great letter writers."

"My half-brother, Malcolm, introduced us. He saw her at a ball in Aberdeen and, characteristically, wasted no time in gaining an introduction. Malcolm always went after anything he wanted and usually got it, but not this time. Una and I fell in love almost at first sight, and to avoid fuss we eloped. My estates near Braemar were fairly modest then, but they are far from modest now. I devoted myself to them throughout the years and built them into the valuable estates they now are. That meant constant attention, constant work, with no time to accompany my wife on her annual visits to Faillie, which were never for more than a week or two to see that all was well with the place. She was on such a visit here when she gave birth prematurely and died."

"And you were not with her? You let her come alone?"

"Against my wishes. But she insisted. The birth was not imminent, she argued, and therefore nothing was likely to go wrong. And her doctor agreed. Even so, I blame myself. When I heard she was ill, I traveled here posthaste, bringing the doctor with me and, thank God, I was at least in time to be with her at the end."

Morag and I had reached the spiral stairs, which were of stone like the rest; consequently our footsteps echoed clearly as we descended, and between the confining walls Morag's bell-like voice sounded louder than I had heard it all evening.

"Be careful of the turn, Miss MacArthur. Sometimes

31

I fear I shall never become accustomed to these twisting steps myself."

A moment later we were in the Banqueting Hall again and I was staring across the room at Calum Huntly's tense face. Was it a trick of light or my imagination which gave me the impression of a pallor that had not been there before? I sensed, rather than saw, the effort it cost him to pull himself together. And when I turned to the stranger myself I found it difficult to conceal my own surprise at coming face to face with this unknown man, right here in Castle Faillie, and learning from his words that his sister had been Calum's wife.

It was obvious that his arrival had been unexpected. A strange and unpredictable man, I thought, first coming upon me unawares beside the watchman's stone and now reentering my life with equal abruptness. I recalled how he had evaded my questions and how curtly he had told me that his motives were his own, and the feeling of mistrust he had awakened in me stirred again.

As I looked at him I was oddly pleased to realize that the sight of me disconcerted him. But that betrayal was only momentary—a flicker of recognition, instantly suppressed.

He bowed to Morag and myself, but it was no more than a polite acknowledgment of Calum's introduction. In return, I inclined my head. If he wished to reveal no recognition, I was quite willing to do the same. Even so, my vanity was slighted. No woman likes to feel that a man forgets her so quickly.

I heard Calum's voice saying, "This is a first meeting for all of us. My brother-in-law has been abroad for many a year. For how long before I married your sister, Duncan? All my dear Una told me was that you emigrated as a boy."

He had recovered his composure, but I knew that Morag Crombie had also detected her cousin's distress, and I guessed this was why she had hurried downstairs. Perhaps she felt, as I did, that the least Duncan Mackintosh could have done was to give warning of his arrival instead of presenting himself abruptly and at such an hour as this.

The man said calmly, "I emigrated when I was eighteen, to the South Island of New Zealand. Sheep farming in North Canterbury at one time, then gold prospecting in the Shotover more recently."

"And successfully?"

"Successfully enough to be able to return home for good, which has long been my dream." He looked about him, as if implying that Faillie was still rightfully his.

"And when did you arrive in Inverness?"

"This morning."

"Then it was good of you to call upon me so soon. A pity it was not earlier—I would have been delighted to welcome you to supper."

"I had to find out whether you were in residence. No one at the inn seemed to know. I am staying at Culcabock—a tiny village, as you are probably aware."

"So you decided to take a chance, and rode out to see if I were here?" Calum remarked.

"Precisely. Hamish admitted me at once; he recognized me despite the long lapse of time. He was part of our household when I was a boy."

Our household, not this household. Again I detected a proprietorial note, as if he regarded his sister's husband as an intruder.

The man turned and smiled at the servant, who still stood rooted to the spot. At close quarters the old man's excitement was undeniable. There was even a glisten in his eyes, suggesting suppressed tears.

"I am glad Hamish did his duty so well." With a nod, the Laird of Faillie dismissed the servant, who shuffled away unwillingly. "Did the lodgekeeper also remember you?"

"I avoided the main gates. There is a side entrance about a quarter of a mile westward, which Una and I used as children. Our old lodgekeeper died some years ago; Una told me in one of her letters. So I knew his successor would not know me and would doubtless have told me to call back tomorrow. I didn't relish such a welcome at the gates of my home."

My home. Not yours.

"Then I hope you will indeed return tomorrow," his brother-in-law urged, "for you and I must become acquainted after all these years."

"Rest assured that I shall. There is much I want to know. And to see. The paintings, for example. I hope they have been kept in good repair. If not, I will make it my business to have them attended to."

"Paintings? What paintings?"

"My family's collection. They have always been here."

"I know nothing of any paintings. Una must have sold them, as she sold many things."

"My sister *sold* them? I cannot believe it! And why should she?"

"For the upkeep of Faillie. Your family fortunes dwindled in your absence, brother-in-law. No doubt she concealed all this from you, knowing that you were struggling for an existence overseas, but it is a pity you failed to strike gold sooner."

I saw Duncan Mackintosh's jaw tighten and the line of his mouth harden. He seemed about to speak, then thought better of it. Instead, he replied curtly, "I will return tomorrow morning, Huntly."

"Pray, not in the morning. I shall not be here."

Indeed he would not; he would be at the mills, at my father's invitation.

"If you can come in the evening," he suggested, "we will then have more time to talk, and I confess that I would prefer to postpone the painful subject of my wife's death for a while."

"As you wish."

Duncan Mackintosh bowed politely and was gone. I heard his heavy tread descending the stairs with the ease of one well acquainted with them and, even after a prolonged absence, remembering every twist and turn. The sound was followed almost immediately by the light steps of my mother and sister coming down from above.

Shortly after that my father returned, announcing that the coach was ready and Iain waiting. "So you will forgive me if I hurry my family away. Ealasaid and I must be up early if we are to be prepared for your visit to the mills."

I heard the Laird of Faillie saying that he looked forward to it. Then he was stooping over my mother's hand, then mine, and, finally, Sheena's. To me, it seemed that he lingered over hers.

As we left the castle my emotions were very different from those on my arrival; no feeling of alarm went with me, no doubt or uncertainty, no fear. I was even unaware of the inky blackness of the bog as we crossed the causeway.

I sank back into a corner of the coach, jerking out of thought only when my father said, "I wonder who the man was who went galloping away so furiously. I caught sight of him as I returned from the stables."

"I saw no man, dear." My mother yawned, not really interested, adding that it was probably only a servant.

"He didn't look like one. He was well dressed and had a fine horse. And a fine temper, too, from the look of things. He flung himself into the saddle and went racing off across the grounds as if driven by the devil."

"Not to the main entrance? Then I am right. He must have been a servant."

I said evenly, "He was Duncan Mackintosh, Mr. Huntly's brother-in-law. He arrived unexpectedly while Mother and Sheena were upstairs and you, Father, were at the stables. He was probably heading for the side entrance."

"Young Duncan! I remember him as a lad—and a wild one he was. You met him, Ealasaid?"

"Yes. Apparently he has been overseas for many years."

"That's true. His sister was Heretrix, and when their father died the boy cleared off. He was always independent, adventurous, hot-blooded. So he's back. What now, I wonder! He won't take kindly to a

35

stranger occupying his old home. They were a proud and clannish family. What did you think of him, Ealasaid?"

I answered indifferently, "I hardly noticed him."

That was all I was prepared, or wanted, to say. I had more interesting things to reflect upon and was glad to let my thoughts wander as Mother babbled on delightedly about Mr. Huntly's charm.

"And it was plain that he was enchanted by Sheena. What an advantageous visit it proved to be all round."

My father reached over and patted my hand in the darkness of the coach, saying softly that I had been right, after all.

"In what way, Father?"

"In that feeling you had—that something good was to come along, associated with patterns and checks and tartans. Doesn't that prove that your reluctance to enter Castle Faillie was entirely unjustified?"

I admitted that it did indeed, and went to bed feeling happy and excited. I also felt so curious about the new owner of Castle Faillie that it was a long time before I slept. His face, his voice, his personality —all seemed to be stamped indelibly upon my mind. I found myself wondering what his wife had been like, and how their runaway marriage had worked out. His grief when talking of her death had seemed genuine, and yet I could not help feeling that, for his brother-in-law's sake, he had been carefully glossing over the truth. Had the marriage not been happy, after all?

Four

MY EXCITEMENT was well founded, for things moved swiftly after that, starting with the burst of activity at the mills, and increasing with Calum Huntly's visit.

My father and I left home early next morning because the looms began to roll at seven. Normally, Father arrived half an hour later, but today he permitted no tardiness, and before the workers arrived I was already seated at a drawing board, reproducing the first design, while my father calculated the proportionate amounts of wool required for each.

By the time the Laird of Faillie rode up to the mills I had sketched several of the tartans, indicating the varied shades in watercolor. Meanwhile, workers prepared and cleaned the looms whilst others selected the requisite colors and wound them onto "cheeses" to be placed in the bank of the warping mill, a tall holder resembling a bookcase containing steel spindles on which the cheeses were arranged according to the pattern to be produced.

Calum was quick to grasp essential details. He was eager to see everything, from the time the yarn was brought in from the spinning room and wound onto pirns, or bobbins, then onto long, narrow ones for feeding the shuttles.

"The cheeses are used for the warps and the shuttles for the wefts," I said, coloring a little, for behind his smile there seemed to lurk a quality I could not analyze. Amusement? Indulgence?

Perhaps he sensed my feelings, for he quoted gently, " 'And all the women that were wise-hearted did spin with their hands.' Tell me more, I beg you. What of the designs themselves?"

When I showed them to him he complimented me, and I told him how, in days gone by, women had used thread-count sticks, on which they wound threads of yarn to give an exact pattern of the tartan ground-work, stripes, and coloring. "But these were thrown away when proscription was enforced. They were deemed no longer useful and doubtless it was safer to dispose of them in case such evidence could be claimed as proof that they planned to weave the tartan in secret. Hence the loss of the original designs."

"You seem very knowledgeable, Miss MacArthur. No wonder your father is proud of you."

"It is I who am proud of him. From the time he became aware of my interest in weaving, he encouraged it. He used to bring me on visits to the mills as a child, so that I could watch the spinning and dyeing and every other process. Even now, I can remember the old Spinning Jenny . . ."

"What was that?"

"An ancient hand spinner, long since discarded, but my father continued to use it after his rivals had dispensed with it in favor of the factory employment of children."

"I applaud him for that decision."

"I too, but other weavers scoffed at what they called his sentimentality. They preferred to dismiss women, even though they needed the work, because children were paid less than half the amount in wages. That was something my father could not tolerate, and when more advanced water-driven machinery came along he was ready and willing to buy it. His workers appreciate this and have always remained loyal to him."

"I am sure no one could be more loyal to Andrew MacArthur than his daughter."

His tone was admiring, and I felt my cheeks flush. Although it wasn't wholly the kind of admiration I wanted, it was at least something.

"And your talent for reproducing designs such as

these solely from theoretical details must surely be unusual in a woman?"

"It was a joint effort. My father has the knowledge and ability to work these things out like a mathematical problem."

"And you the ability to reproduce them——"

My father's voice cut in unexpectedly, "Plus some technical knowledge which she has acquired through the years."

So absorbed had we been that neither of us had heard his approach. Now Aindreas viewed me fondly. "The older I grow, the more thankful I am for Ealasaid's interest in the mills. Most men have sons to carry on their industries; I have no need of one. I shall hand over the banner to her with every confidence, when the time comes."

"To *me,* Father? To a woman?"

"Why not?"

"But she will marry," Calum Huntly intervened, "she will have a home, a husband, children . . ."

"That is in the nature of things, and what I wish for her, provided she finds the right man, but I see no reason why matrimony should prevent her from running the mills eventually."

"Mother would never approve," I pointed out.

"Possibly not, but she will have to accept the situation. I have already named you as my successor. You look surprised, Huntly. Surely you do not subscribe to the ridiculous idea that such responsibility would make her unfeminine?"

"One could never regard either of your daughters as unfeminine, Mr. MacArthur," Calum said smoothly.

"But only Ealasaid has inherited my love for the mills. When she steps into my shoes she will need only my able right hand, James Macpherson, plus an understanding husband and a housekeeper to run her home. But all that is in the distant future. . . ."

When I returned home I came face to face with Angus, walking across the garden from the direction of the library. From the expression on his face, I knew something was wrong.

Against my will, I stopped. I was tired. The day had been long; already it was late afternoon. Nevertheless, I felt compelled to ask Angus what was the matter.

"Who is he?" Angus demanded, with characteristic directness.

I knew who he meant, of course.

"So he called," I said.

"If you mean that proud fair-haired devil with the arrogance of an aristocrat, yes. *And* took her for a drive in his carriage, with your mother's beaming blessing. I saw them from the library window."

I stifled a sigh. My disappointment was as keen as his, if he did but know it.

"Who is he?" Angus repeated.

"Calum Huntly, Laird of Faillie."

"She *is* flying high!"

"Don't say that. I don't like it."

He regarded me quizzically.

"I can never make up my mind whether your affection for your spoiled little sister is one of pride, or purely maternal. You should have a brood of your own, and then you'd stop feeling protective toward her. You wouldn't have the time."

"And you don't feel protective toward her, I suppose? You only feel jealous because another man is attracted to her—and she to him."

"I thought as much. It was obvious."

I moved on. "There is nothing either you or I can do about it, Angus."

He answered. "So you feel rejected, too—I'm sorry about that."

I went quickly into the house and shut the door. Mother came out of the drawing room to meet me, talking excitedly about that charming Mr. Huntly who had called and taken Sheena for a drive.

"Unchaperoned?" I said cryptically, heading for the stairs.

Mother gave her characteristic little ruffle of indignation.

"Mr. Huntly is a *gentleman,* Elizabeth."

"He is also a man," I replied, and went on my way.

"Elizabeth!"

I turned. "Yes, Mother?"

"You are surely not implying that Mr. Huntly would take advantage of Sheena?"

"How can I tell?" I said, trying to hide my own feelings. "It is you, not I, who is the stickler for propriety, so I'm surprised you didn't insist on Ann accompanying them. Was he driving the carriage himself?"

"Y-yes . . ."

"Then his hands should be well occupied," I assured her lightly.

"Sometimes, Elizabeth, your remarks are outrageous!" But she was obviously upset and I went back to kiss and reassure her. I never really wished to shock her and was always ashamed when goaded into it.

Back at the halfway landing I heard the sound of wheels on gravel. I glanced outside and saw my younger sister sitting demurely beside Calum Huntly, who had his immaculately gloved hands upon the reins.

"And here she is, Mother dear, without a hair out of place."

"There! I knew it was perfectly safe for her to go."

And I know this will only be the first time, I thought, as I went on to my room. Mother was sure to invite him in, and I had no desire to meet him again. Not at this moment, tired and somewhat disheveled after a hard day's work. As I pulled off my bonnet and threw it aside, I saw that my hair, as always, had tumbled from its bonds and was halfway down my shoulders. I had watercolor stains on my fingers, and a smudge across one cheek. For a moment I felt a swift pang of envy when I thought of Sheena's perfection, and wished I had been born as she—clinging and dependent, without any restless urge to be doing things, accomplishing things.

Without any gift of the sight, either, although at this moment it was not the sight that made me wonder whether Calum Huntly intended to woo my sister.

While the looms clattered and progress surged forward at the mills, life at home went forward at an inevitable and predictable pace, and my unhappy speculation seemed justified, for within two weeks Calum was a regular visitor. I would return to hear that today he had taken Sheena riding across the moors ("She, who never cared much for it before!" Angus told me wretchedly) or, still unchaperoned because Mother had implicit trust (or because she wished to further his pursuit?), driving in his carriage. He was teaching my young sister how to handle the reins. Once I saw them in the distance, his arm about her shoulders holding her close, with both hands covering hers as he guided them.

I resigned myself to the inevitable, but took pains with my appearance whenever he came to supper, which was frequently. I indulged in new gowns, run up by Meg Grant, the village dressmaker, whom Sheena scorned but who was highly talented and amazingly swift with her needle. All I had to do was pass on my ideas to her. I found I had a talent for dress design as well as for fabrics, and my ambitions soared into realms hitherto undreamed of. What if the day should come when gowns could be made at the mills, to our exclusive designs and materials, and sold direct to stores in Glasgow and Edinburgh and even faraway London?

I announced my idea at supper. It startled even my father, and although I knew that such an idea might well be nothing but a dream, it served the purpose of catching Calum's attention.

"Elizabeth is certainly ambitious," he said, glancing at me with what I felt to be the first touch of real admiration I had ever won from him. I also felt that it was not prompted solely by my ambition. The gown I wore tonight was particularly becoming, and I had taken pains with my hair, brushing it until it gleamed and piling it on top of my head. In the vast dining room mirror above the heavy sideboard, I caught sight of my reflection. Enthusiasm had brought a sparkle of excitement to my eyes; the ruby red of my gown was flattering to my pale skin and black hair, and across my shoulder I had pinned a tartan sash, held by a silver brooch set with Cairngorm stones.

To my surprise, he said warmly, "You look handsome enough to appear at Court yourself, Elizabeth."

I hoped the pleasure I felt was not apparent to the others. In any case, it was brief enough, for a moment later my sister's chatter demanded his attention and I was forgotten. At the head of the table my father appeared to be intent on his meal but, like my mother, I knew he was well aware of all that was going on. At one point his kindly eyes met mine, affectionate and smiling. I felt he was trying to say something that could not be put into words. Comfort? Reassurance? I turned my attention to my plate, although suddenly my appetite had gone. I knew that tonight Calum would ask for an interview with my father, and what it would portend. His one moment of admiration for me had been fleeting.

Evidently my mother anticipated events also, for there was a suppressed excitement about her when she rose and led my sister and me from the dining room, leaving the two men to their port.

Outside in the hall she whispered eagerly, "Sheena, my love, away upstairs with you and tidy that strand of hair which has become misplaced—no, wait, I will come with you and attend to it myself. It is important, *so* important. . . ."

"What is, Mamma?" Sheena asked, all wide-eyed innocence.

"That you should look your best, of course. I predict that right at this moment—but no, I must not; indeed I must not! That just *might* be tempting providence, although goodness knows it is obvious enough. I can tell. Oh, I can tell! A mother always can. . . ."

I went into the drawing room and shut the door as they bustled upstairs to Sheena's room. I sat down beside the fire, struggling to suppress tears. The effort made my throat ache. I had to prepare myself, be ready with smiles and congratulations, brace myself for my mother's torrent of delight, listen to her flood of plans for the wedding—and never for a moment betray my own feelings. I thought of his body lying close to my sister's; the warmth of their bed; the intimacy that would unite them.

I rose and paced the room, and through a blur of tears saw the crimson of my gown swirling about my feet. Much good it had done me, this sudden interest in my appearance.

They were a long time upstairs. I was glad of that, because it gave me an opportunity to compose myself, and by the time the door clicked open I had somehow managed to.

My father stood there. Beyond him I saw my mother and sister descending the stairs. They paused halfway down. Somehow I knew that Sheena was holding her breath.

As for my mother, she was looking at my father with blatant expectancy—but he was looking at me.

"Andrew?"

He didn't even hear her. The eager question in her voice was lost in the vast well of the hall.

Then my father spoke. I heard astonishment and concern in his voice.

"Ealasaid—Mr. Huntly has asked for your hand in marriage."

Five

IT WAS STRANGE that at such a moment all I should consciously hear was the loud ticking of the drawing room clock, beating like a drum in my ears, and all I should see was my sister's face, pale as a cameo against the dark paneling of the staircase wall. Then my mother's features swam into focus, rigid with shock.

I tried to speak, but no sound came. I felt my lips move, but that was all. Even now I cannot analyze exactly how I felt.

I sat down weakly. My father stooped over me and said, "The answer must be yours, Ealasaid. I'm not a man to contract his daughters in marriage. You can say no, if you wish."

Say *no?*

My head fell against the back of the armchair and stayed there, dizzy with joy. To wed him. To live with him. To be loved by him. To become a woman through him.

Say no to all *that?*

I sprang from the chair and went running from the room, forgetful of everyone. There was no modesty in me. I flung myself through the open door of the dining room and saw him standing, his back to the fireplace, waiting.

"Why?" I demanded. "Why *me?*"

"Because I love you. Why else?" he replied.

"You've shown no sign of it!"

He said with suppressed excitement, "Come here, and I will show you now."

I heard approaching footsteps—my father's, following me. I thrust the door shut and went across the room with shameless eagerness, meeting Calum's outstretched hands, unresisting when he drew my body to him and feeling a leaping response as he pressed me close. Dear God in heaven, I never dreamed it could be like this—the hot quickening in the blood which was so much more than a mere instinct for mating.

It was cruel of my father to open the door at that moment.

"I take it she's said yes."

I turned within Calum's hold and looked back at my father. I knew my face was flushed and that there was no need for words. It was only then that I realized how well I had concealed my feelings from the moment I met Calum. Neither my parents nor my sister had had the slightest suspicion. But Calum must have had. There had been no surprise in his face when I raced into the room; he had been waiting confidently.

"I think," said my father, "that you'd best see my wife and younger daughter tomorrow, sir. If you are the man Ealasaid wants, then you are the man I want for her, but in the circumstances you can hardly expect congratulations from Sheena, nor from my wife —not at the moment, anyway. Catriona will come round to it, of course, for she will desire Ealasaid's happiness as much as I, but as for Sheena . . ." He gave an expressive shrug, then a sigh. "She is young. She will get over it."

I saw concern in Calum's eyes.

"If I have given her any cause to imagine—"

"Let us say hope, shall we? I am well aware, as is everyone, of the time you have spent with her, the attentions you have paid to her . . ."

"Time, yes. Attentions, no. She is like a little sister to me; Elizabeth's little sister. I have taken her riding and driving solely because Elizabeth was not available. Surely that was obvious?"

Not to me. Nor to Sheena. Nor to Mother. Nor to Angus. Nor, apparently, to my father.

I drew away, but Calum's hand shot out and caught mine.

"You, too?" he said quietly.

I nodded.

"I too. But I'm glad I was wrong. Be happy for me, Father. I love Calum."

His kindly face smiled for the first time.

"Come here, lass."

He kissed me on the brow, giving me his blessing.

I couldn't sleep. I sat beside the window of my room, gazing out on the Beauly Firth. There was a moon tonight, palely gleaming, but inside me there was a fire. Who could sleep on such a night?

Stay here, and I would think of nothing else. Go to bed, and I would be reaching for him in my mind, anticipating the future. Let it come quickly, please God! Meanwhile, I had to escape from tumultuous thought.

It was very quiet in the house as I crept downstairs, so quiet that the drawing of the bolt echoed loudly in the hall, and then I was hurrying down the gravel drive and out into the night, walking through a village which slept, up the hill to the watchman's stone. Even in the dark I could have found my way to it. But now moonlight picked out the path and the boulder ahead of me. But it was not bare, as usual. A man sat there.

I knew who he was before he spoke. He was the last person I wanted to see and I halted instinctively. I didn't like his disturbing personality, and at such a moment as this it was far from welcome.

"So you come here at night, too?"

"Why not?" I parried.

"Only witches walk abroad at night."

I felt that he was mocking me in some way, and resented him even more because, after pretending not to know me, he now condescended to do so.

"The inn at Culcabock locks its doors at ten-thirty," I remarked coldly.

He laughed. "I have a key." As proof, he dangled

it before me. "The landlord obliged me. He trusts me, you see, which is more than can be said for you."

I shrugged.

"I neither trust nor mistrust you. In fact, I give you no thought."

"Ah—you are angry. Because I pretended not to know you when my brother-in-law introduced us?"

"That didn't perturb me in the least. Why should it?"

"For the same reason that any other woman would resent it. Wounded vanity. Hurt pride. No woman likes the idea that a man could forget her so soon. Put your mind at rest—I didn't forget you. I merely thought it circumspect to conceal our meeting because it would be frowned upon if it were known that a girl of your upbringing went around talking to strange men."

He had an irritating habit of making me feel foolish.

He continued blandly, "I imagine taking solitary walks at dead of night would also be frowned upon. Do you do it often, or only when disturbed in some way?"

"I am not in the least disturbed."

"Excited, then. I can sense it. Something has happened to stir up a restlessness in you—although I imagine that even normally you are a restless young woman. How does a girl of your temperament tolerate a quiet, humdrum life in the country?"

"I don't have to. My father encourages my interest in the family business."

"Ah, yes—the MacArthur Mills. I remember them from my boyhood; they have grown considerably since then. In what way do you participate? I cannot imagine the proprietor's daughter operating a loom."

"I know how to, nevertheless. And more besides. I am interested in the whole running of the mills and shall take over one day."

In the moonlight, I saw the quick interest in his face.

"I knew you were an unusual young woman the moment I met you."

"And you disapprove?"

"On the contrary. I admire a woman with character and spirit. Many gold prospectors' wives had the same qualities, back in Queenstown, although few could tolerate the hardship of camping in caves down by the Shotover bed. The aim of almost everyone was to get back to Britain. My aim, too. It was for this that I sweated my guts out year after year."

"And now that you have achieved it?"

"I shall remain, of course."

"No other achievement in mind?"

"One in particular. The biggest of my life."

"To claim Castle Faillie . . ." I said slowly.

"Naturally." He added dryly, "Any objections?"

"Calum might have, and well might he be entitled to, having inherited it from his wife."

"Who died childless, in which case it should revert to her nearest relative. That is the Mackintosh tradition. You may not have heard of the Clan Chattan Declaration of 1672, wherein the Lord Lyon declared, in law, that he would give none of the other families of the clan any arms but as cadets of the Laird of Mackintosh's family, whose predecessor married the Heretrix of the Clan Chattan. It is not unusual for inheritance to descend in such a way in Highland families, as I am sure you know, but when the female line is broken, it must revert. This law prevails in my own family, which is closely affiliated to the chief of the Mackintosh clan. It was from an early chief that the original Heretrix in my family came into possession of Faillie, and my sister eventually inherited in her turn."

"And now she is dead, you deem yourself the rightful successor. Would you have returned if your sister had not died?"

"Naturally. For no other reason did I endure that life in New Zealand's South Island."

"I thought gold was an ultimate aim in itself."

"It was for most men, but I went into that gold jungle for one purpose only—to get enough to return to the Highlands. Not merely for my passage home—I'd

49

made enough for that when working the sheep farms as a hired hand—but to return well set-up for life, to buy or build a home here and invest my fortune well. And when I arrived, I learned of my sister's death. I knew then that there was no need to build or buy a place for myself. Faillie would be mine."

"But her husband was her nearest relative."

"But not a Mackintosh. As I told you, it has to revert to a Mackintosh. When I emigrated as a boy it was right and proper that Una should have our home eventually. Then she married. I was glad of that, but now—"

"Now you are not so sure. Why do you dislike Mr. Huntly?"

"Let us merely say that I don't respect him for holding on to property to which he isn't entitled. That is as good a cause as any for dislike."

"He is entitled to it if his wife bequeathed it to him," I answered defensively.

"Una wouldn't do that. As Heretrix she would automatically hand on our property to the next member of the family: a woman, if there were one, a man if not. I am that man."

"She could have changed her mind."

"I doubt it, unless he persuaded her to."

He could do that easily enough. Calum could make any woman yield to him in any way he wished, but I judged him not to be the kind of man who would use his influence in the way Duncan Mackintosh suggested.

"He wouldn't do that. He wouldn't even need to. He has estates of his own on Deeside."

"Then he can move out and go to them."

"But *I* wouldn't—" I broke off. I had been about to say that I wouldn't wish to move to Deeside because it would mean living so far from the mills, but I wasn't yet ready to tell this man about my forthcoming marriage.

I was aware of his deep, intent gaze and turned away from it. Below us, the waters of the Beauly Firth shimmered like silver. It was very quiet up here beside the watchman's stone.

"But you wouldn't—what?" he asked quietly, and I knew then that it was useless to be silent.

"I wouldn't wish to."

His hand shot out and grasped my wrist. I gave a little gasp which was more in surprise than pain. He jerked me around to face him.

"*You* wouldn't wish to? Are you telling me that you are going to marry this man?"

"Yes. I am."

He dropped my wrist, declaring vehemently that he didn't believe it.

"You must. It is true."

"And you expect me to accept it gladly?" he asked, in rising anger.

"Why not?"

"Because I—" He broke off, as if thinking better of what he had been about to say, then finished curtly, "Because he isn't the man for you. Don't ask me how I know or why I say that."

"I have no intention of asking you anything. I know my own mind."

"*And* heart?"

"That too."

He said urgently, "Don't do it, Ealasaid. How long have you known him? No time at all, if my landlord's wife has her facts correct. According to her, Calum Huntly never settled at Faillie until after my sister's death, which was a comparatively short time ago. Did you ever meet her?"

"No. We didn't move in the same circles. And, from all I heard, she rarely left the castle on her annual visits. In the circumstances it was hardly necessary for her husband to leave his own estates to accompany her."

"I can see he has won you over." There was bitterness in his voice.

I said coldly, "I bid you good night, Mr. Mackintosh."

"Not yet." His solid figure blocked my path. I could feel the unyielding determination of the man and thought how unwise it would be for anyone to make an enemy of him.

He said forcefully, "Don't do it, Ealasaid. Don't marry him. Wait awhile. You do not know the truth of his character."

I refused to heed his words. I would allow nothing and no one to discourage me once I set my heart on something, and my heart was set upon Calum Huntly. No outsider's advice and no inner voice could have the slightest effect upon me now.

I turned away abruptly, but this time I was seized by the shoulders and held fast.

"Must I shake some sense into you? I'm capable of doing it—and more besides, believe me! Calum Huntly isn't the only man who could match the passion in you. Do you think I haven't been aware of it since the moment we meet—you, with your witching green eyes and generous mouth and a body no normal man could overlook? You're hot-blooded and hot-headed—the same as I. The astonishing thing is that you have remained unwed, and the only explanation is that you are fastidious. You have allowed no man to touch you, have you, Ealasaid? But not through coldness, I'll warrant. And now you're going to throw yourself away on a man you know nothing about!"

I jerked free and answered furiously that he had no right to say such things, but even in my own ears the words sounded ineffectual.

"You're jealous!" I cried finally. "Jealous because he owns Faillie and you covet it!"

"You're damned right I'm jealous—but not for that reason. But go ahead and believe it if you wish. Go your own hot-headed way and hang yourself! I do covet Faillie because I have a right to the place, but that isn't—" He broke off, steadied his voice, and finished with an effort, "But I promise you one thing, infuriating and exasperating though you are—as long as you live there I will make no attempt to claim it, or to turn you out. When you choose to leave voluntarily—come and tell me. I'll be waiting."

It was he who turned his back this time and strode angrily away from the watchman's stone.

Six

WE MARRIED almost at once, despite the fact that Calum had been a widower for a very short time. I knew my own mind and sharply turned away any memory that Castle Faillie boded me ill.

The wedding was private. Only my parents were present. Sheena remained at home, and not even Calum's half-brother attended. "To tell you the truth," Calum confided, "I haven't the faintest idea where Malcolm is. He was always a bit of a roamer, and after I married Una we lost touch. I don't think he ever forgave me for cutting him out where she was concerned, besides which we never had the slightest thing in common. Like many half-brothers, we were always totally different."

And so I came to Faillie as its mistress, a position which seemed incredible after my almost lifelong aversion to the place.

In the whirl, the question of a honeymoon never came up for discussion. I had wondered briefly whether Calum would take me to Carrisbrae, his estate near Braemar, but in my impatience to marry him—an impatience which matched his own—nothing else mattered, and when he remarked one day that he was anxious to have me at Faillie as soon as possible because it would then begin to seem like home to him at last, I just naturally fell in with his wishes.

As we drove across the causeway, our quiet arrival

seemed appropriate and right. Equally appropriate was the day's brilliant sunshine. It lightened the gray stone walls and sparkled among the trees, completely banishing my former impression. On this sunny afternoon, Faillie was welcoming, not sinister.

Morag Crombie welcomed me too, holding out both hands and kissing me upon both cheeks. I was faintly surprised, and even more so when she said, "Welcome to Faillie, Cousin Elizabeth."

Cousin Elizabeth?

Of course. She was distantly related to Calum, and therefore related to me now, but I had thought of her only as a housekeeper here. She was a strange and disturbing sort of housekeeper who might prove to be a problem unless put firmly in her place from the beginning, but not a person with the right to embrace me, call me Cousin, and kiss me on both cheeks. But Calum merely looked on, smiling, and I realized I had to reshape my ideas. Morag belonged here, and now she was graciously admitting me. Establishing myself as mistress of Faillie in her place was likely to be difficult, so the earlier I tackled it, the better.

She linked her arm in mine, emphasizing our new relationship. It was almost as if she was receiving me as a guest who had come for a visit.

"Let me show you to your room, Elizabeth."

I was nonplussed, but fortunately Calum burst out laughing.

"My dear Morag, you are talking to my wife! *I* will take her upstairs."

He put his arm about my waist and led me away and, as always when he touched me, I forgot everything else. Morag no longer mattered and her condescension was as unimportant as she. I had nothing to fear from her; she had been made to realize already that I was mistress of Faillie, Calum's wife, and that put me beyond her in rank and in precedence. No longer would she act as hostess here, or occupy that chair at the long dining table. . . .

Neither Calum nor I looked back as we climbed the spiral steps leading from the courtyard up to the Billeting Room, but as we walked the length of that room toward the next flight I heard her following, her steps quick and light upon the stone treads. If one could have heard a cat hurrying along behind, that was how it would have sounded.

We had reached the next spiral when she called peremptorily, "Supper will be served at the customary hour, Calum."

He paused, still with his arm about me, and looked back. "Supper, my dear Morag, will be served when I ring for it—and in our room. You surely don't expect our company on our wedding night?"

Without waiting for an answer he led me up the stairs and along the corridor above the Banqueting Hall. I don't know what made me glance down through the last spy slit of all. Morag Crombie was standing exactly where we had left her, and even from this distance I knew that her eyes were stone cold.

But again I forgot her as our door closed behind us. Our private quarters consisted of a large bedroom, off which led Calum's dressing room and my boudoir. The whole suite was situated at the end of a passage turning right at the termination of the corridor: a cul-de-sac leading only to us. Previously I had been no farther than the room in which my mother, sister, and I had shed our cloaks on our first visit; the room in which Mother and Sheena had excitedly discussed the evening's success whilst I had looked down from one of the spy slits and overheard Duncan Mackintosh's question about his sister's death.

The recollection of that incident lent a chill to my homecoming, like the intrusion of something unpleasant, best forgotten. And I quickly discarded it as my husband unbuttoned my gown. One by one, my garments slid to the floor and I stepped out of the cluster about my feet, eager for his touch, as eager as he to give and to receive, for neither of us could wait for the night to come.

In the ensuing days I blossomed beneath my husband's love. In every way I now experienced the fulfillment I had been unconsciously craving, and had no time now for fancies and imaginary premonitions. Life was too full with this exciting and demanding husband.

"The only moments I find intolerable are those you spend away from me," he said across the breakfast table one morning. "I even resent your occasional visits to the mills, few as they are now. Sometimes I wish I had never been responsible for this tartan revival at Mac-Arthur's."

"If you had not been, we would never have met."

"Oh yes, we would. Someway, sometime, somewhere. We were meant for each other. I believe it can sometimes be like that between a man and a woman."

"Was it not, with Una?"

"Not for long."

The answer was abrupt, almost in a tone with which I was becoming familiar. He used it to Hamish, to grooms and stable boys, sometimes even to Morag, but this imperiousness was never turned upon me. It was absent now, but the subject of Una was dismissed. When he was ready to talk about his first marriage, he would choose the moment himself, and I was content to let it be. But I could not help recalling my impression when overhearing his conversation with Duncan Mackintosh on that memorable first visit to Faillie—the impression that, in talking about his marriage, he had been glossing over the truth. I wondered again whether that whirlwind elopement had resulted in unhappiness, and whether this was partly the reason why Calum had never accompanied Una when visiting her old home.

Inevitably, I speculated about the girl who had died bearing his child and whether the passion between them had been as great as ours. I loved Calum jealously, and in doing so had even greater compassion for Sheena, who showed no signs of quick recovery. Overnight her face seemed to have changed into a pinched little mask. I had cheated her, defrauded her, and our easy communication had changed to stilted politeness. Whenever we met, I was possessed by an unhappy sense of guilt.

Still, the future would take care of Sheena's heart,

and all I could do was let her see that she meant as much to me as ever, and that when she was ready to thaw toward me, I would be waiting and welcoming. Beyond that, there was nothing I could do. In time she would remember that in all my twenty-three years I had never been so pretty or so admired as she; then she would not begrudge my happiness.

"You are far away, my love. What are you thinking?"

Calum's voice jerked me back to our room and the breakfast table set for two. This was a treasured hour of the day; he in a long quilted robe with broad satin revers, and I in his favorite *peignoir* of peacock silk ruched at throat and wrists. My wardrobe was extensive now; closets overflowed with elegant gowns and cloaks and lingerie, hats and riding habits, shoes and accessories. The girl who once sat upon the watchman's stone wrapped in a homely dark cape was far removed from the woman sipping gruel in the finest bedroom in Castle Faillie, wearing an elegant night-dress beneath an elegant robe.

I replied quite honestly that I had been thinking of Sheena and wondering how long it would take her to forgive me.

"She has nothing to forgive. If the child misconstrued my attentions to her, she had only herself to blame. Stop worrying about her. She must learn to grow up."

I knew he was right, and tried not to think too much about my sister.

Our room commanded a wonderful view of the surrounding countryside, marred only by the sluggish bog within Faillie's grounds. As I gazed on it now, I was filled with a compulsive desire to do something about it. Drained, cleared, and filled with fresh water, it could become a moat again, ablaze with water lilies. My father had rewarded me generously for my recent services to the mills, and here was a way in which I could put the money to good use. I had nothing else on which to spend it, for my husband deprived me of nothing, and I needed no further additions to my lavish wardrobe.

"I have lost you again," Calum said gently. "Where are your thoughts roaming now?"

"Down there, in that unsightly bog. I intend to have it cleared and transformed into the moat it must once have been."

"Other things need priority. You must leave the management of Faillie to me."

"But your place on Deeside—"

"—is well looked after by my factor and staff. My dear Elizabeth, all I ask of you is that you shall be decorative and devoted. Morag can run this establishment and I can attend to its renovation."

"And I? Am I to be useless?"

"Your father doesn't find you so, more's the pity. Despite the short time you have been my wife, I suspect he would like to have you back at those mills more or less permanently."

I laughed.

"You were reproaching yourself just now for helping us to revive the tartan, so if he does, you indeed have only yourself to blame!"

He reached across the table and kissed me, and the tenderness which was ever-present between us stirred again. But as he raised his arms there was a knock at the door.

It was Morag, armed with menus. Nothing could have been less welcome, nor more prosaic, but I had brought this upon myself by asking to see them daily, a request which I had presented carefully, having quickly learned that this was the only way to approach Morag. The welcome she had extended to me on arrival had frozen into hostility following Calum's indication of my priority over her. But the question of the menus had not represented such a hurdle as our first supper together. That was an event I would never forget.

At the head of the long dining table was Calum's tall-backed chair, made of oak and heavily carved, and at the opposite end was a replica of it for the mistress of the house. In this second chair Morag had always sat. As the three of us entered the Banqueting Hall on the night following my arrival at Faillie, she went to it automatically—but so did I. Even now I could recall the astonishment in her hooded eyes. For a second she hesitated. I did not. This was my rightful place, and I waited only long enough for Calum to withdraw the chair for me. As he did so, his eyes had flickered toward her, relegating her to a lesser seat. She had had no choice but to accept it, but throughout the meal I felt a stirring of malevolence toward me. This was something stronger than her reaction on the previous afternoon, and far more frightening.

I had forced myself to dismiss it with the thought that in time we would become adjusted to each other, and I felt so safe in the warmth of Calum's love and so sure of his support that I was unworried. This feeling was justified, for he upheld me in everything—until the day that I remarked, in the privacy of our room, that I wished we could take our meals alone together.

"So do I, my love, but Morag is one of the family and, although she must now yield to you in most things, we cannot banish her to the servants' hall, nor suggest that she eat in her own quarters."

He was right, of course; nor did I wish to antagonize the woman further by deliberately slighting her. Tact was the keynote, but so was firmness, and just as it had been necessary to assume my rightful place at the dining table, it was equally necessary to emphasize other points too. The choice of the day's menus had been one.

"I know you plan excellent meals, Morag, but I should enjoy participating."

Beneath such subtle flattery she expanded a little—and promptly made me feel that I was an inexperienced young wife who needed to be taught. This impression I quickly overcame. My mother, like any true Scotswoman, had brought up both her daughters with a knowledge of housewifery and cooking, and I was soon injecting my own ideas into Morag's menus.

But knocking on our bedroom door to present them was an unprecedented intrusion.

"My dear Morag," Calum said, "surely you know that you should show the menus to Elizabeth in the morning room, when she is ready?"

He could not have told her more plainly that she was intruding, and that a husband and wife had the right to remain in their bedroom for as long as they pleased without being disturbed.

She murmured an apology, then looked directly at me and said, with what seemed to my ears to be a hint of sarcasm, "Perhaps you will be so kind as to summon me there—when you are ready to come down?"

When the door was closed again, Calum said with some annoyance, "Morag should know better than to knock on our bedroom door at this hour of the day—or at any hour."

"If we had risen earlier, the intrusion wouldn't have been necessary." I felt a trifle guilty. She had reminded me that there was more to being a wife than the hours spent in bed with a husband.

Calum yawned, stretched, and said fondly, "You are entitled to lie abed as long as you wish, my darling. I can think of no place which I so much enjoy sharing with you, and we will rise as late as we wish until you are back in harness at the mills."

"But I shan't be. That was only temporary, when Father needed me on the designing side."

"He will want you back, to design more."

"But all the setts you passed on to us are authentic and we have no need to add to them, whatever other weavers may be doing."

"But MacArthur's must keep abreast of competitors, and a clan tartan is no less of a clan tartan because it is newly designed. Every clan has a right to adopt another sett as their own if an original pattern is lost. The only thing they cannot do is adopt one which is being used by another clan. You could create dozens of new tartans for those who cannot officially claim one as their own."

"But not yet. It isn't necessary."

"It will be. For the time being, MacArthur tartans are well launched, but the market will grow. I wouldn't like to see your father taking a back seat."

I laughed. "If you imagine he would be content to, you don't know him."

Calum smiled. "Luckily for me, I do know his daughter—and am more than content for our honeymoon to continue, even though we choose to spend it at home. That is why Morag should have more tact than to knock on our door so early—particularly since she was once married herself."

"To whom? And how long has she been widowed?"

"A few years, I think. I have never been interested enough to ask, nor to inquire whom she married. To tell you the truth, I know very little about her."

I said, suddenly feeling sorry for the woman, that perhaps she had forgotten the rapture of early marriage and for this reason we should be more tolerant, with which Calum disagreed.

"One of the family she may be, but she must realize where she stands in this household, and that is not at our bedroom door early in the morning."

"But it isn't early; we are disgracefully late. And I think Morag is finding it difficult to accept me as mistress here."

"She will do so in time."

As the days passed, I learned many things about the household. Apart from Hamish, who had lived here all his life, most of the staff had been engaged since Calum's arrival, carefully selected by Morag. In Una's day, the place had been maintained by a skeleton staff, headed by Hamish, whose daughter had come over from Cawdor village each day to cook when the Heretrix was in residence, but Morag had dispensed with her services after Una's death. The girl's talents were too limited, she explained. Homely food was all right up to a point, but not really good enough for Calum's table, and since cooking was a talent on which Morag prided herself, Hamish's daughter was superfluous now.

This was all very logical—but not, I guessed, to Hamish, who wasn't the type of man to take kindly to his daughter's dismissal, nor to being supervised or dictated to by a woman who was not his employer by right, as Una had been. No doubt he considered me in the same light, but he would have to accept the new regime at Faillie, whether he liked it or not.

To this new regime I adapted myself well, and as the days slid by I began to feel very much at home in my new surroundings. I took a lively interest in Calum's improvements and carried out some of my own, including the removal of encroaching woodland on the southern side, which let in more sunlight so that the castle interior was brightened considerably. Of this Calum thoroughly approved, as he did of the rock garden I planned in a sheltered corner of the grounds. The creation of a moat would be a longer and more costly process, but I was determined not to abandon the idea. Meanwhile I was content to take a step at a time.

But for all my domestic bliss, I lost none of my love for the moors, and gradually Calum came to share it, although he was more accustomed to the gentleness of Deeside than to this rugged country. We rode together often, from Meall Mor to Creagon Glas, from Assich Forest to Cawdor Wood.

"Someday," I declared, "you will know every valley and hill as far as Nairn and Fort George and love them as I do."

"And you will learn to love Deeside," he promised.

"When will you take me?"

"As soon as I have accomplished all I wish to accomplish at Faillie."

"That will take a long time!"

"Possibly, but my own estates are well run; these are sadly neglected. An occasional visit to Carrisbrae is all that is needed, for it is well looked after by a man who has been with my family for as long as Hamish has been with Una's, and a man who is a great deal more conscientious. If it were not disloyal to my late wife, I would get rid of Hamish."

"I doubt if he would go. He looks upon Faillie as his rightful home."

"And so it is," Calum said fairly. "His father before him worked for the Mackintoshes. One has a duty to family retainers."

"As now you feel you have a duty to Una for not appreciating her pride in the place? Is this your reason for wanting to accomplish so much at Faillie?"

"You are perceptive, my darling. And what you say is true. I want to make amends to her, even at this late hour. To be honest, I want to salve my conscience. God forgive me, I was often impatient with her."

Gently, I asked why. We had crested a hill and now looked down on the valley of the Nairn. Calum reined in his horse, and I drew alongside, waiting. His profile was toward me, the pale hair shining silver in the sun as he removed his hat and let the breeze blow through it. It seemed to me that he found the wind soothing. Not for the first time, when Una was mentioned, I sensed some inner turbulence of his mind.

He said slowly, "Unfortunately, the Heretrix of a clannish family can sometimes be—shall I say, tyrannical? Spoiled, at any rate. Una was accustomed to having her every wish indulged, and in the beginning I made the mistake of carrying on the practice. In time, my patience wore thin. I have many faults, Elizabeth, and chief among them is the desire to dominate—never to be dominated."

"I could not admire a man who was willing to be. But I have seen no sign of your wishing to dominate me."

"Ah—but I love you so much more than I loved Una. Ours was a swift affair, the attraction of opposites and inevitably, I suppose, it died as swiftly. You, on the other hand, have never been spoiled. You have never become imperious or demanding."

"I have never been in a position to be."

"But Una was. She was born to it. We clashed very quickly. Perhaps it was unavoidable between two

63

people who had both inherited estates on which they desired to live; neither would yield to the other. I was greatly at fault. I insisted that she should make her home at Carrisbrae."

"That seems right, since a woman's place is beside her husband."

He reached out and took my hand. His grip was tight, and grateful.

"I should have compromised, even so, but because she was willful and stubborn, I was stubborn too. I even urged her to sell Faillie when it became obvious that her income was unequal to its upkeep. At that time Carrisbrae was not prospering to the degree it is now, and I was concentrating my time and energy on seeing that it did. In the circumstances it was not surprising that Una became resentful. I couldn't have been the easiest of husbands."

"And now you are reproaching yourself. Darling, don't. You had your own responsibilities to think of."

"Of which she was one."

"But her property was not your responsibility."

"Believe me, I would have made it so, had I been able to afford it. The sad thing is that now I am in a position to, it is too late—except by way of atonement."

"There is her brother . . ."

"No! It is up to me. I owe it to her. I could not live with my conscience unless I restored Faillie as she would have wished. I am ashamed to say that I was always thankful when she paid her annual visit here and left me alone at Carrisbrae; she had become increasingly neurotic—always ailing, complaining, fretful. Then, when she was expecting a child, she declared that when the time came it should be born at Faillie, not Carrisbrae. She also set her heart on having a daughter so that she would be the next Heretrix. She hated the thought of the succession passing into her brother's hands. I don't think she ever quite forgave him for decamping overseas."

"I don't think that was his intention. He felt that Una was rightly entitled to Faillie and everything

64

that went with it, and that he should fend for himself."

"How do you know that?"

"He told me."

"I wasn't aware that you knew him well enough for confidences."

I found it difficult to answer. Recalling our last conversation by the watchman's stone was not something I wished to do, for that meant recalling Duncan's warning not to marry Calum.

"He made no secret of the fact that Una was entitled to everything and he to nothing," I repeated. "If she felt that he had deserted her in some way, I am sure he has no knowledge of it."

"The fact that she bequeathed the place to me speaks for itself, and so he should realize. Possibly he does, but won't admit it. The bequest placed a trust upon me which I cannot pass on to someone else. You understand, don't you?"

"Yes, Calum."

"I knew you would. But I also want you to understand why I don't really like you spending your money on the place."

"But you have allowed me to clear those encroaching woods and create a rock garden."

"To humor you, my love."

"Thank you, Calum. But the moat—"

"The moat," he said firmly, "will be a big and costly project. I am sorry, my darling, but it must remain the last item of all." He glanced westward. The sun was beginning to move from its zenith. It would be light for several hours yet, for in this northern hemisphere darkness came late and dawn early, but to my disappointment Calum said it was time to return home. He had correspondence to deal with concerning Carrisbrae. "But there is no need for you to come too. Enjoy an evening ride—I know how much you love it."

I watched him ride away, his tall figure erect in the saddle. My love for him seemed to have taken on a new dimension, and my picture of Una was now vivid.

I rode on down the valley, across the waters of the Nairn, and up the opposite slope, so absorbed in thought that I paid no heed to direction until a massive boulder at the junction of four lanes made me realize where I was. This was Cumberland's Stone from whence it was believed the fat German had directed the infamous battle, and far in the distance was the Prince's Stone, from where his cousin, Charles Stuart, had done the same. How had they felt, those two closely related young men who had never met each other, the one so handsome with a weakness for drink, and the other so fat with a weakness for food? What had they thought as they witnessed the slaughter brought about by their enmity?

I regretted coming this way at a moment when I had been feeling happy. Since marrying Calum I had been untroubled by fancies or premonitions, but now I wanted to race back home to him for reassurance.

I passed the old cottage of Leanach hurriedly, because the sight of it recalled too vividly the battle which had raged around it and the part it had played. Some of the butchered had crawled inside for safety, only to be massacred by blood-crazed soldiers when the fighting was over. This was the beginning of the horrifying aftermath, but by some miracle the thatched bothy had survived whilst for miles around others were burned with their inhabitants and fugitives within.

Looking up, I now saw nothing but gray sky. All brightness had gone from the evening. I headed quickly toward Daviot, turning down to the valley again and back across the river. Dusk was descending as I passed through Craggiemore. I could see Daviot Church upon its hill, with the house called Daviot Lodge a little beyond.

As always, I glanced at the lodge as I approached. It was a mellow stone house, about the size of a small

English manor, and I had always liked it. A man named Alex McKenzie had lived there for many years, a prosperous merchant with a family of children older than myself, all long since married and scattered overseas. After his wife's death, old McKenzie had spent the rest of his life there, tending the gardens with pride, a contented man, grateful for all that life had given him. But now he was dead and I missed my frequent visits.

I halted for a moment outside the tall wrought-iron gates which the local smith had forged to the old man's design. In my imagination McKenzie's personality still lingered about the place, although it now stood empty, awaiting new ownership. I hoped it would be bought by someone who would love the house as McKenzie had done. Whoever they were, they would be our nearest neighbors and I would be able to visit them as of old.

"Good evening to you—Mistress of Faillie."

The voice startled me. I stared at the man who had opened the gates. It was Duncan Mackintosh.

"You look surprised," he added.

"I am indeed. What are you doing here?"

"Examining my property."

"*You* have bought this place?"

"Why the dismay? Is the thought of my living so close to Faillie distasteful to you?"

I had nothing to say. How could I admit that he was right? The proximity of this man would serve one purpose only—to remind me constantly that I was living in the castle which he considered rightfully his. Despite his assurance that so long as I lived at Faillie he would make no attempt to claim it, his nearness would be like a hound baying at my heels.

"When you choose to leave voluntarily, come and tell me," he had said. Such a thing would never happen. My marriage was happy; Faillie was my home and I would live there so long as my husband remained in possession. And Calum would never give it up. Why should he? I thought defensively.

"I hope you will be happy in Daviot Lodge, Mr.

Mackintosh. It has always been a happy house. I know it well."

"Then I trust you will renew your acquaintance with it whenever you wish—Mistress Huntly."

Not during *your* occupation, I thought passionately. I wanted to remember the place as it had been, ruled over by a friendly and welcoming old gentleman, not by this critical and watchful man.

I wanted to ride away quickly, but knew that my retreat must be dignified and polite. Anything less would betray my uneasiness, and to let Duncan Mackintosh know that he had the power to disturb me was something I wanted to avoid at all costs.

"You have been riding hard," he observed. "Perhaps you would care to accept my hospitality now and give that fine horse a chance to rest? The house is empty as yet, but we could sit in the garden awhile."

I thanked him, but declined. "He is a strong animal and we have only a short distance to go." I regretted the remark immediately, partly because it emphasized the proximity between this house and Faillie, and partly because it also emphasized my desire to be gone.

"As you wish, Mistress Huntly." His tone was indifferent. I was glad of that, for it gave me the opportunity to end the conversation. I murmured a polite good-evening and turned away. Then his voice arrested me.

"That is a very becoming habit you are wearing; I presume the material is a MacArthur weave. It would interest me greatly to know how your father obtained that tartan pattern."

"Why?" I asked coldly.

"Because it closely resembles an ancient one which has not been seen for many a year."

"That is not surprising. We are reviving authentic tartans at the mills."

"And from where did you get hold of them?"

"From a very reliable source," I retorted.

"That confirms what I thought," he answered cryptically.

I refused to ask what he meant, although there seemed to be an implication in his words which demanded it. Instead, I took my leave decisively.

"Beannachd leat, Mr. Mackintosh."

Farewell—as he had said to me after our first meeting. Nothing could be more final than that.

To my fury, he laughed.

"Beannachd leat, Witch of the Watchman's Stone." Then he added deliberately, "Haste ye back."

It was all I could do not to ride away furiously, but at least, I reflected as I departed at a deliberately slow and indifferent pace, I had turned my back upon the man.

Seven

CALUM WAS NOT in the least perturbed.

"We must invite him here, my love. There is absolutely no reason why the three of us should not be friends."

"I can see plenty of reason! He covets this place. He would have us out, if he could. He will be forever watchful of all that goes on."

"How can he be? Faillie is overlooked from no point whatever and, even if it were, he could only be pleased by all we are doing to it. Come now, you are letting your imagination run away with you."

"That sounds just like Mother! Letting my imagination run away with me was a pet phrase of hers. I feel that Duncan Mackintosh has bought Daviot Lodge solely to embarrass us."

"Then he is wasting his time. The property is mine. He has bought that house because he realizes he has no chance whatsoever of claiming Faillie, so Daviot

Lodge represents the next best thing. We can even afford to feel sorry for the man."

"You are too generous. He resents your ownership."

"At first he did, but by now he must have accepted it. And whether I am echoing your mother or not, I repeat that you are letting your imagination run away with you. You must accept him as a neighbor and as a friend. Dismiss from your mind all this nonsense about his motives."

I wished I could, but knew intuitively that in some fashion Duncan Mackintosh threatened my future.

I also knew that eventually I would have to do as my husband wished: welcome his brother-in-law to Faillie. Not only did Scottish hospitality demand it, but to do anything less would indicate my antagonism and mistrust.

But for the time being the matter could rest. He had not yet moved into the lodge; until he did, I could forget him. In this I was helped by an unexpected visit from my father the next evening, on a matter which drove everything else out of my mind. He arrived when we were changing for dinner.

I was surprised, for I believed him to be in Edinburgh. For the first time in years he had allowed himself to be lured away from Inverness to Scotland's capital city, Mother and Sheena accompanying him, but it was not for their sakes that he had gone. The King's visit was growing nearer. With it, demands for tartans were increasing, and talks with retail suppliers and tailors demanded his personal attention. So he had torn himself away from the mills, leaving James Macpherson to hold the fort.

When Hamish tapped on our door and announced that my father waited downstairs in the Billeting Room, I told Calum that I would go down to greet him, for my husband was busy with his neckcloth, a procedure which demanded prolonged attention.

"I didn't know you were expecting your father," Calum remarked absently, absorbed in his task.

"I wasn't, but I am delighted he has come." I hesitated, trying to calculate just how long that neckcloth

70

was likely to take tonight. "Hurry, won't you, darling? It is more than two weeks since we saw him . . ."

Calum was too engrossed to answer, and I deemed it wiser not to disturb him during a task of such supreme importance. As I turned away again I caught sight of my reflection in a long cheval mirror and was reminded of an occasion when Sheena had described me as striking and dramatic. For a fleeting moment I saw myself as my sister had seen me for, as then, I was wearing black—velvet, this time—my neck and shoulders bare. It was a style which became me well, and in that brief glance I observed the poise which marriage had so quickly given me.

But all this was dismissed from my mind when I saw my father. His face was serious. He kissed me affectionately but briefly, wasting no further time with greetings. "Ask your husband to be good enough to speak with me at once, my dear."

"What is it, Father? What is wrong?"

"Just fetch him, there's a good girl. Tell him the matter is important."

I went at once, feeling vaguely troubled.

Calum looked surprised and rather unwilling. "Why the urgency, Elizabeth? You know I cannot deal with my neckcloth hurriedly."

I refrained from pointing out that he had devoted nearly half an hour to it already. Instead, I offered to help, at which he brushed my hands aside, saying that the matter was one for masculine concentration. I had soon discovered that my husband had certain little vanities, of which this was one, but now I felt a stirring of impatience.

"Please hurry, Calum. Like Morag, Mother chafes if a meal is delayed. No doubt this is the reason for Father's urgency." But I had a definite premonition that it was far more serious than that.

He put what I hoped were the final touches, then stood back and surveyed his handiwork, which apparently satisfied him for he then turned to me with a contrite smile.

"Forgive my irritation, darling, but do try not to interrupt at such a vital moment again."

"I imagine my father has something much more vital on his mind. I haven't seen him look so serious for a long time."

Even then one last touch was necessary to complete my husband's toilet, the application of cologne, and as he attended to this further ritual he remarked indifferently, "I expect it is that flighty young sister of yours. No doubt she has been up to some caper in Edinburgh and he wishes to talk it over with another man. Since I am his son-in-law, it is natural that he should consult me on family matters."

But Sheena was not the object of Father's concern. He came to the point at once.

"Did you know the Sobieski Stuart brothers are in Edinburgh?"

"I did not, but I am not surprised. I imagined that might be their ultimate aim. Why the concern, sir?"

"Because the city is agog with news of this Latin manuscript, about which they are boasting but refusing to allow anyone to see."

"That also fails to surprise me. I told you at the outset that I had paid well for the contents."

"Some of the contents, I understood you to say."

"That is correct."

"And now these men are supplying tartan designs to other manufacturers, all outlined in their ancient manuscript and named for individual clans, or so they claim."

"And you are worried in case they clash with yours? They cannot, because they no longer possess the ones they sold to me. As I predicted, you are first in the field with them. Your apprehension is quite unfounded. Since you have these particular designs exclusively, no other manufacturer can produce tartans bearing the same names."

There was logic in Calum's argument, but my father merely replied that he had already thought of that. "Nevertheless, I am anxious. Their claim to Royal birth is of no interest to me, but their claim to possessing irrefutable knowledge of ancient clan tartans, the source of which they now decline to show to anyone, most definitely is—particularly since it is the source from which our own designs came. And I gather they have been in Scotland some weeks, battening onto Edinburgh society and doing very well for themselves. Where did you say you met them? And when?"

"In Austria. Vienna, to be exact. A year or more ago." There was a chilly note in my husband's voice, but he continued civilly, "I assure you, you have no cause for anxiety."

"I wish I could be so certain. Under pressure, the brothers allowed Sir Walter Scott to see just one page of their alleged document. He pronounced the Latin as 'dubious.' I don't like the idea of any MacArthur designs emanating from such a doubtful source. I want to see that manuscript myself. It may surprise you to know that I, too, can read Latin."

"It doesn't surprise me in the least. I have the greatest respect for your scholarship."

My father shot a keen glance from beneath his bushy eyebrows, as if suspecting that my husband mocked him, but Calum's clear regard reassured him.

"You desire me to arrange a meeting with these two men? That is the object of your visit, I take it."

"That is correct."

"I shall be pleased to do so. I will travel to Edinburgh tomorrow and seek them out. They will not refuse; they are under too great an obligation to me. Nor would they wish it to be known that at one time they were in such an impoverished state that they needed my financial help."

I was shocked into protest.

"You mean you would threaten to spread that story? But that would be tantamount to blackmail!"

"No, my love. Business."

"I have never used threat of any kind in business," my father rapped out. "Arrange a meeting with them, by all means, but not by any despicable means."

Calum rapped back, "I have given you my promise to arrange a meeting. I will keep that promise."

73

"*And* that I shall see the entire manuscript, not merely one page of it. The meeting will serve no useful purpose otherwise. And I would also like to see the actual pages you purchased from these men."

"Alas, in that I cannot oblige you. I destroyed them after transcription, for they served no further purpose. But rest assured that I shall do all I can to set your mind at ease."

My father accepted this reassurance with a curt nod, turned on his heel, and marched from the room. I remained quite still as his heavy footfall faded into silence.

"Come, Elizabeth, we must dine. Here is Morag, waiting patiently. As you yourself remarked a few minutes ago, she hates a good meal to be spoiled."

And there she was, standing discreetly in the shadows. How long had she been there?

I felt my husband's hand beneath my elbow and made no resistance when he led me to the Banqueting Hall, although my instinct was to draw away. In my heart lay a foreboding stronger than I had experienced for a long time.

Eight

THERE WAS A constraint between us for the rest of the evening, and I was convinced Morag was aware of it. Although she kept up her usual flow of smooth conversation (it was at mealtimes that she made me very much aware that she was one of the family), I was conscious of the perceptiveness of those opaque eyes. I was also conscious of Calum's unusual silence, and knew that she was too. Her glance continually slid from one to the other of us, as if sizing up the situation and speculating upon it.

When at last we were alone in our room, Calum said gently, "Don't look so unhappy, my dear. I shall set your father's mind at rest."

"I know but it distressed me to hear the two of you quarrel. I care for you both very much."

"But more greatly for me, surely? Therefore, my viewpoint must come first with you."

Somehow I felt I was being cornered.

"I care for you in a different way. My father and I have always been very close. Marriage makes no difference to the quality of affection between a father and daughter."

"But it does make a difference to her loyalties— or should."

"You make that sound like a reproach. I don't recall taking sides. I saw both."

"That is unfortunate, for I expect you to see only mine."

"Isn't that being selfish?"

"I don't consider it so. It is a wife's duty to concede to her husband's views—"

"—and to have no mind of her own?" I interrupted.

"I wasn't going to say that. In any case," he added affectionately, "I knew when I married you that you were a young woman very much with a mind of her own, but now you are my wife I consider you should put my views first."

"But I could see my father's viewpoint also."

"Even his mistrust of me?"

"He has never mistrusted you. Nor does he now, I am sure."

"But he doubts me, which is the same thing. I find that insulting."

"He doubts those two men. They may be genuine, they may be adventurers—who can tell? As for insulting you, my father has never insulted anyone. He is too kind."

"Even so, when I allay his doubts, I shall expect an apology from him."

"Won't allaying his doubts be sufficient satisfaction?"

"Don't spoil your lovely face with a frown, Elizabeth."

"Don't give me cause to!"

He kissed me, but I was in no mood to respond. The thought of his demanding an apology from my father displeased me too much, and I was still troubled with a sense of foreboding which refused to be stifled.

Calum gave me a long, hard look, then put both arms about me in a grip so strong that I could not escape. His lips came down upon mine again, compelling surrender, and because I could never resist him I finally yielded.

"Sometimes I wish I didn't love you so much," I murmured at last.

"Don't ever love me less," he warned.

But love such as mine gave him too much power over me. The thought came spontaneously, shocking me a little. He seemed to be demanding total allegiance to the exclusion of everyone else.

"You surely cannot be jealous of my affection for my own father?"

"Of course not, so long as your first loyalty is to your husband."

But I had other loyalties too, and saw no reason why they should conflict. Tonight they had.

I wasn't totally happy when we went to bed, but Calum loved me so passionately that any lingering trace of doubt or anxiety was dispelled. And with it went my feeling of foreboding.

Before he left for Edinburgh, my husband insisted that I was to worry in no way at all. "And try to reassure your father. I am sorry for losing patience with him—like you, I do understand how he feels. I should have controlled my reaction. You must forgive me, Elizabeth."

The shadow between us might never have existed. I kissed him warmly and begged him to return soon.

"As soon as I possibly can, that I promise. This

76

parting isn't something I look forward to. Nor do I like the thought of your being lonely in my absence."

"I shall keep busy. I shall go to the mills. Father will like that."

"An excellent idea. And make him see how totally unfounded his anxiety is. Make him trust me, Elizabeth."

"I've told you—it isn't you he mistrusts."

My father was already striding down the long weaving shed when I reached the mills.

"Look at them!" he shouted, above the clatter of the looms. "Have you ever seen so many working at once? Soon we will have to install more. The problem is how to make room for them."

"We must extend the premises, sir." It was James Macpherson who spoke. As he did so we left the clatter of the shed behind us and sought the quieter region of his office. Beyond it was my father's. Between them, they were responsible for the entire running of the mills.

Mugs of strong tea were brought in and I suddenly realized how glad I was to be back. Marriage had absorbed me but with Calum away—how lucky I was to have this place to come to!

When we had finished our tea, I walked with my father through the checking room, where rows of women carefully scrutinized every yard of woven material, rectifying by hand any slightly misplaced thread or minute fault, discarding any fabric that did not completely match up to MacArthur's standards. These lengths would be sold more cheaply than the rest, and lesser retailers would travel for miles to buy them direct from the mills, for the amount of material slightly below standard was limited and competition to get hold of it was keen. Few mills were as meticulous as ours. I knew well enough that material rejected by MacArthur's would have passed muster elsewhere. It was on our pride in perfection that our reputation had been built.

This integrity was at the root of my father's present

concern, and when we reached the final room where new weaves were on display, I well understood it, for there hung the tartans in all their glory, colors warm and glowing as only pure vegetable dyes can produce. Some Lowland weavers were already experimenting with chemicals which, they predicted, would eventually replace all vegetable dyes, but the results were vivid and harsh, not soft and muted as real tartans should be.

"What do you think of them, Ealasaid?"

"They are beautiful! You have every reason to be proud, and absolutely none for concern. Looking at this array is almost like looking at the whole pageant of tartan history."

"Has Calum gone to Edinburgh?"

"He left first thing this morning. He has your interests at heart."

"I know. I know. He must forgive my agitation last night."

"I am sure he understood it." I jerked my memory away from the feeling of alarm which had haunted me after my father's visit and recalled only Calum's assuring words when he departed this morning. "In any case," I continued, "tartans are tartans, even if newly designed. You know as well as I that a clan tartan is no less of a clan tartan if, for any reason, a design is lost and a clan adopts another, or has another created for them." I broke off realizing that I was actually quoting Calum.

"But we have announced that we are producing designs of genuine antiquity," my father insisted

"And so we are. And Calum will prove it." I pointed out that we had been sufficiently convinced when examining the delineations of the various setts. "Perhaps it would have been better to have demanded stronger proof at that time, instead of embarrassing my husband now."

My father tugged his upper lip in a slight shamefaced fashion, glanced at me from beneath his bushy eyebrows in that characteristic way of his, and nodded. "Are you cross with me, Ealasaid?"

I laughed, threw my arms about him, and hugged him tightly.

"I should be. You upset me last night."

"Didn't mean to," he muttered guiltily, "but in view of all this gossip in Edinburgh, can you blame me?"

"Yes, you wicked man. You should have faith in your son-in-law."

"As you have. You have implicit faith in him, haven't you, my dear?"

"Isn't it natural? Shouldn't a woman have faith in her husband?"

"She should indeed," he agreed. "And now, why not come home with me for the noonday meal? I usually have something with James in his office; his wife brings a good hot meal across, which saves me time and puts something in her purse, but a family reunion would be enjoyable and your mother will be glad to see you."

"And Sheena?"

"She too, if she has any sense. Not that the lass has a great deal, but I think the trip to Edinburgh did her good. She saw old friends, went to balls, and escaped from your mother's dull sisters—which, alas, was more than I was able to do, once the day's business was over."

I laughed. My aunts—Moira and Fiona—were neither as pretty nor as bright as their names. Stuffy, Sheena called them, and stuffy they were.

"Poor Father! Never mind, you are back in harness again."

"Thank God for that!" He led me outside to his phaeton. Later, I would return for my own carriage. I saw Hamish pacing the horses. He looked less surly than usual and his face even brightened a little on seeing my father. He also doffed his hat without displaying any dislike of such subservience.

"I take it Calum has driven himself to Edinburgh?"

"Yes, he likes to. And I'm afraid he finds Hamish rather slow."

"Well, I'm glad to see he still employs the old man."

"Naturally he does. Calum says we have a duty to family retainers, a fact which I sometimes think Hamish doesn't appreciate. He's a surly fellow."

"You must make allowances, my dear. The man has served only Mackintoshes in the whole of his life, and no doubt finds it difficult to bend the knee to outsiders."

"Calum isn't an outsider."

"Anyone but a Mackintosh at Faillie must be an outsider to Hamish."

"Then as far as I am concerned he can go and serve a Mackintosh at Daviot Lodge."

Father handed me into the phaeton, then climbed up beside me and picked up the reins. "Daviot Lodge?" he echoed. "Who has bought it?"

"Duncan Mackintosh, and he has wasted no time in moving in. I saw furniture being installed as I drove here this morning."

"You sound as if you don't like the idea. Why, lass?"

"Because I don't like him."

"For what reason?"

"He has an eye on Faillie. He thinks it should right-fully be his."

"Well, it has always been in his branch of the Mackintosh family, and was once his home. He was born there. Perhaps one cannot blame him. His sister was Heretrix, I know, but she left no children."

"She bequeathed Faillie to my husband. It passed out of Mackintosh hands."

"In that case," my father answered benignly, "you should not resent Duncan Mackintosh making his home nearby." He flicked the reins, turned the horses' heads, and moved slowly across the mill yard. "Personally, I like Duncan. Your mother does too. She has had him to supper several times. I think she now regards him as a desirable suitor for Sheena. A man who has made a fortune out of gold would make a more acceptable son-in-law than a boat-builder who hasn't yet reached the top of the tree and who, moreover, has responsibilities to younger brothers."

"Mother is forever matchmaking!"

My father laughed, agreeing with me. Then he added, "Don't worry about Daviot Lodge, my dear. Duncan will make a worthy successor to old McKenzie."

I made no reply, merely asking him to pause for a moment as we passed Hamish. "He should have something to eat while waiting for me. Perhaps he could have your share of Mistress Macpherson's cooking?"

My father agreed, and told the old man to go along to Macpherson's office.

"It was your mistress' idea, not mine," he added, at which Hamish actually had the grace to thank me with a tilt of the mouth which, with a stretch of imagination, could have been taken for a smile.

It was strange to return to Faillie and find Calum absent. The castle had a desolate air which somehow revived my old impression of the place, and although I had become accustomed to driving across the causeway without even glancing at the bog beneath, I did so now, repelled by its inky blackness. My footsteps seemed to echo forlornly as I mounted the stairs from the Banqueting Hall and turned along the corridor to my room, the emptiness of which seemed to emphasize my loneliness, and when I had shed my cloak and bonnet I went downstairs again and out into the grounds. I was eager to escape from the silence of the castle and now wished that I had persuaded Calum to take me with him to Edinburgh.

I walked briskly across the courtyard and then across a lawn which had been unkempt when I first came to Faillie, but was now improving rapidly. Other things were also improving. Thickets were being cleared and dead trees removed. I paused for a while, watching the men at work, and it was then that I noticed the man in charge: a dark, gypsy-like person to whom I had deliberately paid no attention because every instinct made me wary of him. Now it was impossible to ignore him because he was standing, arms akimbo, staring at me blatantly, a bold look on his face which clearly bespoke strong sensuality. If Calum had been present the man would never have dared look at me like that. He needed to be put firmly in his place, I decided, and so I commanded him to come to me. He obeyed, sauntering over with a leisurely stride and a smirk on his face.

"Why aren't you working?"

"But I am, Mistress. I am Supervisor, not a laborer."

"Then I should turn your attention to the work in hand, since that is what you are employed for, otherwise I shall report your negligence to the laird."

"The laird?" He spoke in a drawl that held too much self-confidence. "But the laird wouldn't dismiss me, if that is what you are imagining, Mistress. I've been part of his household too long."

"His household?"

"Aye, Mistress. I came with him from Deeside." The man touched his forelock with a gesture that should have indicated servility, but somehow suggested insolence. "The laird would never part with me. Never."

I watched him slouch away disrespectfully, and even thought I heard him quietly laughing.

So the man came from Carrisbrae. And yet his manner and air of self-confidence were out of keeping with the position of a servant. Even the way in which he touched his forelock seemed a mockery. I experienced a flickering apprehension, an instinct which told me to watch this man and to beware of him—and, at all costs, never to be alone with him.

I walked briskly to the kitchen garden, where I saw Morag stooping over a patch of herbs which she cultivated with care. This was her own small domain and no gardener was allowed to touch it. She grew mint and parsley, sage and marjoram, basil and orris. There were others, not used in cooking, whose names I did not know, that she grew for medicinal purposes. Calum scorned her belief in tisanes and elixirs, declaring that the smell of her brews alone was enough to make a person feel unwell. "Then she can doctor them and congratulate herself on their recovery!"

It was true that some of her concoctions were slightly odorous, but all herbs gave out certain aromas when infused, and Morag's cures had proved effective more than once. She had treated me for a head cold that cleared in record time with the aid of a particular tisane; she sometimes treated Hamish for stomach troubles—the man was prone to dyspepsia, a contributory cause of his ill temper, I thought—and she had cured a stable boy of warts by the simple process of applying the sap of milkweed.

As I approached, Morag looked up with a smile which had no welcome in it, but I asked without hesitation whether she knew the names of any of the staff at Carrisbrae.

Something flickered in her opaque eyes.

"Carrisbrae?" She jerked. "Why do you ask?"

"Because there is a man supervising outside work here who tells me he comes from there. A dark, insolent man."

"Insolent? I have never found Guthrie insolent. Of course, people adapt their manners to those they meet. No servant would dare be insolent to me."

Not by a flicker of an eyelid did I let her see that the shaft had gone home.

"Guthrie—so that's his name. The man is too sure of himself. I shall ask for him to be sent away, despite the fact that he believes himself to be indispensable."

"He—said that?"

"He said that my husband would never dismiss him, which amounts to the same thing." I turned my attention to the herb garden and asked at random for the names of several plants which were unfamiliar to me. Morag actually seemed pleased, and hurriedly pointed to one saying, "That is hyssop. A very ancient plant, mentioned in the Bible. 'Purge me with Hyssop and I shall be clean,' David said, so if the Bible recommends it, it must be good, don't you think?"

Checking a smile, I agreed, although the idea of being purged held little appeal.

"And this?" My eye was caught by a pretty yellow flower with finely toothed leaves. I stooped and rubbed them between my fingers, as I often did with mint and thyme and verbena, whose fragrance I liked. I sniffed my fingertips, then wiped them immediately on a handkerchief, for the smell this time was bitter.

"Not too pleasant, is it, Elizabeth? But a most efficacious plant."

"What is it called, and what is it used for?"

"Its name is tansy, and it has many uses: the sap for poultices to soothe rheumatic pains and chest complaints, also for reducing inflammation of the skin caused by nettle stings and such, and the leaves for tea in treatment of the stomach. I am afraid the odor will linger on your fingers for quite a while. I should have warned you. It is pungent but perfectly harmless."

"It will wash off," I said. "And this?" I indicated a cluster of flowers which were familiar. "Haven't I seen them hanging up to dry in the scullery?"

"Yes. Chamomile. I have a nightly cup of chamomile tea; it helps me to sleep."

"Are you a bad sleeper, Morag?"

"I have become so, since my husband died."

"And how long ago was that?"

"More than five years. But time is not the great healer it is claimed to be. I still miss him sadly."

I felt a swift pang of pity. She was a lonely woman and, as the third member of our household, was no doubt acutely conscious of being the odd one out.

I said spontaneously, "I think you have lost interest in yourself, Morag. You could——" I broke off in embarrassment.

"Make more of myself? Is that what you were going to say? But I have never been a good-looking woman, like you. The first time I saw you I thought you one of the most striking young women I had ever seen, and so did my cousin—I could tell. I was not in the least surprised that he wanted to marry you."

"Then you were the only person who was not! Everyone thought he preferred my sister."

"How could he? Sheena is a pretty little thing, but Calum prefers women with more character. He would have found such prettiness as hers empty and boring in time. I would rather be like you than any other woman in the world!"

She spoke so passionately that I was startled.

"You underrate yourself, Morag. I am sure that if you made an effort you would be handsome indeed."

"For whose benefit?" she demanded bitterly. "For a dead husband? Or are you suggesting I should try to entice another? You want to be rid of me, perhaps?"

"Morag!"

"Don't sound so surprised. I have been aware from the beginning that you don't want me here."

"That isn't true."

"I'm not so sure. You wasted no time in making it plain that you were now Mistress of Faillie."

"Didn't you expect things to change?"

She evaded that and continued bitterly, "You must surely realize that a woman in my present position can have little opportunity to meet eligible men—except among the servants. A butler? A valet? I would find neither socially acceptable. My husband was a gentleman. Do you imagine I could be happy with someone who was content to serve others; to carry trays, press his master's clothes, or preside over the servants' hall?"

"Of course not."

"Then what other fate is there for me now that I am relegated to a menial position?"

"You are talking nonsense! Your position is anything but menial. You still live as one of the family, dine with us, meet our guests . . ."

"But in the background. I am only tolerated at your table and treated like a superior servant by guests. Before you came, I acted as Calum's hostess."

"Because he was unmarried. Now he has a wife."

"I am very much aware of that. As I say, it has been made plain from the start."

I refrained from pointing out that it was Calum who had first been responsible for that.

"Can't we be friends?" I pleaded. "I want to be friends."

"I can believe that. Every crofter on the moors knows how 'friendly' you are. Every millworker too, I have no doubt."

The sarcasm was unmistakable—also the implication. My anger rose, but I suppressed it and answered coolly that I would take my evening meal in my room.

"Send it up at seven," I added, deliberately refraining from putting the order in the form of a request. "And I hope you will welcome additions to your wardrobe. We are not so greatly different in height or figure, but I know you are clever with your needle and could carry out any necessary alterations."

"You are too kind." The sarcasm was still there, but this time it was defensive. Even so, she could not refrain from adding, with an air of self-martyrdom, that a woman in her position needed few clothes. "A serviceable morning dress, a slightly better one for afternoons, and something a shade more elegant for evening. It is, of course, totally unnecessary for a poor relation to impress your guests, but if a refusal would offend you, I will naturally accept."

On that note of antagonism, we parted. It was plain that my desire for friendship was not reciprocated.

I felt restless, disturbed, and unable to settle to anything as I went indoors, so I decided to explore the unoccupied Keep, which I had not yet seen.

The plan of the castle was compact. From the Banqueting Hall one could proceed to the battlements by way of a heavy, studded door near the top of the spiral stairs leading to the upper floor, our bedroom floor. I opened this door now and stood on the ramparts awhile, looking down on the main forecourt with its arched entrance leading from the causeway. This entrance had once contained a portcullis. When the portcullis was lowered, the besieged withdrew and held the inner fortress. Calum had explained this to me during one of our evening walks. To view the sunset from the battlements was something we both enjoyed, but walking here alone was not to my liking, and I turned away.

In doing so, I looked across an inner courtyard to the Keep, now empty. The turrets were badly in need of repair, and the long flight of steps that had once led up from the courtyard to the entrance was completely broken away, leaving a high drop above rough stony ground. One would need a ladder to climb up there, and a dangerous approach it was, for the ancient door hung agape, broken on its hinges. But then I recalled that the round tower could be reached by a passage from within the castle. I retraced my steps to this passage, which was approached through a door directly facing the top of the stairs. The corridor was angled and flanked on one side by bedrooms, the other consisting of a stone wall containing mullioned windows overlooking the inner courtyard. Both the passage and the bedrooms leading from it formed a sort of bridge linking the Keep with the main part of the castle.

Like the door leading onto the battlements, the inner entrance to the Keep was also of studded oak, with large iron hinges and a heavy iron lock in which a rusty key looked as if it had not been turned for centuries. But it was unnecessary to turn it, for the door was unlocked.

It groaned heavily as I pushed it open. A smell of mustiness, damp, and disuse met me, and I knew at once why Calum had never brought me here. I had emerged into the top room of the tower, which was bitterly cold, with parts of the floor rotten with age. I stepped carefully as I descended to the rooms below, all of which proved to be empty, and as cold as the main one above. It was hard to believe that at one time maintenance supplies had been housed here.

I shivered, disliking the atmosphere, and promptly retraced my steps, but mounting the stairs was as alarming as descending them, and I stumbled more than once as pieces of stone fell away beneath my feet. I had been stupid to venture here alone, and if I sprained an ankle I'd have only myself to blame. I could picture myself lying amid fallen masonry, my cries unheard, slowly freezing to death. Mother was right. My imagination had always been too vivid.

But it wasn't imagination that alarmed me when at last I reached the door leading back to warmth and safety.

It was locked.

At first I was too stunned to believe it; then incredulity gave way to annoyance. I hammered upon the solid oak, calling for help until I was beating with both fists in frustration.

I took deep breaths to steady myself. Giving way to panic would be senseless, for someone must rescue me. Beyond that door was an entire household; I would be missed, searched for, and found. All I had to do was to keep on calling and hammering . . . calling and hammering . . .

I did so until my fists were sore, my shoulders aching, my voice hoarse. Temporarily, I gave up, leaning my back against the door to rest. It was then that I saw the window on the opposite side of the round room. It was set in a small Gothic arch, half broken. From that side of the tower it must overlook the inner courtyard. If I could reach the deep sill, haul myself up, and shout through the broken lead lights, one of the grooms or stable boys must surely hear me, for their quarters were down there.

But light was fading rapidly. I had not realized how much time had passed. Judging by the quality of the light, the hour was late. Why had no one missed me? Darkness was descending, making it all the more difficult to pick my way across the rotted floor. One false step and I would fall through it to my death, crashing to the stone floor of the lofty room below.

Somehow I reached the window. I could touch the sill with my fingertips, but could get no grip to haul myself up; tall as I was, that window eluded me, for it was placed high in the wall. I stood below it, calling helplessly. Ahead of me spread the long, dark night, imprisoning me in this horrible place . . .

A sound jerked my head round. I could see nothing, but the sound was followed by another. And another. Something brushed against my foot. I screamed as rat after rat scurried across the floor in the darkness, and every story I had ever heard of the savageness of these creatures came back to me, triggering off hysteria.

"Get me out of here! Get me out of here! GET ME OUT!"

A shout from below penetrated my terror. Was it an answering call, or my imagination playing tricks?

"Mistress! *Mistress!* Where are ye?"

It was Hamish, calling from below. I cried out in answer and he shouted to me to stay right where I was. "We'll be there in no time, Mistress!"

But it seemed nearly an hour before the key grated in the lock and light from a flickering candle spilled a path toward me.

Morag held it, and behind her stood Hamish. He pushed past her unceremoniously, his hands held out to me. Carefully, he led me from the place and Morag closed the heavy door behind us. I was back in a warm, safe world again.

"My dear Elizabeth, whatever made you venture there?"

The concern in Morag's voice seemed genuine, but I felt too spent to answer. I passed a shaking hand across my face and pushed back my disordered hair, only realizing when I looked at my hands how much dirt I had collected.

Hamish snapped, "This is no time to ask stupid questions, woman. Get the lass to bed."

Even in my shaken condition I was aware of Morag's anger; no servant had the right to speak to her in such a way. But I had the old man to thank for my rescue and, as Morag took my arm and led me to my room, I did thank him, uncaring whether she approved or not.

She helped me to undress, dropping my gown on the floor distastefully. I could hardly blame her, for it was in a worse condition than I had realized—not only dirty but torn. I was altogether a sorry sight and, in such a state, I was also at a disadvantage—the Mistress of Faillie looking like an unkempt gypsy.

A hip-bath was brought in, then wooden buckets of steaming water. Morag departed to brew one of her tisanes; a special one, she said, which would help me to sleep. I sank into the water gratefully, and remained there until I heard her returning. By the time she reached the door I was cocooned in the depths of a big towel. Somehow the situation was reminiscent of a child and its nurse. At any moment I expected to be scolded for my escapade. And I was.

"You behaved very stupidly, Elizabeth."

"The person to be blamed for stupidity is the person who locked that door," I retorted, as I buttoned my long flounced nightdress. In the mirror I saw her eyes taking in every detail of it—the lace and the ribbons and the frills. It was also of very flimsy material, and her eyes didn't miss that, either. Was she envious, or merely disapproving? As always, it was hard to read her inscrutable face.

When I was in bed she gave me the tisane, and I sipped it obediently but absently, for I was still thinking about that locked door.

"I shall find out who did it," I declared. "If it was some sort of practical joke, the joker will have to answer to Calum."

She replied calmly that it was no practical joke. "I locked that door because it was my duty to do so. The door of the Keep is always kept locked. Surely you knew that?"

"It wasn't when I went in. And why should it be kept locked?"

"Because anyone could climb through that gaping aperture leading into the place from outside, and thus into the castle. Before retiring each night I check that all doors leading to outer access are secured. We don't want thieves breaking in."

"And you didn't hear me moving about inside?"

"Through that solid door and those thick walls?" Her eyebrows raised, as if astonished by such a ridiculous question.

"But you must have missed me at dinner?"

"You told me to send it to your room. I sent a tray up precisely at seven—as you ordered."

"Who brought it?"

"One of the maids."

"And she didn't tell you I wasn't here?"

"She probably thought you were in your boudoir."

That was logical enough, but I was still puzzled.

"If the door of the Keep is kept permanently locked," I said, "then *someone* must have opened it and forgotten to lock it behind them. Who could possibly want to go into that empty tower? And why?"

"Hamish. He seems to imagine that his late mistress left him to guard Faillie. He periodically inspects the whole of the castle. Calum humors him. It does no harm. But he should lock the door of the Keep when he leaves the place. I must reprimand him about that. *And* about his impertinence to me."

I handed her the empty cup and thanked her for the tisane, then found myself speaking up in defense of Hamish. "But for him I would have spent the night in the Keep, for I would certainly have been unable to climb down through the open courtyard entrance without breaking my neck. So his abrupt manner should be overlooked, Morag. He was concerned about me." I finished lightly, "With two such able guard dogs about the place, I shall sleep well tonight."

"Guard dogs?"

"Yourself and Hamish."

But she didn't share my small joke. I felt that nothing I ever said or did would either please or amuse her.

As I expected, the days were happier than the nights. I saw more of my father, more of my family, and Sheena's manner toward me eased somewhat, although I felt we would never regain the intimacy of our earlier relationship. But at least Angus Fraser was hopeful once more.

"She does spare time to talk to me occasionally. Not here in your father's library, of course—your mother's eagle eye prevents that—but sometimes she walks through the village and lingers at the boatyard."

"You love her very much, don't you, Angus?"

"I have never loved anyone else, nor ever will. If any man hurt a hair of her head, he'd have me to reckon with."

"And I suppose you consider that *I* hurt her?"

"Not deliberately. It was no fault of yours that you married the man she wanted."

"But you condemn him."

"He should never have raised her hopes—for that I condemn him, yes."

It was useless to point out that Calum had done so unwittingly. The past was past; only the present and the future were important.

I paid daily visits to the mills, which pleased James Macpherson as well as Aindreas. "Your father has missed ye, Miss Elizabeth." James still called me Miss Elizabeth as of old, and I didn't mind, for I knew that this was how he and other workers at the mills would always think of me.

"I don't know who is the more dedicated—you or my father," I said. "The mills are your life as much as his."

"Aye, they are indeed."

He was a bluff, honest man, an able man, but a man of few words. Rather solemn and somewhat lacking in humor, perhaps, but none the less admirable for that.

On the Sunday following Calum's departure for Edinburgh I decided to go riding with my father after church. It was four days since my husband had gone and all being well he could be back at Faillie before the week was out. This Sunday was likely to be the

92

only one on which Aindreas and I could ride together as of old.

The morning was brilliant, one of those rare Highland days unspoiled by mist, when the hills stood out sharply against the sky and every birdcall echoed like a bell. As Hamish drove me to Clachnaharry I gazed from the carriage as on that evening which now seemed so long ago, feasting my eyes upon the earth I loved. With the hood of the carriage down, I missed nothing.

So it was inevitable that as we descended the hill into Daviot I should see Daviot Lodge. It seemed to have come alive again after a long sleep, its windows open wide to sun and air, just as it had been in old McKenzie's day. Its lawns were trim again and, even though it was the Sabbath, gardeners were at work and Duncan Mackintosh, shirtsleeves rolled up, was digging close to the entrance gates and looked up as I approached. He paused with one foot on the spade. I saw tanned, muscular arms and a strong throat beneath the open neck of his shirt, all evidence of hard physical work in the past.

I was glad he was wasting no time in restoring the gardens which had been the pride of McKenzie's heart, and guessed that he must be paying his workers well, for nothing else would have enticed them to labor on the Sabbath and thus earn the disapproval of their neighbors and the Kirk. Obviously, such disapproval meant nothing to the man who employed them.

His glance was unavoidable. I bowed, and he bowed in return. I detected his usual irony, both in his bow and his smile. Was he challenging the Mistress of Faillie to frown upon his defiance of the Sabbath laws? If so, he was disappointed, for I smiled nonchalantly in return and called "good day" as I drove on. Then something arrested me. I stared at the man working alongside him. It was Guthrie, and his dark face was looking at me with customary boldness.

What was he doing in Duncan Mackintosh's employ, and why should it disturb me? The man was free to work elsewhere in his spare time, and I had no proof that the new owner of Daviot Lodge had deliberately sought him out but, as always, whatever Duncan Mackintosh did made me troubled and suspicious.

Nine

AFTER ATTENDING the ten o'clock service in the little Presbyterian church, I went back to my parents' house and changed into a riding habit I had worn before marriage. It was neither as elegant nor as costly as those Calum had since chosen for me, but wearing it again took me back to my girlhood, for this was the habit my father had liked me in best of all—the skirt of sage green, with a matching jacket in velvet. Of old, I would have let my hair blow free, for I loved the feel of the wind through it, but now I coiled it neatly on the nape of my neck. "It is more suitable for a sedate married woman," I said, at which my father laughed.

"You will never be sedate, my Ealasaid, and I would never have you be. So untie it, young woman, and let me see you as you once were."

"Have I changed so much?"

"Marriage always changes a woman, but in your case not for the worse. It has beautified you."

"Mother has never held my looks in much regard. I hope she thinks a little better of them now."

"Yours isn't a conventional beauty, but the kind a man appreciates. You are a man's woman, and Calum is lucky to have you."

"You are biased in my favor."

"Perhaps—but not entirely. I can view both my children objectively and love them equally. Sheena is still as pretty as a picture, although she has lost weight. But it will come back in time."

"Is she still fretting over Calum?"

"It is hard to tell, which is surprising because at one time her emotions were all too obvious." He frowned slightly and I wondered if he were worried about my sister.

"You mean she is taking longer to get over it than you anticipated?" I asked.

"I fear so."

"But she is seeing Angus again. Not at home, of course, but at the boatyard, a fact which pleases him."

"It pleases me too." Aindreas lifted his face to the sun. "What a beautiful day! And there'll be no deer-stalkers around in weather like this. They need rain and mist to aid them."

It was a wonderful day for a ride, though I was sorry to see my father turn toward the melancholy battlefield of Culloden.

Automatically, we slowed as we passed the graves of the clans. Even our horses seemed to step more softly, as if aware that they were treading sacred ground. Their footfalls were muffled by heather and the screen of surrounding trees.

We scarcely spoke until Culloden House came into view. In the old castle which had once stood on the site, now replaced by a stately new building designed like an English manor, the Prince had snatched a hasty night's sleep on the eve of the battle. The site of this house marked the end of this unhappy stretch of earth, and I expected that my oppression would now lift.

Instead, it deepened. I felt as if a warning hand were reaching out to clutch my horse's bridle and bring it to a halt.

I cried out urgently, "Father—let us go another way!"

He had pulled ahead of me and now looked back over his shoulder in surprise.

"Why, my dear?" Something in my face made him ask what was amiss. "I know you don't like crossing Drummossie," he continued, "but if we go back we must recross it and return the way we came. It will also take longer."

He was thinking of Mother, of course, and the good Sabbath meal awaiting us. Neither should be kept waiting. But still I was reluctant.

"We could turn off here and head toward Meall Mor . . ."

"A detour, and longer still. My dear Ealasaid, what is wrong?"

Nothing, I assured him, unwilling to admit that I had no grounds for changing our route other than a powerful premonition that it was dangerous not to do so.

"Then come," he cried boisterously. "I'll race you to the top of Saddle Hill!"

I had no choice but to accept the challenge, for his horse was dancing impatiently, and mine was restive too. Then both were off and away, breaking at once to a canter and then into a neck-and-neck gallop. I had no time now for fears and fancies and was soon laughing exultantly. As my father flashed ahead I called after him that he had an unfair advantage with a horse like Rufus—a wild creature that he had broken to the bit himself. They made an unbeatable pair, and I was not surprised when the distance between us lengthened.

That was how I last saw my father, coattails flying, gray hair lifting in the wind, thundering ahead of me to the crest of the hill; a powerful man on a powerful beast, vigorous and full of life. Then a shot rang out as he reached the peak. Against the sky, I saw him crash from the saddle.

Rufus, startled, went galloping on, stirrups and martingale flying. Every detail of that moment will be etched on my memory forever: the terrifying screech of the horse and the thunder of its hooves as it fled, and the fearful thump of my father's body as it hit the ground.

He was lying quite still when I reached him. In a flash I was out of the saddle and on my knees beside him. He looked up, tried to smile, and failed. Gently I lifted his head onto my lap.

He gasped hoarsely, *"Some—damned—poacher!"* His voice broke on an agonized cough. His head lolled sideways, his mouth fell open, and a sudden spurt of red splashed across the green of my skirt.

I stared at it. So did he. I could see it, but he could not.

Ten

THE WHOLE WORLD was still, and I with it. A terrible numbness possessed me so that I remained where I was, unconscious of time. It might have been minutes or hours before I looked up from that spreading splash of red upon green and saw a man standing above me, gun in hand.

It was Duncan Mackintosh, and at the sight of him my stunned brain burst into life.

"You did it. *YOU* DID IT!" The words were accompanied by wild and uncontrollable sobs which seemed dry in my throat and harsh in my ears.

He stooped and closed my father's eyes, then laid his head softly upon the earth and covered his dead face with a jacket. His own jacket. I saw his discarded gun upon the ground and, without realizing what I did, I snatched it up and pointed it at him. Calmly, he took it from me.

"It hasn't been fired, Ealasaid. You can examine it for yourself."

I was incapable of doing so. Not only my hands but my whole body was shaking. Duncan opened the gun and said, "You see—not a shot. Not a single shot."

"You could have replaced the cartridge!"

"I could, but I didn't. And when your father is examined, the bullet will prove to have come from another weapon."

"You could have used another weapon and thrown it away!"

"Why should I? And why should *I* want to murder your father?"

I cried hysterically, "Then perhaps it was meant for me! To get me out of Faillie once and for all!"

"Good God—you think me capable of that?"

I had no answer. Instead, I fell upon him, physically beating his chest with my fists until he seized my shoulders and shook me, hard. My head rocked backward and forward until he stopped. Then he took a handkerchief from his pocket and wiped my cheeks with it. I had not realized that they were wet. Shock, grief, and unbelievable horror blinded me to everything but a savage and primitive desire to kill my father's murderer.

When I had achieved a degree of calmness Duncan picked me up and placed me bodily in the saddle, forcing the reins into my hands. Numbly, I watched as he lifted my father from the ground and laid him across his own horse, standing nearby. I had not even noticed the beast before, but now other things began to register too, even the reverence with which Duncan lifted my father and the gentle way in which he handled him. Only much later, when shock began to recede, did I recall his strength and the ease with which he lifted so heavy a body from the ground.

This was the way in which my father returned from his last ride across the moors, with Duncan Mackintosh walking beside him, and I so dazed that it was my horse that automatically followed the route to Clachnaharry. I sat still and silent in the saddle, unaware of the world about me until we passed the foot of the hill beneath the watchman's stone. At that moment something stirred in my mind: the awareness that another of my premonitions had come true.

For a long time the intense grief I felt over my father's death made me refuse to accept it as a reality. It was impossible to believe that I would never again hear his voice, or be enveloped in his warmth and kindness. Such vigor as his could never be snuffed out; a man such as he could never die. Nor could the bond of affection between us be snapped in a single moment of time, leaving me bereft. My heart would forever cry out in disbelief when I thought of him, and the gap he left could never be filled.

Even so, the truth was forced upon me. Despite the fact that weather conditions were wrong, some ignorant poacher had been out—and would never be brought to justice. Accidents had happened on the moors before, and the culprits remained untraced. This was one of the harsh realities of life in these parts, but that knowledge did nothing to assuage my grief.

When extracted, the shot, which had shattered not only a lung but the breastbone, which pierced his heart, proved to be from the type of rifle used almost exclusively by deerstalkers, whereas the gun carried by Duncan Mackintosh had been a much lighter weapon, for he had been after nothing bigger than hare. I should have been ashamed of my wild accusations, but my grief was all-consuming. Also, his sudden appearance on the scene persisted in troubling me. In all that vast stretch of moors it seemed unlikely that chance alone could bring him to that very spot, at that very moment.

Inevitably it fell to me, as elder daughter, to comfort my mother, but little did she or anyone realize the strain such a task imposed upon me when sorrow was like an unhealed wound in my heart. Sheena shed swift and instant tears and I envied her this release, for my own shock so numbed me that I was unable to weep. "Thank God for your calmness, Elizabeth!" my mother wailed. "How I envy your ability to remain unmoved!" How little she knew or understood me; how little she comprehended that sometimes sorrow could be too intense for tears. . . .

Not until I was alone in bed did I yield to pent-up agony; in the darkness of the night, it was unquenchable. I longed to turn to Calum for comfort, but had no means of getting a message to him, for I had no knowledge of his Edinburgh address.

Naturally, I stayed with my mother until after the funeral, at which, according to Scottish custom, there were only male mourners, the women staying at home with their sorrow. Within three days my father was laid to rest in the village churchyard, and people flocked from Inverness to pay him tribute. The church was too small to hold them all, so the overflow stood outside, joining in the hymns which could be heard through the windows of the little kirk. It was Duncan who told me this later. He and Angus sat together with James Macpherson in the family pew.

Rich and poor, young and old, crofters and mill workers, all turned out to say good-bye to Aindreas MacArthur. I wondered if he realized how many friends he left behind, or how greatly he was loved, but undoubtedly he would have comprehended the depth of my own distress.

The day after the funeral, silent and alone, I returned to Faillie. And the day after that, Calum came home. I listened wordlessly when he told me that he had arranged the meeting with the Stuart brothers and then, with an ache in my throat, somehow managed to reply that it was unnecessary now.

As my father had promised, he left the mills to me, with a lesser share to James Macpherson as second in command. Aindreas died a wealthy man, wealthier even than anticipated, for his habits were frugal and his manners those of a man of the people. His widow was amply provided for; she would live in comfort for the rest of her life, and so would Sheena.

Apart from the usual bequests to servants, he made an additional one to Angus Fraser: enough money to enlarge his boatyard and to buy a neighboring property, a disused, detached house which Angus began to renovate as soon as the title deeds became his.

Now August was upon us, and the amazing pageant of George IV's visit to Edinburgh came and went. He arrived at Leith on the fourteenth of the month, in a torrent of rain, and by the twenty-ninth he had departed, recalled to London on "a matter of urgency" which, some said, concerned either debts or women. He left behind him the memory of parades, processions, banquets, and levées, culminating in a gathering at the Palace of Holyrood House, where His Majesty paraded like a corpulent pantomine clown wearing full Highland dress, toasted "The Chieftains and the Clans"—and set the tartan fashion booming. Without realizing it, he had launched Scotland's greatest industry.

I wished my father could have lived to see the success of the MacArthur weaves. I was caught up in the whirl of it, which was a blessing, for it prevented me from thinking about him too often. I had much to learn, and found it all a little overwhelming at times.

Not the least of my problems was being accepted in my father's place. To the mill workers, receiving me as the master's daughter was one thing, but accepting me at their head was another. I should be at home rearing bairns, occupying a woman's place.

Within a few days I was aware of this change in their attitude to me. I felt it as I walked through the sheds, meeting either averted heads or glances which revealed something bordering on hostility. Greetings which had once been friendly and welcoming now became stilted, or merely polite.

"Give them time, lass, give them time," James advised when I confided my disappointment to him. "I've been expecting this."

"Then you might have warned me!"

"What use would a warning have been? It would have made ye apprehensive from the start. As it is, ye've walked in here head high. Keep it that way."

He was my ally, and so was Calum, but my husband was also a great deal more than that. He was lover, protector, and mentor, advising and helping me in all ways. He dealt with the executors of my father's estate, handled my prostrate mother with sympathy and kindness, and became the man of the family upon whom we all depended. But, more than that, he was my refuge after the day's work. In his arms I found peace and comfort and understanding. To him I could pour out my problems in a way which was impossible with James Macpherson, ally though he was, for James was an unemotional man who saw me as a kind of initiate who had to be taught and even bullied when necessary: a pupil placed in his charge whom he was determined to tutor well.

I was already aware that an eye for design, plus a knowledge of the manual side of weaving, was not sufficient qualification for someone in control, and that I had a lot to learn; it was for this reason I submitted to the man's occasional impatience.

"Don't be weak, lass. It's weakness to be upset. Remember, these workers have been ruled by a man ever since the sheds were built. Ye've got to be as tough as your father."

But I had never been tough. Self-reliant, yes. Unconventional, according to my mother's standards, but always sensitive to people's reactions. I often knew intuitively what others were thinking, and I knew now that those beneath me were hoping I would not stay the course. I could feel their silent criticism, feel them waiting for me to make a slip. "The old order changeth" was not an acceptable maxim to their way of thinking.

Calum assured me that this phase would pass. "They will have to toe the line, *your* line, Elizabeth, and it is up to Macpherson to see that they do. I hope that man really has your interests at heart."

"Of course he has! He has been a lifelong friend—"

"—who owes his rise at the mills entirely to your father. He should remember that."

"It was his ability that made him rise. Father recognized it, and encouraged it."

But Calum shrugged that aside. He was interested only in me.

Whenever possible, he drove me to the mills each morning; at other times Hamish took me, but Calum always made a point of fetching me home. Otherwise, he declared, I would forget all about time. "Your devotion to those mills threatens to be as great as your father's."

"I have so much to learn. I knew there would be a lot, but never wholly realized how much. There's a great deal more to being a cloth manufacturer than knowing how to handle a loom or understand the technicalities of a pattern."

"Which is why James Macpherson is there—to help share the load. And I shall keep an eye on him, to see that he does. I'm not having my wife overtaxed by business affairs."

"He would never allow me to be."

"I'm not so sure. You are tired at the end of the day. The hours are too long for a woman. Your father should have thought of that before placing such a burden on young shoulders."

Even the slightest criticism of my father made me prickle, but because I knew that Calum's remark stemmed from concern for me, all I said was that the women working at the mills put in the same long hours.

"They come of common stock, my love, so are born to it."

"I never think of them that way."

"Then you should. You are the wife of the Laird of Faillie as well as being owner of the MacArthur Mills. Both these things you must remember."

There seemed to be so many things I had to remember. My position, my authority, my social status, my husband's rank. I had never felt myself superior to anyone, nor could I now. It was the people in the mills, not I, who had created a gulf between us. I began to yearn for the warm, human friendliness I had known.

But Calum's love made up for it all, and even though I was independent by nature I was feminine and therefore enjoyed his protective attitude. Nothing could ever threaten such a union as ours. I felt so secure in my marriage that even Morag's increasing assumption of authority did not worry me, though her attitude had subtly changed with her virtual reinstatement as châtelaine of the castle. It was she who gave orders in my absence, she who ruled domestically, and I was content to let her. I even began to feel that the friendship I desired might not be an impossibility.

Therefore I was surprised when Hamish spoke to me one morning. That a man so dour should make a deliberate point of doing so was surprising, but even more surprising were his words.

"Mistress—I'd warn ye to watch out for that one."

He was handing me into the coach as I left for the mills. Morag had followed with a rug for my knees; the early mornings were chill, whatever the season. Abruptly, Hamish had taken the rug from her. His manners never improved, but now they left Morag entirely unruffled. With a disdainful smile she went back indoors.

So when Hamish leaned into the coach and spread the rug across my knees, his words startled me considerably.

"What do you mean, Hamish?" I could not keep the surprise from my voice.

"Just what I say, Mistress." And with that he closed the door and climbed onto the box.

All the way to Inverness I pondered on his remark, only forgetting it briefly as we drove past Daviot Lodge. Without realizing it, I had fallen into the habit of glancing at the house, for it was good to see it coming to life again.

I wondered how my mother's matchmaking plans for Sheena were developing as far as Duncan Mackintosh was concerned—unsuccessfully, I hoped, because my sympathy was with Angus, whom I still considered to be the right man for her. But, reluctantly, I acknowledged that if any man but he were to marry my sister, Duncan seemed to have much to commend him. Putting my personal feelings aside and viewing the man dispassionately, I had to admit that in his rugged way he was an attractive, if not a handsome, man.

When Hamish stopped in the mill yard and helped me down I asked again what he meant by his remark about the housekeeper.

"What I said, Mistress. What else?"

Beyond that, he would not be drawn. His lips set in the familiar, stubborn line, and I chose to disregard his words because he was a crotchety old man with an inborn resentment against anyone not belonging to the family he had always served. He also had cause for a personal grudge against Morag, who had dismissed his daughter.

I said, "You know Mr. Duncan Mackintosh is now residing at Daviot Lodge?"

"Aye, Mistress, and if ye be thinking it would be better if I went to work there, let me tell ye that he has already asked me and I've refused. I belong at Faillie, and there I'll remain."

I checked a smile. I was amused by his plain speaking, but at the same time touched by his loyalty, even if it was more to the place itself than to its current occupants.

"I am glad you feel like that, Hamish."

But, as I entered the mills, it was his earlier words which lingered with me. *"I'd warn ye to look out for that one . . ."*

Then the demands of work drove everything else from my mind, and I was astonished when Calum arrived.

I was in James Macpherson's office when he strolled in with the easy, almost proprietary air with which he always entered the mills. But James didn't like it. He took out his heavy gold watch, the watch my father had presented to him to celebrate twenty-five years of service with the firm, and glanced at it significantly. The mills would not be closed for a long time yet, he pointed out.

"I am aware of that, Macpherson, but my wife is

not a mill worker. The hours she puts in here are too long and too late. I intend to call for her at this time each day, and earlier if I feel so inclined."

I saw James open his mouth, think better of it, and close it again. But he was annoyed.

"I must pull my weight as much as everyone else," I began, but Calum dismissed that with a wave of his well-gloved hand.

"The load can be lightened by Macpherson and by me. I understand that he is now responsible for bookkeeping, at which, I feel sure, he has had little experience."

James cut in, "I am sorry to contradict ye, sir, but the late Mr. MacArthur taught me how to look after the books so that I could handle accounts when he was absent. We knew each other's job thoroughly. It was a sort of insurance."

"And *I* want to insure against my wife being overworked. To do this, I am prepared to handle the company's accounts and so release you to undertake other work. Don't look so surprised, my good man. I am accustomed to managing my estates on Deeside, so accountancy is not outside my experience."

"In that case I should have thought ye'd be there, looking after them now."

In a dead level voice my husband informed him that a resident factor was doing that. "Faillie is my chief responsibility at the moment—after my wife, of course. I have the right to look after her welfare. You are overworking her."

James slammed shut a heavy ledger.

"Her father would never have left these mills to Miss Elizabeth unless he thought her strong enough and clever enough to run them. I happen to share his opinion."

"I am not interested in your opinions."

"Nor I in yours! And I'd like to add that no man can walk in here and interfere with my work—or with Miss Elizabeth's. She has her job to do, and I have mine. Ye may be her husband, but as far as this business is concerned ye be an outsider."

106

When Calum became angry, a pulse beat in his temple. It was beating now, but his voice was unruffled as he remarked that his only thought was to lighten my load. "By handing the accountancy over to me, you could return to the foreman's job that you once held and in which, I am sure, you would be more at home."

I pointed out, hastily that Wilkie Robertson had been promoted to the job of foreman and was doing it well, leaving James free for his present work. "This work," I added, indicating the ledgers.

Calum opened one idly, studied it, and frowned. "Your method seems a little out of date, Macpherson."

"It is the method Mr. MacArthur used and what was good enough for the likes o' him is good enough for the likes o' me."

"But is it good enough for mills which are now booming and heading for even greater things?"

"It seems to be working well enough," James answered dryly, "and, with all respect, I doubt whether ye could undertake work of this nature, not being born to it."

"And were you? I understand your father was a shepherd and your mother a domestic servant, whereas I inherited estates which I was brought up to administer."

"Calum!"

He didn't hear me. Nor did James.

"Be so good as to leave my office—sir. I bid ye good day."

Calum smiled, shrugged, took hold of my arm, and led me from the room. Outside, he remarked with a faint yawn that he seemed to have upset the man.

"I'm not surprised! Did you have to be so insulting? I was ashamed!"

I turned on my heel and left him.

He called after me sharply, "Don't expect me to return for you. I will send Hamish to bring you home."

I flung over my shoulder, "Don't trouble! I am sure

James will drive me, and from now on I will do so myself. I know how to handle the reins."

I walked blindly through the mills, head high, blazing with anger. Through weaving sheds and spinning rooms, past dyers and sorters, balers and laborers, with all the temper I had inherited from my father storming through me. I saw heads turn and watch me, and there must have been something that stopped them from looking away again. There were no evasive glances this time. I was Aindreas MacArthur's girl, and, perhaps for the first time, they really knew it. When I stopped to look at their work there were no sullen glances to intimate that in their minds I had no right to. Just silent submission and, to any comment I made, a careful answer. Perhaps I had been treading too timidly, I reflected. A display of wrath seemed to win more respect.

But after marching militantly through the sheds I was in no mood to sit at a desk, staring at paperwork. The quarrel with Calum had upset me. I went into Macpherson's office and apologized for the scene.

"Don't be fretting yourself, lass." He eyed me shrewdly. "A breath of air would calm ye down."

I nodded, went into my own office, and took down my cloak from its peg behind the door. To reap the benefit of water-driven power my father had built these mills beside the River Ness, with the Ness Islands only a short distance away—shady, tree-lined, green oases in the water, linked by bridges. I often walked there in the middle of the day, after sharing James Macpherson's lunch, as my father had done. A brisk turn now would cool my anger.

To my surprise I came face to face with Duncan Mackintosh in the main hall where our latest tartans were displayed. He was studying them intently.

"I hope you are admiring them, Mr. Mackintosh?"

He spun round. Was it really pleasure that lit his eyes?

"I have always admired them, Mistress Huntly."

"Always?"

"Even as a child. I used to gaze up at the portraits,

fascinated by them. I knew every detail, every pattern."

"I don't understand."

"It is simple enough. The portraits were not only of my forebears, but of many Highland chiefs, each in their individual tartans. No wonder you told me that MacArthur's had obtained them from a very reliable source."

"I have never seen such portraits! You will recall my husband telling you that your sister sold them long ago."

"I find it hard to believe. Una valued them. She would never part with them."

"Unless forced to—which, apparently, she was."

"By whom, I wonder?"

"Not by anyone. By necessity."

To hide a swift alarm, the cause of which I refused to acknowledge even to myself, I turned and walked through the main door, across the mill yard, and down the path leading from it to the banks of the river. Without invitation, Duncan followed.

"It is very odd," he said, as he drew alongside me, "but not one of those tartans has been produced by any other weaver, which suggests that MacArthur's got hold of the setts exclusively."

"You are quite right, and there is nothing odd about it."

"I would very much like to know the 'reliable source' you copied them from." When I made no answer, he continued, "Did your husband get hold of them, or your father? If it was your father, he would have no objection to your telling me the truth, because he was an honest man, but your husband—"

"Is an honest man also."

"Is he? Then surely he would tell me where he got the designs from—unless, of course, he wished to hide the truth."

"My husband has no reason to hide anything. Come to Faillie tonight and ask him yourself."

"I should be delighted." We had reached the bridge leading from the riverbank to the first island. He put his hand beneath my elbow and led me across. His grasp was strong.

"By the way," he continued casually, "I visited Edinburgh recently."

"To see the pageantry?"

"Some of it. It was good to see our Highland dress being worn again, even if all the tartans but those produced by MacArthur's were newly created despite certain claims."

His hand had dropped away, but every now and then it came back to guide me over a rough or stony patch of ground.

"Edinburgh, of course, seethes with gossip, Mistress Huntly."

"And do you listen to it? Personally, I dislike gossip."

"So do I as a general rule, but there are two gentlemen in Edinburgh whom one cannot help hearing about—highly artistic gentlemen who are doing well for themselves by producing tartan designs so that those who can lay no claim to one need not be left out in the cold. I see by your face that you have heard of them."

I kept a careful control on my reaction, as I had been forced to keep on my mind during recent days, for rumors concerning these two brothers had inevitably come filtering through. That they had served in Napoleon's army where Charles, the younger of the two brothers, had been decorated for bravery. That they had then come to London, after a spell in Austria, and learned Gaelic under a Scottish tutor before proceeding to Scotland, where they were received with deference, first by Lord Moray, who entertained them at Darnaway, and then by Lord Lovat, who had given them an island on his estates—Eilean Aegus—and was building a house for them there. That Edinburgh society was split into two opposing factions—those who believed in them, and those who did not. That they were charming, talented, and, from the sound of things, plausible. All this had reminded me of my father's concern and awakened in me an instinctive uneasiness which I had sternly suppressed because of my husband's belief in the two men, backed by the skillful tartan delineations. But now an inner voice seemed to cry out in warning. This was the first I had heard of ancient tartans depicted in the missing Mackintosh portraits, and the sooner I faced Calum with this knowledge, the better.

Another island was ahead, another bridge. After we had crossed it Duncan continued, "I dislike calling you Mistress Huntly—Ealasaid comes more naturally. I think of you by that name always."

"You should not think of me at all," I answered, refusing to meet his eye.

"Why not? Is there any Scottish law which forbids a man to think of a married woman by her Christian name? Ealasaid is beautiful, and so are you—and there is no Scottish law which forbids me to tell you that, either."

"I think we should turn back. . . ."

He made no protest.

"You look thoughtful," he remarked as we retraced our steps.

I was indeed thoughtful, wondering whether to tell him from where Calum had actually obtained the designs and therefore to exonerate him from any suspicion of having seen the portraits, then decided it was up to Calum to do so. He could reveal the truth tonight.

We walked in silence until we reached the riverbank again, then Duncan asked negligently how I liked living at Faillie.

"Very much—naturally."

"So you are happy there?"

"Of course. I am happily married."

"I am glad of that." I saw his sideways glance and knew instinctively that another disconcerting remark was coming.

"I saw your husband as I arrived at the mills. He was driving furiously out of the yard. So furiously that my horses shied. I had the impression that he was angry."

I refused to be drawn, but walked on looking straight ahead.

"And curiously enough," he added, "I had the impression, when you and I met, that you were angry too."

"Impressions can be very misleading."

"Or very revealing."

If he had told me outright that he suspected a quarrel between Calum and myself he could not have made it more clear, and if he was hoping that it indicated a rift which would ultimately separate us and leave Castle Faillie empty, he could not be making a greater mistake. Once home, everything would be right again. Calum would be waiting, and we would make it up.

I said good-bye politely and went back to work, but when I left the mills, Duncan was waiting.

"I thought you might need a driver," he said blandly.

Secretly vowing to walk all the way home if necessary, I told him that Hamish would be coming to fetch me.

"I'm afraid not. He visits his daughter on his half-day—Wednesday. And today is Wednesday."

Seizing my arm firmly, he handed me into his carriage. Short of making a scene before the mill workers as they streamed from the sheds, I could do nothing but yield.

We drove in silence until passing the gates of Daviot Lodge, when I complimented him on the progress he had made.

"You mean with the gardens? Yes—the men have worked well."

"And Guthrie—does he work well?"

"So you've noticed him here, have you? Well, why not? There is nothing to prevent a man from working for someone else in his spare time. But if you do not wish me to employ your workers, I will refrain—although since Guthrie has worked for you for such a short period you cannot really expect to have priority over him, or he to have especial loyalty to you."

"Not to me, perhaps, but to my husband."

"And why?"

"Because Guthrie comes from Carrisbrae."

"Carrisbrae! My sister's home on Deeside?"

"Yes. He has been part of the household there for a long time."

"Has he, indeed?"

"Calum brought him to Faillie."

"That surprises me. My impression was that the man was a rolling stone who had joined the gang of local workers your husband employs."

"On the contrary, he had been put in charge of them; I think he prides himself on being a supervisor and not a laborer, so I am surprised that he is willing to do rough work for you."

"Money can always tempt a man." He changed the subject. "I recall that once you were well acquainted with my gardens. I hope you will renew that acquaintance. I often see you, either driving by or returning from one of your rides. I am glad you still find time to ride, despite your responsibilities at the mills."

"My husband is anxious that I shall spend less time there."

"I am glad he is so devoted."

But was it devotion that had made Calum decide to become involved in the business? The suspicion shamed me, but I could not help reflecting that, compared with me, he had plenty of time to spare, and for the first time I wondered what he did with it, in my absence.

"Since you are acquainted with my gardens," Duncan was saying, "you must also be acquainted with my house, which suggests that you were a friend of the previous owner."

"A great friend. He was a dear old man. I used to visit him often." I added without thinking, "I loved that house."

"Then you will be pleased to hear that apart from redecorating and refurnishing it, I am keeping it much the same. I don't think you will be disappointed when you see it, which I hope will be soon."

"My husband and I will be pleased to call upon you any time you wish," I answered decorously.

He made no answer to that, and I recalled his antipathy toward Calum. But surely this man didn't expect a married woman to visit his house alone? Obviously the invitation must be for both of us.

A shade too casually, Duncan Mackintosh then said that I might care to bring my mother and sister one day, and I thought with a touch of amusement that no doubt Mother would be delighted to accept.

"Perhaps you would include Angus Fraser in the invitation," I suggested. "He is very much in love with Sheena."

"I know."

"I think you should also know that both my father and I hoped Sheena would marry him. He is a fine young man with a fine future ahead of him."

"I know that too," he answered, leaving me with absolutely nothing more to say.

We drove in silence across the causeway and through the arched entrance to the main courtyard. Courtesy demanded that I should invite him in, but I added pointedly, "You can then ask my husband where the tartan designs came from."

"So it *was* he who got hold of them. I thought as much."

He followed me up to the Billeting Room, where I fully expected to find Calum waiting, a glass of wine beside him, for we always lingered here for a relaxing half-hour before changing for supper. Therefore, I was surprised to find the place empty.

I pulled the heavy bell rope beside the fireplace and, when Hamish appeared, ordered refreshment. "And please tell your master that I am home."

"He won't be able to," said Morag's voice from the end of the room. "Calum has left for Carrisbrae."

I was too surprised to refrain from asking when, and why.

"Late this afternoon. He thought it time to see if all was well there."

But he was always confident that everything was well. He had told James Macpherson so this very after-

114

noon, so his sudden departure could only be to punish me for opposing him.

I saw commiseration in Morag's face, and found it galling. Sympathy was one thing, pity another, so I said as lightly as possible how unfortunate it was that Mr. Mackintosh would now be unable to see him.

"He believes we copied our tartan designs from his family's collection of paintings. Calum would have been able to tell him how wrong he is."

"*I* am able to tell him," Morag answered as she glided toward us with her soft, catlike tread.

Duncan asked, "Why you, Mistress Crombie?"

"Because I have been housekeeper to my cousin ever since he came to Faillie, and know exactly what this place contained. Precious little. We found only the most essential furnishing here, for the late mistress spent little on the place—perhaps, poor soul, because she had little to spend. As my cousin once told you, if at any time there were any portraits, she must have parted with them long ago."

"She might have parted with other things, but never with those."

"You doubt my word, Mr. Mackintosh?"

"Naturally. Since you now admit that you have only acted as your cousin's housekeeper since coming to Faillie, how is it you are in a position to judge my sister's actions?"

Morag's thin lips curved in a smile, her eyebrows lifted, and the glint of ice in her eyes was reflected in her voice as she replied, "Because Calum confided in me. He confided in me a lot—until recently." Her glance slid to me and away again. "I also visited them frequently at Carrisbrae. That is how I know that your sister was always ailing; a fretful, improvident woman who would not hesitate to sell anything to raise money for this place—new curtains, new upholstery, anything!"

"And yet you say you found only the most essential furnishings here, and precious little else. . . ."

I thought I heard a sharp intake of her breath, but

couldn't be sure. One could never be sure of anything with Morag, whose guard never cracked.

She was saved from answering by Hamish shuffling in with the wine tray, which he placed on the sideboard; then at a nod from Morag, he departed, but before he reached the door Duncan halted him.

"Hamish! You will bear me out. There was once a valuable collection of portraits here, of my ancestors and various clan chiefs. You remember them?"

"Aye, Master Duncan, I remember them well."

"Where are they now?"

"I wish I knew, sir. I've searched and searched and found no trace."

Morag said sharply, "You have been poking and prying around this castle without my permission? So that is what you get up to on your so-called rounds of inspection!"

"I've done no poking and prying, and I don't need your permission, but only the Mistress of Faillie's."

He shuffled off, muttering beneath his breath. Morag gave an artificial laugh, said how trying it was to have to endure bad servants just because they had been with a family for years, and tried to carry off the incident with indifference, but I could see that she was not only disconcerted but angry. She had become too sure of herself since the mills had claimed my attention, and somehow I knew that Hamish felt this too.

Could it be possible that he actually liked me—that dour man who resented the presence of any but Mackintoshes?

Morag turned to the sideboard and removed the stopper from a decanter, but I asked Duncan to pour in my husband's absence. She didn't like that, either. It robbed her of the opportunity to play the part of hostess, and when I moved to my customary seat beside the fire, she subtly intruded and was there first, spreading her skirts with quiet deliberation. Ignoring the incident, I chose the sofa on the opposite side, but when she pointedly indicated Calum's chair for Duncan—with a smooth and gracious smile—he appeared not to see the gesture and seated himself beside me.

"The interesting thing about the portraits," he said, obviously determined not to relinquish the subject, "is that they depicted tartans dating back to 1745. They were the only records left of these patterns, and the odd thing is that despite the sudden flood of tartans onto the market by Lowland weavers and others, only MacArthur's have been able to produce these long lost and genuine setts. No others can be dated prior to 1800, and the vast majority are newly created. So you see, those portraits are very valuable, almost priceless."

"Which is why you are anxious to recover them," Morag interrupted. "What a pity you are unable to, Mr. Mackintosh. Just think of the amount of money they would fetch now!"

"They would have fetched a large amount at any time, Mistress Crombie, which proves that my sister most certainly did not sell them—otherwise Faillie would not have been so badly in need of restoration. How do you explain that, if she was able to sell the portraits profitably?"

She shrugged, sipped her wine delicately, then answered, "Alas, sir, I cannot. And now, if you will excuse me, I have supper to supervise. Dear Elizabeth must be tired and hungry."

Entirely unruffled, she departed.

For a while we sat in silence, then Duncan said bluntly, "Your husband has done pretty well for himself, hasn't he—coming across these ancient tartans in only one possible way, passing them onto your father's mills, and then marrying the heiress . . . and, I have no doubt, selling the portraits in Edinburgh or elsewhere."

To quell my own uneasiness I said furiously, "I think it is time you left."

"And *I* think it is time you stopped deluding yourself. You're intelligent, but blinded by this man. Not that you're the first sensible young woman in the world to deliberately shut her eyes to the faults of a handsome man, just as many a sane man has deliberately blinded himself to a woman's failings when besotted with her."

"I love him! *And* trust him. And you are totally wrong about the designs being copied from portraits. My husband bought the delineations from those two brothers. They were contained in their ancient manuscript."

He stared at me.

"You actually believe that? And your father—*he* believed it too?"

"He found it hard to credit at first, but was finally convinced as I was." I added defensively, "Apart from the fact that my husband's word is not to be doubted, the fact that the two brothers have not produced these patterns among the many they have launched proves it, don't you agree?"

"It only proves that they've never seen my family's portraits, and I am not surprised your father found this story hard to credit at first, but obviously the technical delineations of the tartans were authentic enough to convince him. Even so, he was a great reader, was he not, with an admirable library? Search among its shelves and I am sure you will find records of Prince Charlie's married life. He was a debauched fifty-two when he married Princess Louise of Stolberg, and she only eighteen. Small wonder that she became a notorious adulteress, sleeping with her husband but rarely. The state of things between them could not be kept secret, nor the fact that although he had occasional mistresses he had no strong sexual appetite for women. The only child he had was an illegitimate daughter, by his former nurse, Clementina Walkinshaw, many years his senior, to whom he was bound only by their mutual addiction to drink, by all accounts, until she finally left him taking the daughter with her."

"Charlotte, whom he legitimized, dubbing her Duchess of Albany."

"And who never married—and who died of an inherited disease a year or two after her father's death. She had no children, legitimate or otherwise."

"These two brothers do not claim to descend from

her, and my husband has no partisan feelings about their claim, in any case."

"Only about this Latin manuscript which they will allow no one to see?" He shook his head at me. "I thought *you* were the witch, Ealasaid, but Huntly has laid a spell on you. I'll break it one day. I'll open your eyes. I am determined on that."

"And have us out of Faillie in the end? You are determined on that, too."

"That, too," he agreed, and left me.

Eleven

HE HAD planted a doubt in my mind, and it grew. My dislike of him grew also. I lay awake for a long time that night, remembering every word he had said and seeing every glance of his expressive face. He was a determined man; a man to be afraid of.

Eventually I slept, but fitfully, dreaming in snatches —dreams which I could scarcely recall on waking, but which left me troubled. All I remember was that Duncan had featured in all of them, threatening me, hounding me—once even standing over me with a gun in his hand. I had sat bolt upright then, believing I was back on the moor with my father's head upon my lap and Duncan standing there watching, a smile on his face. . . . "He is the first to go," he said, "because he stole part of my heritage and turned it to his advantage, and you will be next because you have stolen my home . . . you and your husband, whom I will finally dispose of. . . ."

In the dark loneliness of the night the scene had a terrifying reality, but in the cold light of day it receded, as nightmares do. But against my will I was still troubled; his accusations seemed to have logic on their side. Anyone coming into possession of such portraits had, at a time like this, not only valuable property but valuable information.

To wait silently for Calum's return was impossible. As I drove to the mills next morning I resolved to write to Carrisbrae, urging him to come home, but was spared the necessity, for when I returned, there he was, waiting for me.

Without a word, he held out his arms, and without a word I went into them. Immediately all my doubt and confusion fell away; I was safe; he was home; he would explain everything. For now, it was sufficient that he was here, holding me close, our quarrel forgotten.

So Morag's interruption was far from welcome.

"Ah—so you're back, Calum. Hamish didn't tell me."

Without releasing me, Calum replied, "Hamish didn't see me arrive. I've been back this half-hour."

"Then good gracious, why didn't you ring? Surely you needed refreshment after driving so far?"

I thought how extraordinary it was that Morag could make her smallest concern for Calum seem overelaborate and fussy, and yet was totally unaware of how this jarred upon him.

"If I *had* needed refreshment, Morag, I would have rung for it. And now, if you don't mind, I want to be alone with—"

"Is all well at Carrisbrae?" she interrupted blandly.

"Of course. I knew it would be."

"Then why go there?" Without giving him an opportunity to answer she went straight on, "I think you should know that Duncan Mackintosh has been here, accusing you of stealing his family portraits. I don't suppose Elizabeth troubled to tell you. She brought him home with her last night."

I said briskly, "I haven't had the chance to tell Calum anything yet. I only walked in this instant."

She glanced at my bonnet, cloak, gloves and reticule, which I had flung aside as I ran to Calum. Her glance said plainly enough that it must have taken more than an instant to discard them, and the way in which she now picked them up expressed her disapproval of untidiness.

"Please leave them, Morag. I will take them upstairs when I go."

Which I hoped would be soon. Nowadays it seemed that the only place where my husband and I could be alone was our room.

Calum asked, "What is all this about family portraits?" His arm was still about my waist, but his grip had tightened perceptibly.

Before Morag had a chance to reply, I said, "He mentioned them the first night he called here, remember? But Morag is wrong. He didn't accuse you, or anyone, of stealing them."

"Not in so many words, but the implication was there." Morag didn't sniff because she was too refined, but she might just as well have done so. "I am surprised your wife makes excuses for him, Calum. And I must confess I was also surprised that Elizabeth brought him home in your absence."

I cut in swiftly, "It was a natural courtesy. He drove me from the mills. I invited him in because I fully expected Calum to be here."

Why did I have to defend myself, I thought furiously. Too often I found myself doing so, and it was always Morag who trapped me into it.

My husband said he was glad I had invited Duncan in. "Otherwise we would never have heard about this outrageous idea of his. I hope you put him right about it, my love?"

"*I* did," Morag said virtuously. "I assured him that no portraits of any kind had been found at Faillie, and Hamish confirmed it."

"Hamish! Did you allow the man to question even the servants?"

"Of course not. Hamish happened to be present and Mr. Mackintosh waylaid him."

Calum's arm relaxed about my waist.

"A touchy clan, the Mackintoshes—or my late

wife's particular branch of it. But I would like to know what sparked his extraordinary suspicion."

"The tartans," I said. "He believes they were copied from the portraits because the weaves we have produced follow the tartans featured in them—and, he says, no one could have obtained them in any other way."

Calum laughed aloud.

"Then I hope you enlightened him—although even that shouldn't have been necessary. All you had to do, my love, was to remind him that it would need someone with an expert knowledge, not only of weaving but of tartan design, to work out the setts from a picture. And that knowledge I have never had. Only your father—and yourself."

He took me by the hand and led me away to the library, saying he had something to show me. Once there, he sat me in a deep armchair beside the fire, went to his desk, and drew out a document which he placed in my lap.

"Open it," he commanded.

I did so. It was a will.

It was brief and to the point. After the normal preamble, I read, "To my beloved wife Elizabeth I bequeath the estates of Carrisbrae and all of which I die possessed to remain her property exclusively for the duration of her lifetime and thereafter all the said estates and possessions to pass in equal parts to children born of our union."

It was ridiculous that so staid a document should bring tears to my eyes, but I could have had no greater testimony of his thought for me.

I said shakily, "Do lawyers omit punctuation because they have no knowledge of it?—I often wonder . . ."

He laughed and touched my cheek with a gentle hand. "Tears, Elizabeth? Why tears? This is merely the normal provision a man must make for his wife—or any wife for her husband."

"But to think of death so early in our marriage!" I shivered a little.

122

"One must be practical, my love. I don't have to remind you of how suddenly your father went."

Although he spoke lightly, he was serious. And he was right, of course—marriage was a serious state and the future should be provided for.

"I must do the same," I said.

"It would be wise, but you must bequeath your possessions where you will—to our children exclusively, perhaps. You are not to think of me. I have all I need. But of course in the event of your decease—unbearable thought—I should hold your estate in trust for our children and administer it on their behalf until they were old enough to do so. That is why it is important for me to gain the necessary experience by helping to run the mills now. You do see that, don't you?"

I nodded, with half my attention on what he was saying and half on the identity of the solicitors who had prepared the will, and were named as executors.

I said in surprise, "So you haven't been to Deeside?"

"No. As you can see, my solicitors are in Perth. I merely said that I was going to Carrisbrae to allay my cousin's curiosity. Morag is insatiably inquisitive."

"You should make some provision for her, surely?"

"Why? She didn't come into my life until recently, and it was her husband's responsibility, not mine, to take care of her. My duty is to my own wife, not another man's."

"He couldn't have left her very well off if she had to seek a post as your housekeeper."

Calum shrugged. "I know nothing about that, but she has a home with us and is well looked after. We owe her nothing more than that, but if you want to make some small personal bequest to her—jewelry, clothes, that sort of thing—it is up to you, my dear."

Clothes. I had forgotten all about my resolve to pass some clothes on to her. I would attend to that shortly, I decided; I had something more important to think of right now.

"I will make an appointment to see my father's solicitors in Inverness as soon as possible."

"Tell me of your wishes and I will instruct them for

you; then all you need do is sign the will in the presence of witnesses. The simpler you make it, as I have made mine, the better. A complicated or lengthy document means more work and consequently delay in the granting of probate, but the bequests and stipulations must be entirely your own choice, my darling."

"Your choice is my choice. It is the simplest and the best. Will you put it in hand for me without delay?"

He promised to do so, adding that that was enough serious talk for now. Then he gathered me close, saying that in any case he intended to take the greatest possible care of his dear wife. "I promised to love and to cherish her, and love and cherish her I always will. We have a long life ahead of us, together. Let me kiss away that solemn look, my dearest Elizabeth. Smiling becomes you better."

An hour or two later my mother and sister arrived in a flurry of protests and pleas.

"Elizabeth, my dear, tell your sister that she *must* come with me to visit your aunts. I cannot leave her alone at home, and I see absolutely no reason why she should be averse to staying with them!"

Sheena begged, "Mamma, *please!* They are stuffy and tedious, and will be even more so whilst we are in mourning. There will be no fun, no parties, just dull needlework sessions and discussions about people's ailments. I beg you, don't make me go with you!"

"But I need to get away, child. I need the solace of my sisters. Tell her she must obey me, Elizabeth, for I swear she will pay no heed to her poor mother. I am afraid Sheena has become very willful. If only her father were alive!"

"If he were," my sister pointed out, "you wouldn't be seeking solace with your sisters."

At that, Mother sank into a chair and buried her face in an inadequate handkerchief. Calum stooped over her solicitously while I tried to cope with Sheena, who stubbornly refused to yield.

"Would *you* jump at the chance to stay with those

stuffy old aunts?" she pouted. "I would rather stay at home, and it is nonsense for Mamma to say I cannot. Ann will look after me."

Over the black lace edge of her handkerchief my mother looked at me beseechingly. I knew what troubled her—the fact that Angus Fraser was still allowed to use my father's library. The prospect of their meeting and being alone together, with Ann and Iain far away in the servants' quarters, caused her the gravest concern.

She said desperately, "You are the elder daughter and a married woman, Elizabeth. Talk some sense into the girl, for I declare I cannot. She used to be so *amenable*. I don't know what has come over her!"

More or less the same thing that has come over you, I wanted to say: sudden loss, sudden bereavement, shock. I knew what the house was like now at Clachnaharry and my heart went out to both of them, but more greatly to my mother, for never, until her husband's death, had she realized how much she depended on him, nor how skillfully he handled Sheena. I had no doubt at all that my young sister was giving Mother a trying time and Mother, in her turn, was getting on Sheena's nerves. It would be good for both of them to get away from each other for a while.

"There is one obvious solution," Calum said. "Sheena must come and stay with us while your mother has the change she needs."

I saw Mother's eyes widen with relief, and Sheena's with delight. I agreed that it was a good idea, and Mother was profuse in her thanks. As for Sheena, she gave her characteristic joyous little skip, the first sign I had seen of her old self for a long time, and said what fun it would be to stay in a castle, and how much she would love it, and how sweet of Calum to think of it, and was I sure—were we *both* sure—that she wouldn't be in the way? Her eyes settled on Calum as she waited for an answer.

"It will be our pleasure," he said. "And, as for being in the way," he added with a laugh, "even a castle as small as this has plenty of rooms. Come and stay as long as you like, little sister."

Two days later Mother journeyed to Edinburgh and my sister arrived with two immense wicker skips, a large basket trunk, and a capacious reticule containing all the odds and ends she had forgotten to pack. Morag eyed the array of baggage with disapproval. "Vanity, vanity, all is vanity. . . ." At which Sheena stared in puzzled surprise and asked what she was talking about.

I laughed, linked my arm in my sister's and went upstairs with her. Following behind, Morag said that she doubted whether the closets in the guest room would be large enough for such a vast wardrobe, and asked how long Sheena intended to stay.

"As long as she wishes, Morag." I didn't attempt to keep a sharp note from my voice and was satisfied when the woman made no answer. Later, though, she caught me alone and took the opportunity to say, "Mark my words, Elizabeth, you will regret this; the girl is flighty and will prove a handful."

"My sister is welcome here. She came at the invitation of myself and my husband, and you must do everything possible to make her comfortable and happy at Faillie. One extra person in the household can make little difference."

"I see you are on her side, not mine."

"Side? There are no sides. Pray be good enough not to say such things. My sister is young—"

"And spoiled."

I ignored that.

"Losing one's father at the age of eighteen is a distressing experience for a girl."

"He was your father too, and you were closer to him. The experience was a greater distress for you, particularly since you were with him when it happened."

I didn't want to think about that moment and to my surprise, I saw a hint of understanding in Morag's pale eyes. I softened at once.

"Thank you, Morag. But please don't worry about my sister . . ."

"I am not. It is you I am worrying about."

"But why?"

"You will find out," she answered enigmatically, and with that I had to be content.

After the initial rush to fulfill orders in time for the King's visit, James Macpherson and I were able to relax, and I was glad to do so while Sheena was at Faillie for something of our old relationship had returned.

One afternoon I returned from the mills so early that there was ample time for a long ride together. I was looking forward to it and hurried upstairs to change.

Because there was no sign of her below, I tapped on her door in passing. There was no reply. I opened the door and glanced inside. Clothes lay scattered, as if she had changed in a rush. The scene was reminiscent of days gone by, when her bedroom at home had presented similar chaos until Ann scolded her and made her tidy up.

Should I do the same, or tidy the place myself? Better that, I decided, than risk Morag's disapproval should she happen to come in. I was hanging up a dress when a sound from the door jerked my head round. It was Morag, of course.

"Ah—so you are clearing up the mess, I see. Didn't I say she was spoiled?"

"She seems to have changed in a hurry," I commented indifferently.

"She always does when Calum takes her out—which, I might add, is more than frequently. In your absence they are becoming inseparable."

I closed the door of the closet, feeling oddly disturbed. Was Morag trying to frighten me in some way, or merely hoping to cause mischief?

"I knew that Calum would keep her amused," I remarked casually as I walked from the room.

"And I recall that I agreed with you." Was there mockery in that bell-like voice, or was it my imagination? "Don't you want to know where they have gone?"

"I daresay they will tell me when they get back."

I walked straight on down the corridor to our room. From the spy slits the Banqueting Hall spread wide and empty below; then suddenly a man appeared, slouching in a leisurely fashion down the long room. I stopped dead in my tracks.

"What is that man doing within the castle?" I called to Morag.

"What man?"

"Guthrie! He works outside. He has no right to come indoors."

"He has if I command him to. I told him to bring in a supply of logs."

"Then please don't do it again. I don't like him."

"He is a good worker."

"I don't want him in the castle, Morag. Please remember that."

"My dear Elizabeth, do you expect *me* to carry logs?"

"Of course not. Hamish would do so."

"Hamish is growing old. He can carry no more than a few at a time."

"Then let him carry a few at a time. Or use other servants. I don't want a man like Guthrie about the place. I don't trust him."

With that, I left her, went to my room, and changed. I would ride alone, and perhaps by the time I returned Calum and Sheena would be back.

Crossing the Banqueting Hall on my way down I noticed that the log baskets were empty. I also recalled the direction in which Guthrie had been walking—not from the great Gothic fireplace, but from the direction of the spiral stairs leading down from the upper corridor, where Morag and I had been talking.

Twelve

RETURNING from an uneasy and solitary ride, I found my husband and sister taking tea in my sitting room, with Sheena curled in my favorite chair and Calum seated opposite, regarding her with fond indulgence. I would have been insensitive indeed not to be aware of the rapport between them.

Sheena greeted me happily, and Calum insisted he was disappointed to hear that I had returned and found them gone, but I could not suppress a pang of jealousy.

"We've been shopping in Nairn," Sheena cried gaily, "and look what Calum bought for me!" She held out her wrist, from which dangled a bracelet of Cairngorm stones. Not a valuable gift; the sort of thing a brother would buy for a sister, but looking at it, it seemed to convey a greater significance to me than that. From the way she displayed it, it might have been a love token.

I forced a smile, admiring it.

"I shall keep it always, Calum dear—for ever and ever!" Sheena declared, at which he laughed, saying that in no time at all she would forget a trinket like that compared with some of the purchases she herself had made.

"The boxes this young lady made me carry! She needs a footman to accompany her on shopping expeditions."

Sheena screwed up her nose at him enchantingly and went on to tell me how they had then gone down to the shore and walked by the sea.

"And on the way back we visited the Clava Cairns.

Calum has never seen them before, of course. Creepy! The wind rustling in the trees and all those ancient stones piled in great circles, with only a narrow entrance through which to carry the bodies—I would hate to go there alone, but Calum looked after me."

There was nothing to alarm me about that, nothing to indicate that his care for her had been a form of cherishing, but the impression came over me sharply. I fell silent, feeling shut out and suddenly unwanted. I rose quietly and made for the door.

"Where are you going, my love?"

Calum's voice followed me lazily. I looked back at him, lounging comfortably in a deep armchair beside the fire with the air of a man well content, a man who did not wish to be roused from the aftermath of an enjoyable afternoon. He made no effort to rise and open the door for me.

"To write some letters," I answered, not troubling to point out that this was my own private sitting room in which I dealt with correspondence, for it was plain that they did not intend to bestir themselves.

I closed the door quietly behind me, feeling like an intruder.

It was then that I decided to invite Angus Fraser to visit us. I drove to Clachnaharry the next day and sought him out. I hoped he would come as often as he wished. He thanked me, assured me that he would, and our eyes met in perfect understanding.

He came the next night. I wasn't sure that he enjoyed himself, but he came again two days later, and again the following Sunday. Calum accused me of matchmaking and seemed amused, but I could feel no amusement for as Sheena's vivacity increased beneath Calum's encouragement, Angus became quieter, I more concerned, and Morag, it seemed, increasingly watchful. And during these days Calum came to bed later and later.

"It was a mistake, my love. I knew it would be."

Calum stood behind me, watching me brush my hair. I had already prepared for bed, but he had made no effort to, and now, when I made no comment on his enigmatic statement, he announced that he was going down to the library for a final cigar. He stooped and kissed the nape of my neck. "Don't wait up for me, my love. I'll come in quietly, in order not to disturb you."

"Surely one last cigar won't take that long?"

He smiled. I saw his blond good looks reflected in the mirror, and the curve of that mouth which I knew so well.

"I will probably smoke more than one, and have a nightcap to go with it. I also want to glance at your will; it came today from the solicitors. It will be perfectly satisfactory, of course, for they merely had to draw it up, as they did mine."

I paused, hairbrush in hand.

"As they did yours? Calum, you surely didn't ignore our family solicitors in Inverness?"

" 'Our' family solicitors? You mean your father's, don't you? But naturally you must use your husband's solicitors now—*my* family solicitors. You're not a MacArthur anymore."

Slowly, I began to brush my hair again. Calum lifted a tendril and curled it round his fingers, still smiling at me in the mirror. "Come," he said, "don't look so worried. My lawyers in Perth are long established and highly competent."

"I don't doubt it, but I shall be embarrassed if it ever comes to light that I have gone elsewhere, even for a personal matter. The Inverness firm handles all legal work for the mills and acted for my father in everything. But you know this—they were his executors, and you dealt with them."

"And very efficient they were, I grant you." There was an edge of impatience in his voice. "And very fortunate they are to legally represent the mills—a far more profitable business for them than the mere preparation of a will." He turned to the door. "I will examine it now and you can sign it in the morning.

Good night, my love. I may read awhile. With your sister taking up so much of my time during the day, I have precious little left to myself."

"Calum—wait! What did you mean by 'it was a mistake'?"

He looked surprised.

"Inviting Angus Fraser here, of course. Giving the poor devil cause to hope when you know perfectly well that Sheena is not in love with him. Stop thrusting them together, Elizabeth. You can't run people's lives as you do the mills."

He finished on a note of anger and, on the same note, I retorted. "Then *you* stop indulging her!"

He looked at me coldly.

"You are talking nonsense, my dear. I keep the child amused and she, I confess, amuses me. Since you are obviously determined to exclude me from the mills, you can't blame me if I find something else to do."

"That's unfair! The day will come—"

"The day must come. If anything should happen to you, I must be able to take over. Not that anything *is* likely to happen to you, but when you have children you will have duties to them to attend to. Then you will be glad to have me to rely on. And don't tell me you have James Macpherson for that! The work sheds are his sphere. He should go back to them."

"I would never allow him to. He has worked his way up . . ."

"So you have often told me. I find the subject tedious. Good night."

"Calum!"

He looked back through the half-open door and said indifferently, "Well?"

"Please—don't let's part like this."

"Part? Who is talking about parting? Go to bed and to sleep, unless you have something of importance to tell me—such as being ready to let me handle the financial side of the business. You can entrust me with something so trivial as a will, but not with that, apparently. On second thoughts, rather than disturb you by coming to bed late, I will sleep in my dressing room tonight."

He closed the door sharply behind him.

Calum joined me for breakfast as usual, emerging from his dressing room looking as he always did first thing in the morning—blond hair rumpled sleepy-eyed. He kissed me as if no cross word had ever passed between us, asking if I had slept well. I said yes, although it was a long time before I had done so.

"You must have stayed up a long time," I said. "I didn't hear you in your dressing room."

With a rather sheepish smile he admitted that he had fallen asleep in his armchair beside the library fire, and not wakened until the early hours. "The ashes in the grate were stone cold, and so was I! I tried to be as noiseless as possible when I finally turned in."

I asked for the will, and he brought it to me. "You will find it quite in order. Sign at your leisure, my love; there's no hurry. Two of the staff can act as witnesses."

I said I would take it to the mills and get James Macpherson and Wilkie Robertson to do so.

"Morag and one of the servants would suffice."

"Morag is a relative."

"Not close enough—to you, at any rate—to really count as one, and the lawyers aren't to know that Mistress Morag Crombie is linked with you even remotely. There's a foreman outside who can add his signature."

"Not Guthrie. I won't agree to that."

"Why not?"

"I don't like him. He is insolent, for one thing, and I wouldn't want him to know anything about my private affairs, for another."

"When has he been insolent?"

"When you were in Edinburgh. I didn't like his manner. It was almost familiar."

"That doesn't sound like Guthrie. I know him well."

"So he gave me to understand. He told me you brought him here from Deeside."

"That is true."

"*And* that you were never likely to dismiss him."

"What made him say that?"

"I threatened to report him for negligence unless he got on with his work. I didn't like the way he stared at me, nor his tone of voice."

"That doesn't seem like Guthrie."

"So Morag said."

"It sounds as if you got his back up, my dear."

"*He* got *mine* up!" I folded the will and replaced it in its large manila envelope. "I will get James and Wilkie to witness this."

Calum yawned, stretched, and went into his dressing room, saying that if it would make me happier to have them as witnesses, it was a matter of indifference to him. "I will then take it to the lawyers in Perth for you. Today I have promised to take Sheena to Aviemore. It is a long drive, but she enjoys these outings so much that I haven't the heart to refuse."

I had to suppress a sharp feeling of envy. I was having to suppress my feelings a great deal since Sheena's arrival and, to myself, secretly admitted that I wanted her to go home.

Their day was long in Aviemore. They supped at an inn on the way back. "The landlord gave us a private room!" Sheena announced excitedly when they eventually returned.

"Naturally he did," Calum put in. "Respectable young women don't dine in public rooms, and I am sure Elizabeth would have been angry with me had I permitted it."

What could I say to that? Nothing, except that I was glad he had taken such good care of her. I had endured a solitary meal with Morag, throughout which she had repeatedly commented on their protracted absence.

She said now, somewhat caustically, "Well, at least

you are both back in time for our nightcap," and off she went to fetch the usual dish of tea. Calum said he would drink his in the library, and left the three of us to have ours alone. Shortly after that, Sheena yawned, said that the day had been wonderful but quite exhausting, so would I forgive her if she went to bed? I was glad to go, too.

I lay awake for a long time. Shortly after midnight I rose and went into Calum's dressing room. It was empty, so I went downstairs, determined to persuade him to come to bed, but the library, too, was empty.

It was then that I experienced one of the most alarming premonitions of my life.

To my relief and Sheena's chagrin my mother arrived unexpectedly about noon the next day.

"There was no time to get a message to you, Elizabeth. I discovered that dear Moira and Fiona had promised to visit Cousin Meg in Glasgow, quite some time ago, and naturally I had no wish to prevent them, so I started for home the day before yesterday, spending the last night at Pitlochry. Now, Sheena my child, hurry with your packing and you can come home with me. Iain is waiting outside."

"But Mamma, it will take me *hours* to pack!"

"I have no doubt your sister will help you. I am glad you are not at those mills today, my dear Elizabeth. A wife's place is in the home, and your dear father should have realized that."

Morag, who had gone downstairs to meet my mother and brought her up to the Billeting Room, now said briskly that she would send Iain along to the kitchen for something to eat, and then set out a cold collation for us in the Banqueting Hall.

"And while you all enjoy it, *I* will deal with Sheena's luggage."

I let her. No one would pack more speedily and efficiently than Morag, and I had a shrewd idea that Morag would enjoy doing that more than sharing the luncheon.

135

On leaving, Sheena embraced me gratefully, thanked Morag politely for her kindness, then turned to Calum. Suddenly she flung her arms around his neck, kissed him swiftly, and cried, "Thank you for everything!"

It was obvious she was as much in love with Calum as ever, but all he said was, "Good-bye, little sister."

When they had gone Calum linked his arm in mine and said, "Thank heaven, our home is our own again."

I was silent. A deep depression had settled upon me.

"I want to speak to you, Calum."

"Then let us go out onto the ramparts. It is a long time since we strolled there together."

We could have made opportunities, I thought, but allowed him to lead me up the spiral stairs and through the heavy door at the top.

"Now," he said, "what do you wish to speak to me about?"

"Last night."

"What of last night?"

"I looked into your dressing room. You were not there, nor in the library." I tried to keep a note of accusation from my voice.

"And what time was that?"

"Some time after midnight."

"My dear love, you should have looked for me out here. I was getting a breath of air before turning in. Had I known you were awake, I wouldn't have spent an uncomfortable night on that dressing room sofa." He tilted up my chin and kissed me. "Thank God we can be together again now."

And so it was. Life went back to its normal routine and I felt ashamed for having resented the time he had given to my sister, and also ashamed of the ugly suspicion which conmmon sense now told me to dismiss.

We were lovers again, but as the weeks progressed and late summer slid into autumn, I became subtly aware of a change in our relationship, as if, on my husbad's part, lovemaking lacked spontaneity and had become a taken-for-granted thing.

Thirteen

THE WILL WAS SIGNED and Calum took it to Perth on his next visit. I felt restless after his departure and, for the first time since my father's death, rode toward the moors. A late evening mist was gathering.

Daviot Lodge was within sight when I turned off to the valley of Strathnairn, plunged down to the narrow river, and then climbed the opposite bank toward the distant Clava Stones. On an impulse, I used the low surrounding wall to dismount, then tethered my horse and went inside.

Slabs of rock, reminiscent of a miniature Stonehenge, stood like petrified sentinels on the outer perimeter of the field, with spaces in between suggesting that at some time certain stones had been removed or stolen—unless the gaps had been designed to admit burial processions passing to the inner cairns. Some believed that the stone sentinels had been placed there, in the remote past, to watch over the dead, but people more knowledgeable than I had speculated upon the truth and found no answer.

There was no sound but the whispering trees. No birds sang. This was a place of death, to be fled from, but something compelled me to remain. Ahead were the burial chambers—circular walls of massive stones curving inward to domed roofs, with entrances the depth of the thick walls, like short dark tunnels. What had happened to the dead once piled within those cairns? When opened, none were there . . . .

The thud of approaching hooves startled me; apparently I was not the only rider in this lonely area.

The horse's steps were slowing down, and I felt a strange uneasiness, as if being tracked by an enemy.

The uneasiness was justified, for the next moment I saw the dark, sensual face of Guthrie and felt a sickening lurch of apprehension as he halted beyond the low stone wall surrounding the field. He doffed his hat, a surprisingly elegant beaver, I observed. The rest of his clothes were also more costly than I should have expected.

"Good day to you—Mistress," he said with a bold, insolent smile.

I inclined my head coldly.

"And what would bring a lady like yourself to this lonely place—Mistress? And without a groom. How will you remount?" I was annoyed that he should draw attention to my riding skirt, a costume which made it impossible for a woman to mount without aid, but I answered disdainfully that the low stone wall made an excellent mounting block.

He laughed softly and raked me with a glance which seemed to strip me naked. All along I had been aware of this man's unwelcome attention, his suggestive glances whenever we met. Now I felt that his sudden appearance in this isolated area had a sinister aspect; that, seeing me ride away from the castle alone, he had deliberately followed with one purpose in mind. I suppressed a shiver, but I could not suppress the lick of fear in my heart.

I jerked away violently, but as I hurried across the field I could feel him watching me, as if trying to mesmerize me into looking back. I refused to, bending all my will power to drive him away, but it seemed a long time before I heard his departure.

With his going the tension within me eased, and the field immediately seemed less eerie, less threatening. I moved toward the central cairn, largest of all the burial chambers, wondering why they had been placed in such a way—for rank and importance, with lesser ones set apart? Only the silent past held the answer, and I was content to let it.

To admit light, circular areas had been cleared in the

apex of the roofs so that visitors could examine the inner structures but, even so, on such an evening as this it was difficult to see within the restricting walls of the chambers. But curiosity still held me and without hesitation I walked into the central cairn. Instantly I remembered the day in my childhood when I paid my first and only visit here whilst Sheena remained outside the field and I, alone within this silent chamber, imagined myself being slowly and relentlessly walled up, some unseen enemy stacking stone upon stone to block the entrance until I was sealed inside forever.

I had chosen the worst possible moment to recall that macabre drama. It had terrified me even as I made it up, and it terrified me now. I found myself standing transfixed in the middle of the chamber, with emptiness and darkness about me, too petrified to move.

It was then that I heard the sound. A stealthy footstep, slowly approaching. The crunch of dry twigs beneath a heavy footfall. The snap of a fallen branch, loud as a pistol shot, as someone trod upon it. Then silence.

Guthrie had returned. The thick walls of the burial chamber had cut off the sound of his horse's hooves this time, but he had seen my mare still tethered outside and therefore knew I was still here. I was trapped, and confidence deserted me. I had either to walk out boldly and face him, or he would walk in here and do whatever he willed.

Either way, he would do whatever he willed, for the man was stronger than I and no one was likely to pass this way. Screams would float unheeded into the thick Highland mist.

I tried to call out. I would order him away, command him to return to Faillie or it would be the worse for him. But my throat muscles were stiff and from my jerking mouth no sound came.

My legs were stiff also; stiff and numb and perilously weak as I forced them forward, one creeping step at a time. The gap of light through the entrance drew slowly nearer. I had reached it when all light was suddenly blocked out and my body lurched against his within the aperture. I felt his arms go around me in a grip which could have snapped my spine.

"What in the name of hell are you doing in this sepulcher?"

Duncan! Duncan Mackintosh, not that man with the sinister devil's face, but this other with the tough, unyielding one.

I cried, in wild and hysterical relief, "Well, at least you're the lesser of two evils!" and strength returned to me unexpectedly. I pushed at him violently and the surprise lessened his grip. I was free; running across the field between its rigid stone sentinels, and out into the lane beyond; back into the year 1822, my own self again. I heard him call and as I reached the stile where my mare was tethered he caught up with me. To my astonishment, he was laughing.

"What attraction do ancient stones hold for you, Ealasaid? First the watchman's, and now these! Is it the witch in you? Did you come here in some previous life and take part in forbidden rites?"

I threw him a glance which I hoped was contemptuous.

"Allow me," he said, but instead of cupping his hands to make a mounting step for me he put them upon my waist and lifted me up. Halfway, he paused, holding me with my eyes level with his own. For a long moment we looked at each other and then his arms went around me, holding me close. I was powerless to move, not merely because of his strength but because something within me urged no resistance. I closed my eyes, wanting only to remain where I was, conscious of a feeling of security which seemed to have been slipping away from me during the past weeks, but when his mouth came down upon mine the shock of passion went through me and I knew that my lack of resistance was based on something much stronger than a desire to feel safe.

This is wrong. You must not feel this way toward a man who is not your husband. The words shouted in my inner consciousness and made me pull away, ashamed and bewildered, telling myself that my reactions had been due solely to relief at not coming face to face with Guthrie again. But I was shaking, wanting to run away not only from this man, but from myself and from emotions I could not, would not, analyze.

"And now, I suppose, I should apologize," he said calmly. "But I don't."

This time he did cup his hands to make a mounting step for me. I accepted and sprang into the saddle, hoping that his observant eyes did not notice my trembling hands as they picked up the reins.

"I might ask what brought *you* to the Clava Cairns," I asked forcing a casual note into my voice.

"You did. I saw your horse tethered here, and recognized it. As a matter of fact, I saw you approaching my house and then turn off toward the valley. You seemed to make up your mind suddenly. To avoid an encounter with me? Anyway, by the time I had saddled my horse and followed, you were out of sight. I was lucky to find you."

Perhaps I had been the lucky one, despite that disturbing and betraying moment, I thought. Guthrie as an alternative held no appeal.

As we proceeded down the track, Duncan asked, "What did you mean by the lesser of two evils? Were you expecting someone else?"

"Not expecting—but afraid. That man Guthrie passed by earlier."

"Following you?" he asked sharply.

"I shouldn't think so. It was a chance meeting that I had no desire to repeat."

He was thoughtful for a moment, then commented, "So your husband is away." When I made no reply, he continued, "It is a natural assumption, since you are riding alone. I cannot imagine any husband permitting his wife to roam this particular stretch of the moors without his protection or that of a groom."

"I have roamed them all my life. I need no protection."

I shifted my position in the saddle, for my foot was oddly uncomfortable in the stirrup.

"But you were afraid of Guthrie."

I made no answer to that, and when I urged my horse forward Duncan did the same. We rode side by side with the Highland mist eddying about us in an encompassing veil which seemed to both isolate and bind us. I broke into a trot and he did the same—and memory winged back to that terrible morning when my father and I had taken our last ride together, side by side until he went racing ahead to his death. And now I was riding side by side with the man who had later stood over us, gun in hand. A shudder ran through me.

Flicking my crop I broke into a canter. I heard him shout, "I hope you know this ground well, witch! The mist is thickening. . . ." But I paid no heed. I wanted to get away, to get home. Duncan spurred after me.

Leaning my body forward in the saddle to give the mare her head I suddenly put more weight upon the stirrup and the lower one snapped. I pitched to the earth, my ankle twisting, the metal of the stirrup biting into it. I felt a searing pain, coupled with fury because I had made a food of myself before this man—I who prided myself on my horsemanship. So strong was this reaction that I failed even to wonder how I had managed to drag the stirrup away.

I struggled to rise, and failed. He snapped, "Keep still, you little fool, and let me examine your foot."

His words cut off abruptly as he paused with his hand upon my boot. "And how the devil did that happen?"

The stirrup had slid from toe to instep, and lodged there firmly, a piece of broken strap attached to it. Despite pain, I was as puzzled as he.

Gently, he detached it and lifted me into his own saddle. Then he caught the reins of my mare, mounted behind me, and headed toward Daviot, my horse walking alongside. "We'll remove that boot and examine you when we reach my house," he said, his voice close to my ear.

The pain was now so acute that I found it an effort to argue, and when I murmured something about going straight home to Faillie he merely told me to keep quiet. I sagged against him, glad of something solid to lean on, and in this way we proceeded to Daviot Lodge, where he carried me indoors and set me upon a sofa. "Now," he ordered, "off with that riding boot. . . ."

Meekly, I extended my leg and after he had eased away the boot he added, "And now your stocking, Ealasaid—and let's have no modesty about it."

He turned his back, poured a tot of brandy, and brought it across to me. By that time I had drawn the stocking down to my ankle. "Here, let me," he said, holding out the glass. For a man with large hands his touch was gentle as he rolled the stocking the rest of the way. Above my bare foot the flesh was swelling rapidly.

"Sprained, and damned painful, from the look of it. Drink that brandy and you'll feel better."

I drank it at a gulp, and almost immediately felt light headed and uncaring. I rested my head against the cushioned back of the sofa.

"I didn't tell you to gulp it, witch." There was amusement in his voice. "But it won't do you any harm to nod off while I deal with this."

Light-headedness and pain made me close my eyes. I was scarcely aware of his movements, only of his voice calling for cold water and bandages. "Any sort of bandages will do—tear up a tablecloth or something if we haven't anything proper in the house!" Then he came back to me and laid me full length upon the sofa. I floated away on a pleasant cloud, willing to drift off forever, but was brought back from this semi-conscious haze by a welcome coldness dimming the burning pain in my ankle, and the sensation of an inflating balloon subsiding beneath pressure. I opened my eyes and saw him leaning over me, and thought remotely that it should be Calum who looked down upon me with such gentleness and concern. Somehow, their roles seemed to have been reversed.

I sat up, winced, and saw then that my stocking had been inexpertly replaced.

"I must go home . . ."

"Not yet. Not until you've eaten. Then I will take you. And don't imagine you can ride; apart from the fact that no boot would go over that bandaged ankle, you have only one stirrup—the strap of the other has been cut."

I was fully awake then.

"Cut! By whom? And why?"

"I could hazard a guess, but can *you?*"

I shook my head. "The strap must have been faulty, worn . . ."

"The strap was—is—perfectly sound, apart from a neat and precise cut which yielded under pressure."

"But I rode all the way to the Clava field."

"But not hard. You took it easily, no doubt, so the cut in the strap expanded slowly. Or else it was cut while you were there."

"Guthrie! Who else but Guthrie? He had had the time and the opportunity. Instead of watching me, as I had imagined, he could have been causing this damage. But with what motive?"

"Of course," Duncan continued, "I had the time and opportunity also. It is hardly necessary for me to point that out. Either Guthrie—or me. Is that what you are thinking? You were in the central cairn when I came along. I doubt if you heard hoofbeats from inside that place, so you have no idea when I actually arrived. And, of course, I do have a motive—one you have reminded me of before. To drive you out of Faillie. By trying to kill you? It seems a pretty desperate way to evict a person—especially when I intend to do that, ultimately, without risking the hangman's rope. And now, here is some food. When you have eaten we can talk further."

He spoke so practically that he might never have been the man who had kissed me with passion only a short time ago.

A table was wheeled in. I pretended to toy with the food until we were alone, when I set aside my fork and said, "I must examine that strap."

"By all means. I have the stirrup here. It was cut, Ealasaid. Either before you left Faillie, or when your horse was tethered outside the field. You will have to take my word that I didn't do it, and it seems unlikely that it was done before you left Faillie. That leaves only Guthrie. Why should *he* want you to fall and break your neck?"

"Only if he were a maniac."

"Which he isn't. I have employed him. He is plausible and easily bought, but for doing a thing which might endanger your life he would have to be very well paid by someone who would benefit by your death."

My throat went dry. I felt as if I were back in the darkness of the Clava burial chamber, numbed by fear. I tried to convey some food to my mouth, but the fork merely rattled against my plate. Duncan poured wine into a glass and handed it to me.

"Drink slowly this time," he ordered.

The wine was chill, and steadying, and after a second or two the glass ceased to chatter against my teeth.

"What you are saying is ridiculous," I managed to say at last. "Hamish is in charge of the harness room. He would allow no one to tamper with anything."

"So I am right—it must have been done outside the Clava field. For God's sake, Ealasaid, face the truth. Ask yourself who would benefit by your death. *I* wouldn't, because even if you were out of Faillie your husband would still claim ownership. Stop mistrusting me, and look closer to home."

Through stiff lips I declared again that the strap must have been faulty in some way, and that I would speak to Hamish about it. "He is honest and painstaking, but he is growing old and his eyesight isn't too good. It would be the easiest thing in the world for him to overlook slight damage."

Duncan answered indifferently, "Very well, remain blind if you wish to."

I forced myself to eat, determined not to reveal any sign of shock or alarm. I drank the wine, and Duncan suddenly smiled at me across the table.

"What with that and the brandy, you should sleep

well tonight. But for my sake, if not your own, watch out for the future."

"For your sake? What is it to you if I live or die?"

"A very great deal," he answered solemnly. "And does it occur to you that right at this moment you are thoroughly compromised—supping alone with me in my house? If I had sent for a doctor to examine you, the news would have leaked out within the hour and scandal be spreading the length and breadth of Inverness already."

I saw then that there was laughter in his eyes, and was infuriated. First he tried to frighten me, and then he had the audacity to try to flirt with me! It seemed as if I could never have the right kind of conversation with this man, and that any conversation we did have was controlled by him.

I remarked, with what dignity I could muster, that it was time for me to leave. He made no attempt to detain me, merely remarking that he would have a carriage prepared immediately. When he had gone, I sat very still. The coldness of fear had partially diminished; more lasting was a wild and terrible doubt in my mind. One person and one person only would benefit by my death—my husband, who had subtly persuaded me to make a will in his favor, who had tried to insinuate himself into the family business, who wanted to learn all he could so that if anything happened to me he would be capable of taking control, and who had married me quickly after learning that I was to inherit the mills.

Suspicion and speculation were so hideous that, in defense, I called up memories of passion between us and an ardency on his part which could never have been assumed—except by a man easily aroused by women. Any woman? All women who were reasonably attractive? And particularly women like myself, passionate and responsive when in love?

I dared not believe I had been duped. I found myself hating Duncan Mackintosh for sowing such seeds of suspicion and I plainly saw his motive. If he could create a rift between Calum and me and so cause a breakup in our marriage, Faillie would become empty almost at once for, contrary to whatever he pretended to believe, Calum would inevitably return to Deeside and I to Clachnaharry. The man had already admitted that ultimately he intended to get us out somehow.

The door clicked open. "Your carriage awaits you," he announced on a light note which I found singularly jarring. Without more ado, he picked me up and carried me outside.

Back at Faillie Morag was greatly concerned and insisted upon examining my ankle, tut-tutting with disapproval over the amateurish bandaging. Once satisfied that no bones were broken, she announced that it was indeed a severe sprain. That point confirmed, she then scolded me for riding so recklessly.

"Your mistress was not riding recklessly," Duncan said. "She was merely breaking into a canter. That was enough to strain a stirrup already made dangerous."

"Dangerous?" she echoed sharply. "In what way?"

"It had been cut."

I put in quickly, "I'm not satisfied on that point. I would like Hamish to be consulted."

"I thought you said he was shortsighted," Duncan reminded me. "But I am not—and nor are you. Nor, I imagine, is Mistress Crombie." He withdrew the stirrup from the deep pocket of his jacket and held it out. "See for yourself," he said to her. "You will be forced to acknowledge the truth, even if the Mistress of Faillie doesn't want to believe it. Was that rent caused initially by a knife cut, or not?"

Morag protested at once that no one would do such a murderous thing, then added thoughtfully, "Except, perhaps, Hamish. . . ."

I cried, *"Hamish?* Never! Underneath his surliness he is a kind old man . . ."

"Who doesn't want any of us here," she interrupted. "He has never served us willingly, even though my cousin was his late mistress' husband.

And of course, if it comes to that, *you* don't want any of us here, do you, Mr. Mackintosh?"

His mouth curved in amusement.

"As I've already pointed out to the laird's wife, I would hardly risk the hangman's rope to get rid of any of you."

I lost patience then, declared I was tired of all this talk about intended murder. "As you can see, all it resulted in was a sprained ankle!"

But Morag insisted that it could have killed me had I been riding hard. "And it is well known in these parts that you do. I've seen you myself, galloping at breakneck speed across the roughest territory. Oh, you think I don't know what goes on, but many a prayer have I said for you when I've caught sight of you from the ramparts. I, too, enjoy the view from up there occasionally."

"Then perhaps your prayers saved me today," I answered. "And now I'll rebandage my ankle and you can murmur an incantation over it."

"*I* shall rebandage it, after I have prepared a poultice. I can make an excellent herbal one which will take down the swelling very quickly."

I thanked her and struggled out of my chair, saying she could doctor it in my room and that I saw no reason why I couldn't get there without help. I wanted no more from Duncan Mackintosh.

Ignoring my remark, the man picked me up again and marched toward the stairs. "Show me her room, Mistress Crombie, and I'll deposit her there."

Like a parcel—or a tiresome child. I clamped down an angry retort and suffered the indignity of being conveyed upstairs by a man I was anxious to see the last of. Morag went ahead, her soft-footed tread swift and soundless as ever, and to avoid looking at Duncan's face, so close to my own, I stared fixedly at the long wall of the corridor containing the spy slits. One by one they passed, and when we reached the last one of all, memory flashed a picture back into my mind, the first picture I had ever seen through that revealing gap—the picture of this man standing down there in the Banqueting Hall, facing Calum.

With equal vividness his words came back to me. *"I want to know exactly how my sister died. . . ."*

Fourteen

I SUBMITTED to Morag's ministrations. I even accepted a tisane which she declared would give me a good night's sleep. "And mind you drink every drop," she insisted, as she placed it beside my bed. I took a sip to humor her, but after she had gone I set aside the cup, finding the smell unpleasant. It was vaguely familiar, but not until later did I identify it. That was after I wakened with a slight feeling of nausea, and smelled the herbal brew, still steaming faintly in the cup.

Tansy. I remembered rubbing the finely toothed leaves between my fingers, and disliking their pungency, and Morag telling me of the many uses to which the herb could be put. ". . . for poultices to soothe rheumatic pains and chest complaints, also for reducing inflammation of the skin . . . and the leaves in tea for treatment of the stomach. . . ." But surely it was chamomile that she had named as an aid to sleep?

In the morning, Morag was slightly vexed by my rejection of her tisane. She brought my breakfast tray to me personally, and noticed the cup beside my bed. I admitted that I had disliked it. "And I had no idea that tansy helped one to sleep. I thought you used chamomile."

"Of course I use chamomile. Tansy is for stomach upsets. Ask Hamish. I have treated him with it."

Then Hamish should be commended for swallowing such a concoction, I thought, but merely said that I had recognized the smell of tansy immediately.

Morag sniffed the cup. "My dear Elizabeth, chamomile tea has no odor at all, and nor has this. Test it for yourself."

I did, and she was right. I thought it hardly worth while to suggest that perhaps the smell had evaporated as the tisane cooled, so let the matter drop.

Being confined to my room was irksome, but struggling to get up and down spiral stairs without summoning aid was even more so, and I yielded to Morag's advice to rest with my leg outstretched upon a chaise longue beside my window. I could at least gaze at the view, when not occupying my mind and hands with either reading or sewing. I could see the whole of the main courtyard and the causeway spanning the bog—the sluggish bog which irked me so much because it spoiled what would otherwise have been an attractive sight. The arched entrance to the courtyard was picturesque, the stone parapet flanking the causeway equally so, and the vast entrance gates which shut out the world were magnificent. We had spent much money on restoring them, likewise all the stonework within sight, and it seemed false economy not to extend this work to the bog as well. I decided to tackle Calum about it again, when he returned.

I was able to look forward to that event with more peace of mind since talking to Hamish, who had assured me that much of the equipment in the harness room was old and worn. This information made nonsense of Duncan's outrageous implications.

"My late mistress couldna' afford to replace things that were worn out. I had to repair 'em and neglect the rest. Other things needed attention first, she said."

Like the bog, I thought now, gazing down upon its inky blackness. Distant as it was, I was aware of its thick sluggishness stretching out of sight on either side of the causeway, dark, dense, and dank. Water should sparkle there, ripples stirring its surface in the breeze; it should be alive, not dead and stagnant. This struck me as being an' excellent reason for pressing the matter when Calum came home. Stagnant water was undesirable and unhealthy.

But again Calum dismissed my pleas, merely promising to have it cleared when the projects at present under way had been dealt with.

I wasted little time in bringing up the matter after he came striding into the bedroom full of concern, having been greeted with the news of my accident by Morag. It was a relief to see him and a solace to be told that he had missed me sorely. His eyes met mine frankly and openly, so that I was ashamed of having entertained the smallest doubt or fear. Those eyes were too patently honest to deceive, and I now regarded Duncan Mackintosh's wild assumptions with contempt. In doing so, I felt more secure.

Calum examined every item in the harness room, setting aside pieces that could be sent away for expert repair and discarding altogether those that could not. In particular, he examined my stirrup strap and announced that the break in it could have been mistaken for a cut at first glance, but in his opinion it was more likely to have been caused by a jagged hook, probably a rusty one on which it had been hanging. Shortsighted Hamish might have pulled it off with a jerk, and so started the rent, which had finally broken under pressure. He ordered much restocking of the harness room to avoid any such disaster in the future. Calum's anxiety for me was so great that I made no mention of Guthrie, nor my uneasy feeling about the man, until he asked how far I had ridden and, on hearing, reprimanded me for visiting such an isolated spot, and particularly for riding without a groom.

"A woman alone could well be in danger if she

met some untrustworthy ruffian, especially an attractive woman like you."

"I did meet someone. Guthrie, looking very dandified in expensive suiting. On a laborer's pay, I wondered how he could afford such clothes, although I know he supplements his earnings with other work."

"What other work, and where?" Calum demanded.

"In the gardens at Daviot Lodge. I have seen him there."

Calum was annoyed, remarking that the man was employed exclusively by him, and had no right to undertake work for others.

"Then you must make that plain. Sometimes I wonder if you're not too lenient with him. If you allowed him less free time, he would be unable to work for anyone else."

Calum regarded me indulgently. "And who was persuading me to get rid of him altogether, only a short time ago? Yet now you upbraid me for not employing him enough."

I laughed, and admitted that inconsistency was part of my nature.

"A lovable part, my imaginative, spirited wife. And I would not have you different in any way."

One advantage of having a sprained ankle was that for a few days, at least, Calum and I had our meals sent upstairs. For a brief spell we were able to enjoy them alone, but Morag's herbal poultice proved so effective that not only did the swelling disappear as speedily as she predicted, but the pain also. It wasn't long before I was able to put my foot to the ground, stepping gingerly at first and then, day by day, for slightly longer periods. But Calum would not yet allow me to return to the mills; Macpherson, he declared, would have to carry on without me. He also helped by going to the mills himself, whether welcomed by Macpherson or not.

"And vastly interesting it all is," he declared one day. "I can understand the fascination it has for you. I even understand the intricacies of the tartan now. I never realized before just how few colors are actually employed in it, and that each color appears not only in its pure form but in an equal blend with every other color."

"There's a great deal more to it than that," I told him.

"Such as?"

"Well, in the old days, thread-count sticks reproduced the number of threads for each stripe, depending upon the thickness of the yarn used, and on the size of the sett. Formerly, the web must have been about twenty-six inches across, and the sett arranged to fit into this width a definite number of times, with one edge of the web—and sometimes both—coinciding with the turning point of the design."

"I hope I shall grasp it all as completely as you have, my love."

"I was born into the industry, so I've had a lifetime in which to learn."

It was good to be able to discuss the art of weaving with him, and I reflected comfortably that when James observed my husband's very real interest in things he would no longer regard him as an outsider, and all traces of friction between them would disappear. One good thing, at least, was resulting from my sprained ankle, so I was content to let things take their course, and in this peaceful interval the days slid by serenely; my ankle healed; I was happy.

Perhaps it was too much to expect this serenity to continue. It was interrupted with a jolt when Hamish came to me one day, carrying a coiled rope in his hand and with a look of concern on his face.

I was sitting in my rock garden, beside a sundial Calum had bought for me. "You can count the hours of our life together," he had said affectionately.

To see Hamish enter the rock garden was surprising in itself, for he rarely ventured beyond his own sphere

—mainly the harness room and coach house—so I knew at once that something of importance brought him here.

For a moment I was touched with apprehension, and it was hard to keep it from my voice when asking what was wrong.

"This, Mistress." He held up the rope—coiled, dirty, and somewhat sodden.

"Why bring that to me?"

"Because I found it beneath a bush not far from the spot where y'r father was killed."

I saw then that it was the kind of rope a deerstalker would use, and my heart seemed to clench. Had this rope belonged to my father's killer?

"I was coming back from visiting my daughter and caught sight of it, sticking out from under a bush. I don't know what made me drag it out, except that I've been looking for a missing rope ever since that day. This one, Mistress. We keep nigh on a dozen in the harness room. Since that day there've been only eleven. A poacher, mebbe. Some say poachers will break in anywhere, help themselves to anything. O' course, I don't know if a rifle was stolen from the gun room, that being the laird's private place and no servants allowed in. Mistress Crombie dusts it and keeps it clean, but no one else may set foot in there."

"I know." And indeed I did. Morag was very proud because she alone was permitted to enter the gun room, but the fact never troubled me because guns held no appeal. One day Calum had shown me the room: case after case of guns, all acquired by generations of Mackintoshes. A fine collection, he had declared, and I could see then that he was proud to own them, just as he could see my lack of interest. It had disappointed him, although he didn't say so. He had simply remarked that Morag kept the place dusted, so I need not visit there if I had no wish to. I never did. Not even when he retired there alone, as he frequently did, to admire the collection, like a small boy cherishing toy soldiers.

"How do you know that rope belongs to Faillie? It might belong to anyone."

"I know it by this, Mistress."

The rope slid through Hamish's hands for a yard or two, then halted. "I did this repair m'sel', about a year ago. I know my own work, and I know my own ropes, whether folks say they all look alike or not. I did that resplicing with these very hands, *and* that knotting and binding. Someone helped themselves to it that Sabbath Day—and I'd like to know how, seeing as I'd locked the harness room m'sel', Mistress Crombie giving me permission to go to Daviot Kirk."

"You mean—"

"That it must have been taken by someone from Faillie, that's what I mean."

"Or someone who knew how to get into the harness room; someone who knew where you kept the key."

"Aye."

"And who had that knowledge, besides yourself, Hamish?"

"The laird, o' course, but he was away. The housekeeper because she keeps a check on all keys. One or two o' the servants, mebbe, but I know all of 'em and none dare borrow a rope or a gun or a horse or it'd cost them their jobs, that it would. Wouldna dare do it m'sel', Mistress."

"What of the workmen? There are several about the place during the week."

"Aye, I've thought of that, and it seems the only likely thing, though I've kept away from the lot of 'em —a rough crowd they be, these laboring gangs. I've taken care of all my keys with that lot around—*and* good care that none of 'em should see where I put them."

"And where do you put them?"

"On a hook in the small scullery off the kitchen. There's an outside door to it, and Mistress Crombie usually locks it from the inside, but that morning she told me to take the key with me so that I could let m'sel' in when I came back. In your absence the castle was empty. Setting great store by religion, she let all

155

the staff go to the Kirk that day. I eat my midday meal in the kitchen with them, and that scullery door is the back way into it."

"And having locked the door from the outside, you took the key with you, leaving the one for the harness room on its hook in the scullery?"

"Aye, I did so."

"And it was still there when you returned?"

He admitted to being uncertain. He had walked straight through the scullery and into the kitchen, not looking for the key until next day. It had been on its hook then, with all the rest.

"And it wasn't until then that I missed the rope. I wanted to keep busy because the shock had gone deep, Mistress; the shock of your father's death. So keep busy I did, looking for jobs to do. That was why I counted everything in the harness room, and found a rope was missing. This one."

"And you didn't report it?"

He shuffled uncomfortably.

"I was afraid, Mistress. I'm responsible for everything there and that housekeeper can be a tartar—if ye'll forgive me saying so. With the laird away, and y'rsel' at Clachnaharry, there was only she I could report to and I—well, I . . ."

"You were afraid to. I understand, Hamish. Don't worry."

My hands fell limply into my lap. I was totally unaware of the embroidery needle piercing one of my fingers until, later, I saw a fleck of blood on it. All the horror of my father's death had come rushing back and, with it, the realization that if someone within the castle could have taken the key of the harness room they could also have helped themselves to a rifle from the gun room, and a horse from the stables. Horse and gun would have been returned, but the rope could have been lost, and in their hurry to get away they had not paused to search for it. Why trouble, when it had merely been part of their disguise, although usually carried by a ghillie or helpers? This fact alone implied that the person knew very little about deer-stalking.

I asked, through numb lips, how close the bush had been to the place where my father had died.

"Close enough, Mistress, close enough."

"How do you know?"

He answered, somewhat shyly, that he had gone there to pay his respects. "I went as soon as I heard, Mistress, for he was a good man, Aindreas MacArthur. The spot was easy to find, for the earth was still stained. I knelt awhile, and prayed."

I trembled and closed my eyes. I felt his gnarled old hand upon my shoulder.

"Forgive me, Mistress. I'd no mind to distress ye."

With my eyes still closed in a vain endeavor to hold back my tears, I groped for his hand and clung to it. He begged me again to forgive him, adding that he could never forgive himself. "The rope lying there so close, and I not seeing it...."

"Left there by his murderer, Hamish. We know now, you and I, that it was no accident. No deerstalker would have made a mistake at such close range. Someone shot my father deliberately."

Fifteen

I DECIDED to speak about it to no one, and commanded Hamish to keep his knowledge to himself, for I was aware that without further proof I could be accused of jumping to conclusions, or letting my imagination run away with me again—morbidly, this time. Against all this my argument would be weak, so I remained silent, hugging conviction to myself. The time would come, must come, when truth emerged.

Meanwhile, I went over and over in my mind every detail of that fatal weekend. With Calum away in Edinburgh on my father's behalf, who had remained at the castle? Myself, Hamish, Morag, and the servants she had engaged—all local people without any motive for murder. If it came to that, no one had a motive. Aindreas MacArthur had been a man who made friends, not enemies.

But there was also that sinister man Guthrie, who slept above the stables with others of the outdoor staff; a man who would stop at nothing if the price was right, Duncan had declared.

Uneasiness haunted me even when I returned to the mills next day. James grudgingly admitted that my husband had acquitted himself well. "He has an astute brain, Miss Elizabeth." From James, such praise was a big concession.

He remarked that I looked pale. "And tired, lass. That fall seems to have taken a lot out o' ye. Are ye wise to come back so soon?"

Because it wasn't the fall from which I was suffering, but yesterday's shock, all I said was that I felt well enough and that I would feel even better for working again, which was true. To remain idly at home, brooding, was about the worst thing I could do. I had slept little enough last night, my thoughts going round and round in circles, and unless I exhausted myself with work it would be the same tonight. At the end of the day I left the mills reluctantly.

At dinner Morag remarked, as James had done, that I looked tired, and Calum insisted that I go to bed early. I obeyed, and it wasn't long before he joined me, taking me in his arms automatically. But I was too tired to respond and after a while he drew away somewhat coldly.

Again sleep eluded me, and I lay for a long time listening to my husband's breathing, my brain relentlessly asking questions and seeking answers which refused to be found. In the end, I slipped out of bed, lit a candle, and went barefoot into the short passage outside. I would go down to the library and find a book that demanded concentration.

My bare feet made no sound as I turned into the long corridor above the Banqueting Hall, holding the candle high to guide my way. To my surprise, it was not wholly necessary, for through the spy slits light glimmered.

Puzzled, I glanced down—and went rigid with astonishment.

I was staring at the back of a woman, seated in my chair at the long dining table. Dark hair streamed over her shoulders and her face was buried in her hands. She was weeping. On the table beside her stood a four-branched silver candelabrum, its light casting a sheen upon her hair and upon the richness of an emerald satin gown.

I stood rooted to the spot. I was the only dark-haired woman at Faillie, and, unless I had taken leave of my senses, not even my wildest imagination could convince me that I was looking at some vision of myself. A ghost, then? There was nothing so insubstantial about that very human figure giving way to very human emotion.

I remained where I was; watching, wondering, and coming to one inevitable conclusion. Somewhere in this castle a woman lived, hidden from the eyes of the world.

I knew that I had to go down and face her but, even as I took a step forward, she pushed back her chair slowly and rose. The curtain of her hair fell forward, concealing her face as she picked up the candelabrum. With the other hand lifting her voluminous skirt, she walked down the long Banqueting Hall toward the stairs. I waited, watching her retreating figure, knowing that I could do one of two things—go toward the stairs myself and meet her, or wait for her to mount them.

I waited. To come face to face with me on the narrow spiral would be a shock to someone already distraught. As soon as she reached the top and turned the end of the corridor, I would speak to her gently.

As she continued down the Banqueting Hall in a flickering pool of light, I took in every detail of her gown, which was costly and elegant. She was obviously no servant, playing at being mistress of the castle while the real mistress was believed to be abed. She was a woman accustomed to good things; she wore that gown with ease, as if it had been made for her, and on the hand which held the candelabrum rings sparkled brilliantly. I also caught the flash of jewels about her neck.

A moment later she was out of view, and the Banqueting Hall returned to darkness as she started to climb the stairs. I found myself waiting for her breathlessly, counting the treads as she mounted them. I knew there were fifteen in all: fifteen steps; then she would appear at the top of the spiral, turn, and face me.

I was right in only one thing: she did appear at the top of the spiral but, in expecting her to face me, I was wrong. She went straight forward, opened the door of the short passage leading to the Keep, walked through, and closed it behind her. I saw only her side view, with the curtain of dark hair still screening her features.

I hurried after her, anxious to see which room she entered. It had to be one of the bedrooms opening from that passage, although I was surprised that a woman of such obvious means should be accommodated so modestly. On my first tour of the castle, Morag had explained that in the old days, when the Mackintoshes had entertained lavishly, ladies' maids and valets had occupied those rooms. That meant that they would be comfortably furnished, but not luxurious and, from the look of the unknown woman, luxury was something to which she was accustomed.

I had my hand upon the door latch when my husband's voice arrested me.

"Elizabeth! What are you doing there? Come back to bed, my love."

He was standing at the turn of the corridor leading from our rooms. He had pulled on a robe without bothering to tie it. He said again, "Come back to bed at once, or you'll catch cold. Your feet are bare!"

I said urgently, "I saw a woman—an unknown woman!" and as I spoke I opened the door. The passage was empty. Unless I looked in every bedroom I had no hope of finding her.

Calum came striding along the corridor and took my arm.

"There you go, imagining things again! I knew you would overtire yourself by going back to the mills so soon." He closed the passage door and led me away.

"I imagined nothing, Calum, and I am anything but tired. I am very much awake, believe me, and so was that woman. She was weeping. I want to find her. . . ."

He repeated, indulgently, that my imagination was far too lively. It sounded like an echo of my mother in the old days, except that she had always said it with impatience. Now it was I who felt impatient, and as Calum removed my robe and urged me into bed, saying that tomorrow he would send for a doctor, I answered irritably that I had no need of one.

"A sprained ankle doesn't cause illness," I declared crossly, "nor am I suffering from delusions. I saw a woman sitting down there in the Banqueting Hall, in *my* place!"

Slipping into bed beside me Calum asked me to describe her, and the elaborate patience in his voice almost goaded me to fury.

"She wore a beautiful gown. Emerald satin. Her fingers sparkled with rings. There were more jewels round her neck—I saw the flash of them through her hair, which was long and dark, flowing over her shoulders. The gown must have cost quite a deal of money. And she carried a four-branch candelabrum."

"And her face?"

I confessed I had not seen that. "She was weeping, her head in her hands."

He said mockingly, "And you didn't go down to her—this poor, distressed woman?"

"You don't believe a word I've said!"

"Do you really expect me to?"

Furiously, I declared that I was speaking the truth.

"I didn't see her face because her long hair concealed it."

"Long, and dark?"

"That's right."

"Like your own, in fact."

I bit back an angry retort, and he laughed gently as he reached across and snuffed out the candles. Then he put his arms around me, cradling me against him, but I lay stiff and unyielding.

"You surely don't expect me to take this seriously?" he said. "And you mustn't be hurt by my teasing."

"I am hurt—because you won't believe me. But what I told you is the truth. When she rose, she picked up the candles, and walked away from me down the Banqueting Hall toward the stairs. I knew then that I would meet her when she reached the top."

"And did you?"

"No. She didn't turn along the corridor. She went through the door facing the stairs, opening onto the short passage leading to the Keep. I was about to follow when you called to me."

"But you did open the door, and the passage was empty."

"Yes."

He stifled a yawn.

"You've been reading too many melodramas, Elizabeth. What are you imagining now—that I keep a secret mistress somewhere in the castle?" He finished impatiently, "You must have been sleepwalking, and dreaming into the bargain."

"I tell you I saw her and I heard her weeping, and the rustle of her skirts as she walked. I heard the latch lift as she opened the door, and I heard it shut behind her."

"Come to your senses, Elizabeth. Only one person sleeps along that passage: Morag, who is mousy-haired and impoverished."

"It certainly wasn't Morag."

"Then we must have a ghost at Faillie! I hope I may have the pleasure of meeting her sometime, especially if she is a beautiful damsel in distress in need of comfort. . . ."

I said no more. What was the use? He fell asleep, still amused, still disbelieving, still convinced that I had imagined the whole thing. Eventually I slept too, and in my dreams a faceless woman walked toward me, carrying a rope. The rope was long and the ends of it trailed at her sides; in the center, suspended between her outstretched hands, was one part carefully repaired. As she neared me she lifted the rope toward my throat and I, numbed and helpless, waited for inescapable death. Then a man appeared, carrying a long-barreled rifle, and took the rope from her. He then focused the rifle on me, and the faceless woman stood by and watched. The man had the figure of Duncan Mackintosh, but Calum's features.

"You are going to join Sheena," he said. "She is in the field of the dead."

Duncan's figure, Calum's face—and Guthrie's voice. I saw then that we were surrounded by the Clava Stones, with the yawning mouth of the main burial chamber waiting to receive me. And I knew that something tragic had happened to Sheena, and that when I found out what it was I would recoil from the pain of it.

I wakened violently, cold all through, and remained awake until dawn. In the light of day the background details of the nightmare faded, but the terrible feeling I had about Sheena remained. It was as if some message had been trying to get through to me; some premonition that I wanted to resist, but the awareness was as vivid as last night's incident. The woman I had seen had been real enough, and so was my bewilderment, which was with me still.

After breakfast, I told Morag about the woman. Like Calum, she didn't believe me and looked at me in astonishment, as if I were slightly mad.

As I prepared to leave for the mills, I heard the sound of wheels rattling across the causeway but I paid little heed. This was the time of day when deliveries from the mail coach, which arrived in Inverness nightly, were brought out by local carrier, so I was not surprised to see Calum reading a letter when I went downstairs. He was frowning.

"Not bad news, I hope?"

He crumpled the missive and threw it in the fire. "Unfortunately, yes. I must leave for Carrisbrae at once. Grant, my factor, has been taken ill."

I glanced outside. "This is no weather for travel. Must you leave today?"

"The sooner the better. Someone must carry on in his place."

"The rain is heavy and, from the look of the sky, promises to be worse. If you are likely to be at Carrisbrae for some time, couldn't I come with you?"

"I don't recommend it in weather like this. You would be lonely and confined indoors. Don't fret, I will return as quickly as possible. And Grant's wife is something of an alarmist; I have no doubt she has exaggerated the situation." He pulled the bellrope beside the fireplace and, when Morag appeared, asked her to pack a grip for him at once. "And see that Elizabeth gets to bed early each night."

I retorted impatiently, pulling on my gloves, "Good gracious, I'm not ill! You've made a lot of unnecessary fuss over that fall. Believe me, I am glad to be working again. Idleness bores me."

I was indeed glad to be back at the mills. The rattle of looms, the smell of wool, and the sight of colorful bales of cloth lightened my heart. It also seemed that the workers were pleased to see me, for I no longer met evasive glances or unwilling answers.

The weather worsened throughout the day, and as I drove across the causeway on my return I saw that the bog had swollen considerably. By morning it was worse, and I thought with satisfaction that I now had a justifiable excuse to put the clearing in hand in Calum's absence. On reached Inverness the next morning I did so, arranging for a team of workmen to come as soon as the bad weather eased.

Meanwhile, Morag's company was far from enjoyable. At dinner she seemed distraught and morose. I had grown accustomed to her moods, but found this one particularly trying. I noticed she had not even bothered to change from her plain afternoon dress, and her hair was pulled back haphazardly from her brow, as if untouched since morning.

I retired to my sitting room and tried to concentrate on a book for the remainder of the evening but the identity of the unknown woman still bothered me. Whatever Calum or Morag cared to say, she had been no phantom of my imagination. After a while I laid aside my book and, glancing at the fob watch pinned to my bodice, saw that it was nearly time for the nightly dish of tea which Morag always served beside the fire in the Billeting Room. I went there reluctantly, knowing that she would be offended if I did not. I was relieved to find the room empty, for had she been waiting I would have suffered her displeasure.

I paced the floor restlessly; as I did so, my glance fell on the leather mailbag that was kept on a small table near the head of the spiral stairs leading down to the main entrance. The flap had fallen open; letters were inside. I took them out, presuming that Calum had overlooked them. To my surprise, they proved to be letters I myself had written a day or two before, and which should have been collected by the carrier when delivering. It was his job to take them into Inverness and put them on the next mail coach. When no deliveries came to the castle, Hamish took all letters into Inverness and arranged for their dispatch.

I turned at the sound of Morag's step, asking why the letters had not been given to the carrier when he called.

"There was no delivery either today or yesterday."

"Indeed there was. Calum received a communication from Carrisbrae yesterday morning. His factor's wife had written urgently. That was why he asked you to pack a grip for him at once."

I had an inexplicable feeling that she had resented not being told the reason for Calum's departure. She liked to be aware of everything that went on, and perhaps for this reason made a show of indifference now by shrugging her shoulders and saying that Hamish must have forgotten to give the man our outgoing mail.

I pushed the letters back. They were not important. But it was the first time I had known Hamish to forget.

We sipped our tea in silence, Morag's preoccupation like a cloud between us. My concern for her deepened, and I decided that before retiring I would choose some gowns and leave them in her room.

I left her staring into the fire. She scarcely heeded my good-night. I felt that she was likely to remain there until the embers were dying, but I knew it was useless to urge her to bed. When I took the clothes along to her room, I was not surprised to find it still empty.

It was a comfortable place, well furnished, with a deep closet built into a wide recess. I decided to hang the gowns inside, so dropped them upon the bed and opened the closet doors.

It was stacked full. Cloaks and gowns, all carefully protected by holland covers, hung beneath a wide shelf on which an array of bonnets stood in bandboxes, and beneath the holland covers protruded deep hems of velvet and fur, and flounces in muslin, silk, and satin.

Emerald satin.

I snatched at that one, and pulled away the cover. The gown was unmistakable. I stood with it in my hands and my eyes went to the shelf above, seeking —and finding—a wigstand. It was at the far end, pushed toward the back, but the long dark tresses it supported were as recognizable as the gown I held.

I didn't hear her step. As always, it was soft as a cat's. How long she had been there, I had no idea, but suddenly I was aware of her presence. Her pale eyes watched me from the door, more malevolent than I had ever seen them.

"Why?" I demanded.

She knew what I meant.

She glanced at the clothes upon the bed and a faint smile stirred her thin lips.

"You can take those away, Elizabeth. I don't want your charity."

"Nor do you need it! Why pretend to be impoverished when you have a wardrobe like this——and why parade in drab clothes, like a poor relation, when you are obviously nothing of the sort?"

"You wouldn't understand."

"Self-martyrdom? I admit I find that hard to understand." And then I remembered the weeping figure in the Banqueting Hall, and my heart softened.

"You are unhappy, Morag. Please, tell me, let me help . . ."

"I have nothing to tell you that you have not already heard. I mourn my husband."

"Is that why you were weeping last night?"

"Why else?"

"And—that?" I gestured toward the long dark tresses at the back of the shelf.

"An indulgence." She gave a faint shrug. "Once my hair was long and dark, like yours. My husband loved it. He used to brush it before we went to bed. He loved to stroke it, and he loved to see me beautifully dressed . . ."

"And bejeweled."

"Jewels?" she echoed sharply. "I have no jewels."

"But the rings you wore? I saw them sparkling on your fingers. *And* when your fell forward I saw more jewels about your neck."

"You imagined them. I tell you, I have no jewels."

I swept up my clothes and walked to the door.

"I'm sorry you are unhappy, Morag, but at least let us have no more charades, no more dressing up in secret. I insist that you get rid of those drab garments you've been parading in. You will be a great deal happier in the others. You will also stop feeling sorry for yourself."

"I have good reason to be sorry for myself."

"If every widow indulged in self-pity, she would make those about her very miserable."

"You can afford to be complacent."

"Can I?" I thought of my father; of his blood staining

my skirt, and the unquenchable grief I still felt for him. I thought of the unanswered question mark which seemed to hover over his death. I thought of my broken stirrup strap, and Duncan's strong warning to watch out for the future. And suddenly I thought of the Keep, and the door locked upon me, and the broken floor through which I could have fallen to my death.

I left the room abruptly, and was just in time to see the door of the Keep open at the end of the passage. A man walked through, carrying a lantern.

It was Guthrie.

Momentarily, I stared, then burst out, "Who gave you permission to enter here?" I whipped round then upon Morag. "I thought you made sure all doors were locked at night? And don't blame Hamish for forgetfulness this time!"

"I was about to check the door of the Keep when I heard you in my room. Naturally, I paused."

She was never at a loss for an answer. I spun back to Guthrie and saw his dark, sensual face smiling with secret amusement, as if the prospect of two women in combat entertained him.

"You haven't answered my question, Guthrie. Your territory is outdoors, not within the castle. You are trespassing."

"Your pardon, Mistress. The laird is planning to restore the Keep, and asked me to carry out an inspection."

"At this time of night?"

"Unfortunately, my duties outside prevented me from obeying his instructions until this evening. The Keep is in a bad state. It has taken a long time to go over it—hence the lantern."

He was very glib.

"The weather today has been too bad for outdoor work." I spoke sharply, determined to put the man in his place, but he was impervious to snub and answered blandly that bad weather was never any deterrent to him.

"Then you should have made your exit by the way you came in, which was presumably from the outer entrance of the Keep—using a ladder, since access to it is impossible in any other way."

"Unfortunately, Mistress, the ladder fell away as I took the last step climbing in." He finished smoothly, "I am sure you are too kind to wish me to risk my neck over such a drop."

"So without even knocking for admission, you used this door—conveniently unlocked."

"I was fortunate to come across it—Mistress. I had no idea where it led to. As for knocking, I thought the household would be abed. I had no wish to disturb anyone. My intention was merely to find an exit through the castle, and so back to my quarters above the stables."

"Then do so." I reached behind him and, with one hand, turned the heavy iron key and dropped it in my pocket. "Mistress Crombie will show you to the kitchens—unless, of course, you know the way already? This is not the first time I have seen you within these walls."

I saw a flicker of surprise in those black, arrogant eyes; a darting glance to Morag and away again. Her pale eyes made no response, still and opaque as ever. I felt a gathering rage. What sort of a fool did they take me for, these two unlikable people? But of what could I accuse either, when every accusation I made would be skillfully side-stepped? I could be as suspicious as I liked, but without evidence I could produce no grounds for it.

I turned to Morag then. It was hard to appear dignified when clutching a pile of clothing over one arm, but I was not going to retire defeated.

"I told you never to admit this man into the castle again."

"I did not admit him. You have heard the explanation of how he found his way in here, and I confess that his reason seems logical to me. Would you indeed wish him to risk his neck?"

I felt at that moment that I would dearly like him to break it, and because I also desired to maintain supremacy over both of them I asked Morag coolly for the true reason for Guthrie's visit to the castle that first time.

"Or perhaps it was not the first time? Has he been here before, without my knowledge, ostensibly to check the log supply? But that was merely an excuse, wasn't it? When I saw him, he was nowhere near the fireplace in the Banqueting Hall, but walking away from the stairs leading down from this floor. Did you think me stupid enough not to notice that?"

Guthrie put in quickly, "Mistress Crombie had been giving me instructions. She stood at the foot of the stairs and asked me to attend to the log baskets."

"He speaks the truth, Elizabeth. After that, I came up and met you. You seem a trifle distraught tonight. Perhaps you should go to bed."

They would protect each other against all questions. Very well, I decided, I can wait. Let them underestimate me, if they wish. Perhaps it will be to my advantage to let them do so.

That there was some sort of alliance between these two I was convinced—but the nature of it baffled me. I could not imagine him as her lover. He was the type of man who would desire a more lusty mistress. But I was no longer deceived by Morag's pose of grieving widow, although her weeping last night had been genuine enough.

That brought me to yet another unanswered question, and when I put it to her I was glad to see her disconcerted.

I asked, "Just why were you sitting in my chair at the dining table after we were all abed, dressed up in your finery and jewels? Were you imagining yourself as mistress of Faillie?"

Quick as a flash, Guthrie's black eyes darted at her and remained there, while her pale skin flushed. For the first time in my recollection, she was at a loss for an answer, and she vented her chagrin on Guthrie by saying sharply, "You will find the back door through the kitchens. You can reach them through the far end of the Billeting Room."

"Take him, Morag. You will need to lock up be-hind him. He can hardly do that himself."

She went with apparent nonchalance, but I knew instinctively that the last thing she wanted was to be alone with this man. Somehow I had betrayed some secret to him, and she would hate me for doing so. I cared little about that; I was too busy speculating on the nature of that secret. It seemed to me that Guthrie's attention had been particularly caught by my mention of the jewels which Morag stubbornly denied possessing.

As they went below I made sure that they heard my footsteps going to my room, but once there I tossed the clothes aside and sped softly back along the corridor and out onto the ramparts, making my way to the part that looked down into the inner courtyard. Clouds were still heavy, but between them sliced a glimmer of moonlight; enough to reveal the gaping entrance of the Keep, and the fallen ladder which lay upon crumbled stones from which steps had once risen to that high outer door.

So the ladder had indeed fallen, as Guthrie had said; unless he had deliberately kicked it away. He was a man who would always cover his traces and, if he had an assignment within the castle, his only means of access was through the Keep—once the castle was locked for the night. It was an expedient arrangement, for to admit him through the main rooms involved the risk of being seen or overheard; whereas an unlocked door at the end of a shut-off passage involved no risk of betrayal. But theirs was no amorous assignation. Morag's demeanor throughout the evening had been anything but that of a woman impatiently awaiting a lover.

Before going to bed, I took the heavy iron key from my pocket and hid it away in my boudoir, well concealed beneath layers of underclothes. No one was likely to find it there, for I myself attended to my clothes, as I had been brought up to do. Once the key was hidden, I felt better, for I was determined that the inner door to the Keep should never be opened again.

Morag's secret dressing up in her gowns of former years, in a pathetic attempt to recapture the personality her husband had loved, moved me as much as her denial of the jewels puzzled me, but she herself was an enigma which I could never hope to solve. I stood by my bedroom window before undressing, pondering on her strangeness. Undoubtedly I had seen the sparkle of stones on her fingers and neck. Perhaps they were her secret insurance for the future, about which she wanted no one to know. Perhaps they were artificial and, because of her desire to be a woman of elegance and position, she did not want it known that she would wear anything but the genuine article.

As I pondered, I found myself watching the night clouds scudding across the face of the moon. Light and shadow played across the grounds, sometimes outlining the stone balustrades flanking the causeway, sometimes the high arch leading to the main entrance of the castle, and then, unexpectedly, focusing on the family tomb which stood some distance away. I had never visited it, but now—as clearly as on the day when I had sat upon the watchman's stone and known that something momentous was about to happen —I knew that I had to go down there, that the place held a message for me and that I should waste no time in heeding it.

Flinging a cloak across my shoulders I slipped quietly out of the castle and, half afraid, half excited, raced across the damp grass to the tomb, a circular stone building with a conical roof not unlike those which must once have covered the Clava Cairns. The excitement I felt was that of expectancy mingled with dread, impossible to turn away from however greatly I might want to. It was a compulsion that had to be obeyed.

Steps led down to the door of the vault which, as I knew from Hamish who took care of the place, was never locked. He had also told me that a light was always kept burning there—a Faillie tradition. Consequently no gloom met me when I entered, and I saw that the steadily burning light came from pieces of stick about six inches long, smeared at both ends with brimstone and balanced on iron brackets. They had come into fashion in Edinburgh at the end of the eighteenth century and were still sold by street hawkers as firelighters, called Spunks. Damping the sticks in the middle made the flames burn more slowly and provided, as now, a steady light. Skillful use of the tinderbox was required to ignite them, at which Hamish was adept. I was grateful for his skill now, for the flames banished any sense of chill or eeriness.

I glanced around curiously. The interior of the building was not unusual. Around the walls ran stone shelves on which the coffins of former Mackintoshes stood, carefully dusted and reverently cared for, but in the center of the room a new one stood upon trestles, isolated and alone. I knew at once that it was Una's.

I walked toward it slowly, my eyes fixed upon the polished brass plate with its recent inscription bearing her name. And it was then that I knew what had brought me here, and the message that awaited me.

It was as if a voice spoke loud in my ear, telling me that her casket was empty.

I was suddenly cold. Suddenly, too, that strange feeling of detachment that always possessed me when some uncanny premonition touched me, vanished as quickly as it had come. I was back in reality, a frightened young woman who took to her heels and ran.

Sixteen

AFTER MY UNCANNY EXPERIENCE I was glad to submerge myself in work next morning, but an ominous feeling remained with me and refused to be banished. It was with me still when James thrust his head round the door of the checking room, where I was inspecting the newest lengths from the looms, and announced, "Yon Angus Fraser to see ye, Miss Elizabeth. I told him ye were busy, but he insists the matter is urgent."

I hadn't seen Angus since Sheena had stayed at Faillie and he had come to sup with us. My mind immediately jumped to the conclusion that something was wrong at Clachnaharry.

"Is it Mother?" I asked, as soon as I saw him. "She's not unwell, I hope?"

"Your mother's fine. Sheena's not."

My ominous feeling deepened. I had never succeeded in forgetting my dream warning about Sheena, although I had resolutely tried to. Now I had to force myself to ask what was wrong.

Angus glanced at the dividing door between James's room and my own and, satisfied that it was firmly closed, said bluntly, "She is with child."

My legs went weak. I sat down slowly, unable to speak, but after a while I managed to ask, "Are you the father?"

"You must know I'm not. It would be better if I were."

Through my numbed senses I heard my voice asking remotely, "Why would it be better?" but even as I spoke I knew the answer and something inside me seemed to die.

"Because I am free to marry her, and marry her I would."

"But—the father—is not?"

Angus nodded. His face was tight and controlled, but I could feel the heat of his anger, anger coupled with hatred. Yet beneath it ran compassion and I sensed that the compassion was for me.

"You need tell me no more," I answered dully, remembering the empty pillow beside my own; the hours I had spent waiting for Calum to come to me; the crumpled couch in his dressing room after he had finally entered it in the early hours of the morning— and the hideous suspicion which I had deliberately thrust down.

At last I forced myself to ask Angus why he came to me. "To hurt me, shock me? You have never quite forgiven me for distressing Sheena by marrying Calum, have you? Is that your reason for bringing the news here first—to wound me in return?"

"No! Never that, Elizabeth. She was besotted with the man, and I besotted with her, and all I could care about then was how *she* felt. Later, I was glad that it was you and not she who wed him. I thought she would get over it, forget him, turn back to me. She was on the verge of loving me when he came into our lives. But when I visited the castle and saw you all together, I knew how things were. So, I suspect, did that housekeeper. She's no fool, and nor am I. But you were. You wouldn't see what was under your nose. Sheena was as infatuated with him as ever—more so. And he encouraging her, and enjoying it!"

"Stop!" I crossed to the window and stood for a long time, staring out into the mill yard, but seeing nothing.

At length, Angus said more gently, "I didn't want to come to you at all. I've been to Faillie, but he's not there. Morag Crombie told me he'd been called away; she didn't say where to, and because I didn't want to arouse her curiosity—which is avid enough I suspect—I didn't ask. That is why I've come to you. I'm sorry, Elizabeth. This is hard on you."

"But harder on Sheena? That is what you are thinking, isn't it?"

"Well—it's true. You're a stronger person than she is. You have courage and independence. And the mills. If your marriage falls through, they'll become your abiding interests, as they were your father's."

How little he knew me! He had never been able to understand any woman but Sheena, and very often he failed to totally understand even her because although he had a heart he lacked imagination. He saw her only as weak and vulnerable, and so she was—but I was vulnerable too. Independence was no protection against being hurt.

I managed to say, "If Calum denies all this, what then?"

"Then he's the liar I believe him to be."

A liar? An opportunist? A schemer? Or merely a charmer who could get any woman he wanted? I would rather believe him that. A woman who married a handsome man laid herself open to hurt of that nature, but it was preferable to marrying a man who was crooked. Infidelities were easier to forgive than downright wickedness, because infidelities hurt only one's pride. In time, most men outgrew them, and the scars they left on a woman's heart could slowly heal.

But to be unfaithful with my own sister, and under the same roof! The pain of that went deep. Later, when I was alone, I would weep because of it, but not now, and not here. Tears were meant to be shed in private. I took a deep breath and asked, "Where is she?"

"At my house."

"Does Mother know?"

"Not yet. Sheena came to me. I was glad of that."

I pulled on my cloak.

"Take me to her," I said, knowing that, painful to me as it was, the problem had to be faced.

He had moved from the small house in which he and his brothers had been born, and now lived in a larger one facing his expanding boatyard. It was the first time I had visited it, and even in my shocked state I was aware of the marked improvement in his affairs.

As we walked up the path leading straight from the High Street to his front door, I commented mechanically that he seemed to be doing well.

"Well enough, but not as well as I intend to do."

"And your brothers?" I asked. (Anything to avert the real and distressing issue.)

"The elder one is off to St. Andrews when the new term opens. The younger one will follow. I aimed to put them through university, and I'm doing so, but they can choose their own careers."

It seemed ironical to be talking of such mundane matters with a crisis like this facing us, but at least it aided self-control, which his hot temper needed as much as did my emotional distress. When he opened his front door and ushered me inside, I had to force myself to enter. Was it courage or pride that helped me?

Sheena was in the living room, sitting tautly in a high-backed chair. Her hands were clenched in her lap, her eyes stricken, her face white, but when she saw me she started in surprise and her cheeks slowly dyed a deep crimson.

She cried, "You shouldn't have told her! Not *her!*"

"I had to. Huntly is away."

"So that is why he didn't answer my letter!" There was relief in her voice.

"What letter?" I managed to ask. "When did you write to him?"

"Two days ago. I sent Iain with it, saying it was for you. The old man can neither read nor write, so I knew the name on it would mean nothing to him. He had merely to hand it in."

"Early in the morning?"

"Yes." Something in my voice or in my face made her add tensely, "Why?"

"Because in that case he did receive it. And it was that which drove him away."

Although I spoke the words aloud, I was really talking to myself, understanding now his hurried departure and the lying excuse he had given.

Sheena cried, "I don't believe you! He wouldn't leave, when I asked him to come to me!"

"Did you tell him why you wanted to see him?"

"Of course. The child is his. He had to know."

I had run out of words, and of the ability to delude myself or anyone else. But Sheena launched on a tirade of fury and grief. Outraged, she declared that Calum would never turn his back upon her. He loved her: *her,* and no one else. He had told her so.

"But he turns tail and runs away when you need him," Angus said contemptuously.

All the contempt he felt, I felt also, but not merely for Calum's cowardice—for my own stubborn belief in him, too.

Sheena answered wildly, "Perhaps for some reason Calum didn't get my letter, although I did insist that Iain should on no account hand it to the lodgekeeper, but take it up to the castle personally."

"And so he did. I heard the sound of wheels outside, but thought it was the carrier bringing mail from Inverness." If the scales had to be stripped from my eyes, they had to be stripped from Sheena's also. "He received your letter, and put it on the fire," I told her. "Then he left hurriedly." The words sounded callous, but they had to be uttered and there was no way of softening them because this was precisely what he had done, his calculating brain swiftly inventing an excuse for departure. But I knew where he had gone, and I knew that I would go to him, and bring him back —but first, Sheena had to decide for herself whether she still wanted him, and it was no use pretending that he was the Prince Charming of her dreams.

To my astonishment, she rounded on me.

"You are jealous. Jealous! I know him better than you do. I always have. He only married you because you were to inherit the mills. Don't imagine I'm so naïve that I can't see through him. What he wants, he takes. He wanted me, so he took me—and I wanted him, so I let him! There, now it's in the open and I'm thankful, and if you are shocked, I can't help it. And if you are disgusted, Angus—well, I'm sorry."

She burst into tears, and I marveled at the way in which the tears of a pretty girl could affect apparently the strongest of men, for all his anger dissolved into pity and he gathered her to him protectively. I looked on in silence and then said the only thing that could be said—that if Calum wated to marry her, and if she wanted to marry him, I would step aside.

"He has to marry me!" she stormed. "I am having his child."

"That hasn't always persuaded a man to marry a girl, and it wouldn't be the first time an unmarried woman has given birth to a child and made the best of the situation," I answered dully.

"But Mamma . . ."

"Mother would have to accept it, as I am accepting things now." I added, "I suppose you are sure?"

She answered bitterly, "Oh yes, I'm sure. It is early yet, but there is no doubt."

"And you *want* to marry Calum?"

"Of course I want to!" she wailed.

I turned to go, but Angus, holding her by the shoulders and looking down into her tearstained face, said, "You don't have to, Sheena. You can marry me, and I'll make a better husband, that I'll warrant."

"Oh no," she answered sadly, "I wouldn't do that to you. Not you, of all people. And especially not now."

I was thankful to learn she had that much decency left.

Angus wanted to drive me back to the mills, but I declined. It was essential that I be alone so I walked from Clachnaharry, as I had done in the old days, but I no longer felt like the carefree girl I had then been, and the self-control I had exercised during the last hour faltered as I approached my old home. I had left it so short a time ago, radiantly happy; now I dared not go inside, for to face my mother at such a time as this was something I could not inflict on either her or myself.

I crossed to the other side of the road, turning my

face away as I hurried past the house in case she or Ann Ross should happen to glance outside, although at this hour the noonday meal would be waiting in the dining room overlooking the garden at the back, and Mother, no doubt, would be growing impatient because Sheena was absent. Poor Mother; I would leave her to such small anxieties for the time being. She would have bigger cause for distress when the truth could no longer be hidden.

I forced myself to walk briskly in an attempt to calm down, but as I skirted the banks of the Ness the waters looked blurred. I brushed the back of my hand across my eyes. It would never do to return to the mills showing signs of tears. Nor was I capable of facing James Macpherson without betraying myself, so I sought refuge on the islands until such time that I could return without offering explanation or excuse to him. At length I was forced to sit down, my mind inescapably fastened on Sheena.

Eventually I rose and walked slowly back. I could hear the waters of the River Ness flowing to the gigantic loch ahead, the longest and the mightiest in all Scotland; so many fathoms deep that some said it was bottomless, the haunt of spirits whose home it had been since the world began. The splendor of Loch Ness was as eternal as the Highlands.

At last I was sufficiently calm to re-enter the mills, but shock made me incapable of working any more today. I was wondering what excuse to offer James, but he took one look at me and said, "Ye'd best be off home, Miss Elizabeth. Something has upset ye, I can tell." He asked no questions as he turned back to his work, but when I left he looked up from beneath shaggy eyebrows and gave me one of his rare, warm smiles.

I had taken to driving a pony trap to and from the mills; I enjoyed it, and it made less demand upon Hamish. I was particularly glad to be doing so now, for it occupied my mind during the journey. Concentration was needed on the winding route home, and particularly through the rising streets of Inverness.

Approaching Daviot, a coach overtook me and I

saw Duncan Mackintosh seated within. At the same moment that I saw him, he saw me, and called to his driver to halt. Reluctant as I was to linger, a meeting was unavoidable.

Removing his hat, he sprang down and stood by the roadside, one hand upon my pony's bridle, but the smile with which he greeted me suddenly changed, and he said quickly, "You look stricken, Ealasaid. What has happened?"

"Nothing, I assure you. I feel slightly unwell, that is all, and am on my way home."

"Then perhaps I should keep my news until you are better prepared to hear it."

"What is it?" I asked indifferently. Nothing he had to tell me could equal the distressing news I had already received.

"I have been to Edinburgh," he said.

"Indeed?"

"I was introduced to the two men claiming to be Prince Charlie's grandsons."

"How interesting," I replied, still indifferent.

"Neither recalls ever meeting your husband."

"They could have forgotten, could they not?"

"They also deny ever selling extracts from their Latin manuscript to anyone."

"That seems feasible, too. I imagine they would not wish it to be known that they were once so desperately in need of money."

"They appear to have no hesitation in accepting both hospitality and money from all and sundry, so I imagine pride doesn't enter into it. And, incidentally, they now claim to have regrettably lost that manuscript."

"Which proves them to be as unreliable as their word."

"Possibly, although they have also announced their intention to publish a treatise called the *Vestiarium Scoticum*, outlining all clan tartans for posterity."

"Obviously, a pair of talented young men."

He smiled wryly.

"That is my impression, too."

"You will forgive me if I say good day, Mr. Mackintosh."

But his hand still retained the bridle.

"I have brought a guest home with me. I hope you and your husband will come to dine with us before he leaves. I have a particular reason for inviting you."

I jerked the bridle and his hand fell away. "I will consult Calum," I answered evasively. "Thank you for the invitation. And now, if you will excuse me . . ."

He bowed, and let me go. As I pulled out to overtake the stationary coach I glimpsed his guest, an aging, white-haired gentleman, and received the impression that another figure was within, but the impression was fleeting, and I was only aware that Duncan remained by the roadside, watching me go, as concerned and puzzled as he had looked when I jerked away from him.

I drove straight round to the inner courtyard to seek Hamish, praying that he was there and not busy inside the castle, where Morag might chance to overhear. Fortune was with me, for it was Hamish himself who came to help me down.

I asked in a quick, low voice whether he would be prepared to drive me to Deeside. "It is more than a full day's journey; we would have to spend a night, perhaps two, at some country inn. Do you feel equal to undertaking such a drive?"

"Aye, Mistress. D'ye think I'd let anyone else take ye?"

"I need to get there as quickly as possible. The going might be hard."

"I am accustomed to hard journeys, Mistress, born and brought up in the Highlands. How soon do ye wish to leave?"

"As soon as I have packed a grip. You must do the same. Overnight things, no more. As for food, we will eat on the way. And Hamish . . ."

"Yes, Mistress?"

"Wait here with the carriage, not at the main door."

He nodded and asked no questions.

I was glad to meet no one on my way upstairs, but I had scarcely arrived in my room before I sensed that someone had been there—not merely to clean and tidy it, but on some mission of their own. Papers had been disturbed in my bureau, pigeonholes had been upset, drawers riffled through. In my boudoir, my dressing table had been searched; so had the tallboy containing underwear, the clothes pushed back more or less into place, but not as neatly as I had left them. And at last the seeker had found what was sought. The big iron key of the Keep was gone.

There was no time to think about that. It merely confirmed that Guthrie and Morag needed, and intended, to keep private contact with each other. What did it matter now? I was ready to leave Faillie voluntarily, although the last man to hear of it would be Duncan. I would never subject myself to the further humiliation of telling him personally that, as far as I was concerned, he had won. Nor was I allowing myself to think so far ahead. Calum might well deny everything; indeed, I was confident that he would, and in the face of his denial, how would I act? Walk out of the castle like an outraged wife? I would look a fool if it was he who spoke the truth, and not my sister.

But as I hastily packed my grip I remembered again his empty pillow and it was Sheena whom I believed.

I walked downstairs and out of the castle, knowing that had I met Morag it would not have deterred me, but glad that I was not to be hindered by any questions.

Hamish had the carriage ready and waiting. He stood holding the horses, gazing up at the Keep. As I approached I saw that his glance was fixed on a small window slightly to the right of it; a gun slit now glazed with lead lights belonging to a room linking the Keep with the coach house and stables. These rooms, I knew, were used for stores.

At the sound of my step, Hamish turned and took the grip from me. The carriage steps were already lowered and a moment later I was inside. Hamish folded the steps and closed the door, and as he did so Guthrie's voice echoed clearly across the courtyard.

"Surely you should collect your mistress at the front of the castle?"

The man had not been there when I stepped into the carriage, nor could he have seen Hamish deposit my grip within, for the open door had been on the opposite side from where Guthrie stood. The man must have arrived within the last few seconds, so I was more annoyed than perturbed by his unexpected appearance.

Hamish ignored him, but said loudly, "Your pardon, Mistress, for being late and causing ye to seek me out."

I put my head through the open window, forcing a smile and saying with an effort that the drive to Clachnaharry was but short and that my mother's good catering would not spoil for the waiting. Then we were rumbling out of the courtyard and past the main doors of the castle, beneath the arch and over the causeway.

It was not until we made our first stop for refreshment that I asked Hamish why he had been looking up at the windows above the inner courtyard. "Was Guthrie spying on us?"

"As to spying, Mistress, I couldna' say, but he was standing by the window of a room he had no right to enter. Mistress Crombie seems to let that man ferret where he wills. I still don't trust her. Nor Guthrie, neither."

Bad weather returned and we were two days and nights over the journey into Aberdeenshire and along Deeside to Braemar, but I did not mind the delay. In my heart I was reluctant to reach Carrisbrae at all. I dreaded the meeting with Calum, and repeatedly rehearsed the way in which I would conduct it, knowing all the time that he was more than likely to take control for I had no experience of withstanding him, always too vulnerable in my infatuation to resist him for long. I feared that I might be equally vulnerable now; too hurt to yield to any overtures of love, but too tired to withstand the strength of his will. To accuse him of wrongdoing was one thing; to prove it, another.

The important thing was to persuade him to return to Faillie with me. As yet, I need not look beyond that, for it was the purpose of this unhappy journey.

After endless hours spent on rough roads and sleepless nights in uncomfortable inns, my face felt drawn with fatigue, and I knew I should present a sorry sight on arrival. That would be a bad beginning, for something told me that the picture of a distraught woman was not likely to touch his heart. Calum would be more impressed if I sailed in, elegant and self-confident, ready to take the wind out of his sails.

We crawled into Braemar late in the afternoon. All we had to do now was find my husband's property, and this should be easy since it was prominent in the district. Large estates were known to all country inhabitants, so I told Hamish to call at the main village shop, and inquire. It was a wise decision, for when he returned he announced that Carrisbrae was a couple of miles ahead. "A small gate, on the right. It bears the name."

That would be the tradesman's entrance, of course; the entrance the shopkeeper used when making deliveries. There were similar entries at Faillie, used by the staff as well as tradesmen. Find that, and we would soon find the main entrance to Carrisbrae. When the carriage halted, I was composed and ready.

"This be it, Mistress."

I glanced at the wrought-iron gate. It opened upon an unkempt path, curving to a door well out of sight. I could see the roof of a house and one or two upper windows, but little more, for the place was shrouded in trees. "This must be the lodgekeeper's entrance, or the gardener's," I remarked. "Drive on, Hamish, until we find the main one."

There was no other.

We went back, and Hamish let down the steps and then opened the gate. It squealed loudly on rusted hinges. I walked slowly along the path, which wound to the front door of a much neglected house. It stood in a tangled garden and had the air of a place that had long stood empty.

I walked back briskly. There had to be another place, a much larger one, called Carrisbrae. This house had no doubt taken its name from Calum's eminent estate.

Hamish looked at me sadly, and shook his head.

"No, Mistress. There is no other. The woman told me. The first gate ye come to on the right, a couple of miles beyond Braemar, Mr. Huntly's place, she said. She told me I couldna' miss it, and I haven't." He blinked in an endeavor to keep back tears. "My poor Miss Una—that she should exchange her rightful home for this!"

Seventeen

A LIAR. An opportunist. A schemer. A man with a tongue so plausible that even my father had been deceived by it.

Oddly enough, the knowledge aided my resolution, for it was a weapon in my hand. I marched back along the path, lifted the heavy door knocker, and wielded it loudly. If the house was really empty, I would have no hesitation in exploring as much as I could, forcing a window if necessary.

There was a flicker of light, the shuffling step of someone of advancing years, the sound of bolts stiffly yielding, and the groan of hinges as the door slowly opened. An old man stood there, holding high a flickering candle. Beside him, a darkly paneled hall yawned like a chasm.

In the wavering light, I saw surprise in the man's face. He had not expected to see an unknown woman on the doorstep.

I asked for Mr. Calum Huntly. "He is here, is he not?" I asked, knowing full well that wherever my husband was, it was not in this neglected house. Calum, with his love of luxury, could never tolerate this now that he had become accustomed to Faillie's standards. He had set the scene with his dinner party and his Highland regalia, aided by his cousin's willingness to play the role of housekeeper; backed up with his valuable information about ancient tartans, he had successfully bought his way into my life.

And when I died, he would inherit all, as he had inherited Faillie on his wife's death.

I was cold again, too numb to be aware that the old man was looking at me in concern, until Hamish said gently, "He is asking ye to step inside, Mistress. Ye'll be warmer then."

But I was not shivering because of the weather.

"Mr. Huntly is not here?" I managed to say.

"No, Mistress. He has not been here since he went to Castle Faillie."

"Then thank you—I will come in. You are Grant, I presume?"

He was surprised that I knew his name. "Aye," he said, "and I've worked for Master Calum ever since he brought his young bride to this house—and before that, too. Man and boy, I've worked for the Huntly family."

"Your wife also?"

187

"During her lifetime. Alas, she passed on ten years ago."

So this was the resident factor for the Carrisbrae estates, with the alarmist wife who frantically summoned their lord and master because her husband was ill! Why did the lies have to be embroidered so elaborately, I wondered bitterly as I walked into the shadowy hall.

Obeying the unwritten laws of Scottish hospitality, despite the fact that, as yet, he had no knowledge of my identity, Grant was hurrying ahead to open a door; a smell of disuse came from the room beyond it, dry and musty, but soon a wood fire was crackling in the hearth, and then the man departed for the kitchens and returned with piping hot tea and hunks of bread, apologizing for the humble fare. "But it is the best I can do, alas. I have a roof over my head and a bed to sleep in, which is much to be thankful for, and Mr. Huntly gave me a sum of money to tide me over when he left. But he has never returned and the money has long since run out. My sister in Braemar gives me tea, and bread, and butter too when she can spare it."

I said in distress, "You should have written to your master. You know the address of Castle Faillie, surely?"

"Aye, that I do, my late mistress coming from there, and visiting it once a year, and talking about it the way she did, near all the time. But ye must know that there are many in the Highlands like me'sel, who canna read nor write."

"But you do know your mistress is dead."

He nodded. "Dr. Craig came back with the news. Mr. Huntly sent for him in a hurry——"

"*Sent* for him?" I interrupted, clearly recalling Calum's statement that he had driven posthaste to Faillie, taking the doctor with him.

"Aye, Mistress, but by the time Dr. Craig reached Faillie it was too late to do anything for the poor lass, or to save the bairn." The voice wavered. "My mistress was a good woman, and devoted to Master

Calum. That was why she would never go to Faillie more than once a year. She hated to leave him even for a short time, although I always believed her heart was there, more than here."

"He could have gone with her," Hamish growled.

"It is not for me to judge my master. He preferred to remain here while the mistress departed to see that all was well with her old home. If ye had seen this house then, ye might understand better. Beneath the mistress's eye it was well cared for, and the gardens also. But the gardener ceased coming when his wages didn'a arrive. I'm afraid that be Master Calum all over. Forgetful, that's all. One day he will return and settle our wages—and all the bills as well." He nodded to a tall escritoire, a very fine one, I observed. It stood open, and on it was a small stack of paper that had the unmistakable look of bills.

"I will settle those," I said, "and your wages too."

"You, mistress? But I—I . . ."

"But you don't know who I am. I am the new Mistress Huntly, and my husband's obligations are my obligations."

For a moment he was too astonished to speak, then he mouthed incoherently, "So soon? He married again so soon?" It seemed as if a blow had been struck at all his illusions.

He shuffled away then, shaking his head in bewilderment. I felt sorry for the man, but other thoughts were more pressing, chief among them being the question of Calum's whereabouts. Edinburgh, Aberdeen, Glasgow? Who knew, and how was I to trace him?

I was grateful for the tea. Combined with the heat of the fire, it was reviving, and the leaping flames lit up the room which, I now saw, held some good pieces of furniture. When Hamish followed Grant to the kitchen quarters, I looked around with interest. An oil lamp had been placed on the table beside me and its glow spread into the farthermost corners. Beneath a woman's hand the room must have been pleasant, for it was reasonably spacious, with tall windows overlooking the wilderness of a garden. That, too, must once have been quite lovely, but not even with a stretch of imagination could this house be classed as anything greater than a modest, if once pleasant, country home.

It was sad to see a place deteriorate under neglect and I found it impossible to forgive Calum for allowing it to. But it was impossible to forgive Calum for a great many things, including his lies. How many more had he told me besides the mythical story of his vast estates, his wealth, and his unhappy marriage?

Without warning, I knew I should not yet leave this house. It was as if a voice urged me to stay, or an unseen hand halted me as I reached for my cloak and bonnet. Like every premonition I had ever had, it came upon me suddenly and with conviction.

Simultaneously a knock sounded on the door, and in answer to my summons Grant entered.

"You will be remaining here—Mistress?" Unlike Guthrie's mocking pause, this one was due to the strangeness of using that form of address to an unknown woman, and perhaps a reluctance to regard any but Calum's first wife in that capacity. I liked the man, and sympathized with his feelings, saying that I would be glad to stay for the night, but that in the morning I must return to Faillie. I knew it must seem very odd that I should come all this way to look for my husband, but Grant was a well-trained servant and revealed no curiosity, merely saying that he would fetch his niece from Braemar, and she would quickly have the bedroom ready again.

"She worked here also?"

"From the age of twelve, Mistress."

"But found other employment when her wages failed to arrive?"

"For a while, but now she is wed to the blacksmith's elder son."

I guessed there were no horses in the stables and that Grant would have to trudge to Braemar on foot, so I decided to send Hamish with the carriage. He could then bring back food and other necessities, as well as Grant's niece.

When Hamish heard that we were to remain, it was obvious that he would have preferred to find lodgings elsewhere, and I guessed the reason. This house represented a downward step for the young woman whom he had known since her childhood.

"We will be more comfortable here than at an inn," I insisted, as I gave him money and told him to purchase ample supplies, and when he returned with Grant's niece I made good the girl's outstanding wages, whereupon she went to work with a will. By that time Grant had lit a fire in my bedroom and when at last all was ready I retired willingly, convinced that as soon as my head touched the pillow I should sleep.

I did not, for something in that room disturbed me. The feather bed was deep and comfortable, and even the thought that Calum had slept here with another woman did not trouble me. I had no doubt that he had slept with many women and would do so again. Hurt as I was, and distressed as I was over Sheena's pregnancy, I was not kept awake by thoughts of my husband's infidelities and deceptions, nor even by Duncan's warning, now actively recalled, to watch out for the future. What troubled me was something indefinable, but powerful, that reached out to me the moment I entered this room.

The first thing I had seen, looking down from the wall facing the bed, was a picture of a young woman; dark as her brother, with the same blueness of eye and the same direct glance, but whereas his features were rugged, hers were finely chiseled and decidedly pretty. I had known at once that this was Una and, holding the candle high, had studied her portrait with interest.

As I disrobed, my eyes had returned to the canvas again and again, for her face haunted me, and as I lay in the darkness now I was still aware of her eyes looking down from the wall, just as I had been aware, as I moved about the room, of the way in which they followed me. Something told me that the artist had caught her with uncanny skill, and that the clear gaze shining from the portrait was exactly as it had been in life.

I knew then the cause of my wakefulness. There was a feeling of life in the room, almost as if someone was trying to talk to me. In the glow from the fire I could see Una's clear eyes, and the faintly parted lips which gave me the feeling that she was about to speak, but when I lit a candle the picture once more became merely a portrait on canvas.

Still the strange sensation of not being alone in this room persisted. If inanimate things could talk, I felt that the young woman in the portrait would talk to me now, and if I remained very still, somehow her message would get through. . . .

A long-case clock in the corner ticked away the minutes, chimes marking the quarter-hours and finally striking midnight. Beyond my door, the house was silent, with Grant and Hamish sleeping in distant rooms. If I were to explore the house barefoot, no one would hear me.

I pulled on a robe, picked up the lighted candle, and stepped quietly out onto the landing. In the center, the well of the stairs disappeared into that chasm of dark paneling from which the living room opened. I descended carefully, pausing on every creaking stair and ridiculing myself for such alarm. If Grant heard, and came to determine who prowled about the house, it would be simple enough to say that I was on my way to the kitchen for a beaker of milk. But no one stirred, and I walked from room to room, finding nothing to explain the impulse that had brought me from my bed. There was nothing on the ground floor but the drawing room in which I had sat, a dining room which reflected long disuse, a morning room, similarly lonely, a very masculine study which, I could see even by candlelight, was kept dusted in case its owner unexpectedly returned, and a somewhat gaunt kitchen in which the most comfortable thing was a deep wicker chair pulled close to the wood-fired stove.

I went back upstairs. There were few bedrooms, all shrouded in dust sheets, and I knew as I opened each door that none held the slightest interest for me. The compulsion which had sent me on this search came from elsewhere, and all that remained were the attics above. I trod even more carefully as I made my way up the narrow staircase leading to them, for the attics would be the servants' quarters where Hamish and Grant now slept.

There were only four doors up there. From behind the first I could hear loud snores; from behind the second, nothing. Was the room empty, and should I risk turning the knob to find out? My hand was upon it when I heard the creaking of springs as someone turned in bed. I jerked away, and the candle flame wavered sharply. It would be more difficult to explain my presence on this landing were Grant to open his door and face me now.

I stood rigid. Silence again behind that door; snoring from behind the other. Farther on were two more, and when at last I forced myself to go forward, one proved to open onto a small box-room, and the other onto a larger one containing oddments of furniture, basket trunks, and all the bric-à-brac accumulated by an average household.

This was the last room of all.

I went inside, closed the door behind me, and held the candle high. What I was looking for, I had no idea, but something compelled me to remain, stepping carefully between the clutter to avoid knocking anything over and thus waking the occupants of the adjoining rooms. I had almost reached the window when my bare foot stepped on something hard. I winced, then stooped and picked it up. It was a small stick, carefully wound with thread.

I set the candle down abruptly. Without doubt, the thing I held was a thread-count stick, woven in the replica of a tartan sett, and I recognized it instantly as one we had manufactured at the MacArthur Mills.

193

Nor had it been wound in the days preceding proscription, for the colors were bright and fresh, despite a layer of dust.

But we had produced more than one tartan from Calum's designs, so there were likely to be other thread-count sticks in addition to this one—and sure enough, on a dusty table, I found a batch of them. From the jumbled heap in which they lay, it was obvious that they had been thrown down hurriedly or casually, which was why the one I held had fallen and rolled away.

I recognized every sett. They matched all we had produced.

Suddenly Duncan's voice echoed clearly in my mind: *"Neither recalls ever meeting your husband."*

I knew then that those two men in Edinburgh had been telling the truth. It was not from their controversial Latin manuscript that Calum had obtained these designs; that was just another of his stories, as plausible and convincing as the rest. No doubt he had heard of their sensational arrival in Edinburgh and they had served as a convenient catalyst for his scheme. The real source of the tartans could only have been the valuable paintings in the Mackintosh gallery, and in my heart I knew that I had suspected as much for a long time.

I felt no surprise when I found the canvasses stacked with their faces to the wall. As I expected, all the tartans featured in them matched the thread-count sticks, which had been wound by an expert and then carefully delineated on paper. But not by Calum, though they had been in his handwriting. In copying these ancient tartans, someone had aided him, someone with a knowledge of weaving, and in that case it was likely to be a woman, because weaving was a woman's skill.

I could think of only two, Una, or Morag, and since it seemed unlikely that Una would have hidden her family's collection of pictures, that left Morag, of whom I knew so little.

The candle spluttered; it was burning low. I gathered up the sticks and made my way softly and swiftly to my room. From the wall Una's clear blue eyes greeted me again, but they were unreadable now. No message seemed to linger there, no desire to communicate. She was a portrait on canvas again; no more than that.

I hid the thread-count sticks in the bottom of my grip, and as I climbed back into bed the candle finally spluttered, and died.

Surprisingly, abruptly, as if a shutter had come down in my mind, I slept.

Eighteen

BEFORE LEAVING next morning I took Hamish to the attic and showed him the portraits. I had no need to ask if he recognized them. His face was sufficiently revealing.

"Now you know why you failed to find them, Hamish. They were removed from Faillie and brought here. When did you first miss them?"

"Not until after Miss Una's death, for most of them hung along the corridor above the Banqueting Hall, and the rest in her sleeping quarters. My duties didna' take me further than the stables and kitchens in those days, but my daughter attended Miss Una personally and often talked of her pride in the family collection. 'She'll never part with one of them,' Jessie often said, 'no matter how hard pressed she is.' Everyone had heard of the portraits, everyone knew how valuable they were. When Jessie was dismissed after poor Miss Una's death, I had to take over more household duties, and naturally looked for the paintings.

But I saw no sign of them. So one day I asked Jessie where they'd been kept. 'Same place as they've ever been,' she told me. 'Along that corridor with the spy slits, and in that big bedroom where she sleeps.' They were never displayed in the Banqueting Hall or the Billeting Room; I suppose because they would have attracted attention there and even the most trusted visitors might've attempted a robbery."

"Was that the object of your occasional tours of the castle?"

Partly, he admitted. "It's true that in Miss Una's time I had to see that all was locked downstairs, but nowhere else. When she was gone and Master Calum settled in, I told Mistress Crombie it'd always been my duty to go over the whole castle, including the Keep, and she let me carry on. But never a sight of these paintings did I glimpse until now."

"Then how do you come to recognize them?"

"I saw them once, as a boy. My late master—Miss Una and Master Duncan's father—sent them away to Edinburgh to be reframed, and when they came back they were lined up in a row in the Billeting Room for him to examine. Even now I can remember the pride in his face when he looked at them. He sent for everyone at Faillie, from the highest to the lowest, to come and see them. He trusted us all, and for good reason. Not one would've betrayed as good a master as he. And there the portraits were, all propped along one wall, looking at us the way they're looking at us now, but more alive, if ye know what I mean. Not dirty and tired the way they look now."

"That's because they are in need of restoration, and perhaps that is why your late mistress brought them here."

"Why here, with the nearest place being Aberdeen?"

"Which is closer than Edinburgh, and therefore a shorter distance from which to hire someone."

Hamish looked surprised. I doubted if he had been much farther than Inverness or Nairn in the whole of his life.

"The paintings could have been restored right in this house," I told him. "An expert could have been brought here to do the work, and since your late mistress lived here more than at Faillie it could have been carried out under her supervision, very conveniently."

I knew the old man was not convinced, and I shared his doubt, but not for the same reason. I believed the portraits had been brought here so that the tartans could be copied. It was significant that I could now follow the workings of my husband's devious mind with an almost calm detachment.

I heard Hamish asking if I wished to take the portraits back to Faillie, and that if so the carriage would be overcrowded and uncomfortable. I declined. For the time being they had to stay here. That was important. Why it was important I wasted no time in speculating; sometimes one had to follow an instinct, and a strong instinct told me to leave things as they were. The thread-count sticks were enough to take with me, and when I produced them—if I produced them—I would watch Morag's face.

A sound from the door attracted my attention. It was Grant, inquiring whether I desired refreshment before departing. I thanked him, but said we would halt for some on the way, and that from henceforth weekly supplies would be delivered here from Braemar. "And your wages will also arrive regularly; I will see to that myself." His gratitude was touching. By fulfilling what was, in my eyes, an obligation, I had won his loyalty without in any way intending to, but now his loyalty stood me in good stead for I knew I could ask him a straight question and get an honest answer.

"Can you recall when these paintings were brought here?"

He stared at them blankly. Plainly he had no recollection of ever seeing them before.

"I niver come into this room, Mistress, except to air the place."

I turned one of the paintings to a better light, and

knew at once that it was of a former Mackintosh, for the strong square features and keen blue eyes of Duncan looked out from the tarnished frame. I think it was then that I knew why I was not taking the paintings back to Faillie, and to whom I was going to reveal their whereabouts after I had confronted Calum with my knowledge.

But first, Calum had to be found. The thought brought me back to reality with a sickening thrust, and I scarcely heeded Grant's renewed avowal that he had never seen the portraits before. I knew he spoke the truth; more important was how they came to be here, who brought them, and when.

"Have you ever left this house for any length of time? I mean, for more than a night?"

"Only once, Mistress. The day the mail coach brought a letter from Master Calum, with the news of the mistress' death. Since I canna' read, I had to take it to the manse in Braemar, for the Minister to read."

"But you had already heard from Dr. Craig?"

"Aye. Not that he told me personally, mind. It was in the bar of the Golden Hind that he blabbed about it. Stricken with remorse, he was, for arriving too late to help the poor lass, and so he should aye be. That was what everyone thought, knowing too well that he'd be stopping for a dram all along the road. If Master Calum had iver shown his face here agin, he'd a met with the wrath of everyone around for sending for the likes o' Dr. Craig, and from such a distance."

So Craig had been a drinker, and unreliable; the last doctor to attend a woman in labor. The ugliness of suspicion rose again.

"Where does Dr. Craig live? I would like to call on him."

"Ye canna do that, Mistress. He's here nae more, to the surprise o' nobody, for it was aye certain that he'd go the way he did—either that way, or some other."

"You mean . . ."

"He be dead, Mistress. Run over by a passing coach a week or so later. Iveryone knew he'd not been sober for an hour since he got back, so it weren't surprising that he staggered and fell into the road on his way home, and a de'il of a night it were, with a bitter wind driving down from the Cairngorms. That was why I was glad to stay at my sister's place, even if Master Calum hadna' written telling me to shut up the house until he decided what to do with it."

"He told you to leave the place empty?" I asked swiftly.

"Aye, he did so. The Reverend Ferguson read the letter to me clearly and glad I was to obey, for without the mistress and Master Calum, Carrisbrae weren't the same house, and niver has been since."

"But later you heard that you were to return?"

He nodded. "I thought it meant that the master were coming back, but as ye know, he didna'. But mebbe ye'll persuade him, Mistress? It wae'd be good to hae the house occupied agin."

I gave some reassuring but noncommittal answer, and went out with Hamish to the carriage. He was about to jerk the horses into action when a sudden thought arrested me. I halted him, and called to Grant as he closed the gate behind us, "What of Guthrie?"

"Guthrie, Mistress?"

"He worked here. My husband took him to Faillie with him."

Grant shook his head. "No Guthrie ever worked here, Mistress. Only Wallace, the gardener, my niece, and mysel'. Wallace now works as an under-gardener at Balmoral, and has a cottage near Craithie church. He'll be able to vouch that no Guthrie ever worked for Master Calum."

I felt no surprise. All my worst fears were being confirmed.

"Do you recall a woman named Morag Crombie?"

"A distant relative of Master Calum's? Aye, I ken her. She came to see them once or twice after she was widowed."

Well, one thing was true, at least.

We traveled home via Aviemore and were beyond the Cairngorms when we made our first halt. It was then that I asked Hamish if he had seen the doctor who attended his mistress. Again, I felt no surprise when he replied that he had not.

"I'd been unwell," he explained. "My old stomach trouble which Mistress Crombie has treated since she came. Miss Una thought it would be good for me to visit my sister at Fort Augustus for a while. 'I'll be all right here at Faillie, with Jessie coming daily to get my meals, and if I wish to go anywhere, one of the stable boys can drive me.' That's what she said, and she meant it. And that's what puzzled me, Mistress. If she'd known her husband was coming, she wouldna' ha' let me go; she'd ha' needed me. Last time I saw her she was sitting by the fire in the Billeting Room, looking just as she always did—healthy and well, with color in her cheeks. Of course, a woman can be taken suddenly if she gives birth before her time and, as Jessie said later, no one would ha' suspected it. She could only ha' been a very short time gone, for she showed it not at all."

"A woman can miscarry easily in the early months, Hamish. The third month is the most likely time."

"Aye, but not the most dangerous. At seven months it's a different matter. If she had miscarried then, I wouldna' ha' been surprised to return and find her gone but, as I say, she weren't that advanced. But when I came back to Faillie, she was in her grave—and the laird had arrived. It was he who broke the news to me, and I'll grant that he was griefstricken. It was the first time I or any of the servants had ever met him, the first time he'd shown his face at Faillie after their runaway marriage. Miss Una once told my daughter that her husband was a home-loving man who didn't like being uprooted from his own place. We knew she lived with him at Deeside, despite her love for Faillie, because a wife's place is with her husband. Of course, we were often curious about him; everyone was. But I'll grant that he's tried to make up for it since, with all he has done to the place. Between the pair o' ye, Faillie is almost as it was when Miss Una was a lass."

We made good time on the rest of the journey. After one night's halt, we traveled well, but I had ample time in which to think during the hours I spent jolting along. I was bolstered by the knowledge that I was returning to Faillie with information that could be a weapon in my hand. At the same time, I had to be careful when and to whom I revealed it. Display my hand too soon, and I could be silenced forever. As we neared home I went over in my mind, item by item, all the things I was now certain of; that my husband had lied about his acquaintanceship with the Stuart brothers; that he had removed the paintings from Faillie to his house near Braemar after his first wife's death, making sure that Grant was absent when he deposited them there; that he had then used the ancient tartans depicted in the paintings to scrape acquaintance with my father, possibly with the idea of selling the delineations, until a better idea presented itself—that of marrying the daughter who was to inherit the mills, and then persuading her to prepare a will in his favor. And in signing that will I might well have been signing my death warrant.

The other things—his despicable behavior with Sheena, his pretense that he had been called to his estates on Deeside, his lies and plausible excuses and grandiose pretensions—all revealed the type of man he really was. And on top of that he might be a murderer.

I had to accept that horrifying possibility, for it was as inescapable as the rest. I had only his word that at the time of my father's accidental death he had been in Edinburgh, and I judged now that this had been one of the most blatant lies of all, considering he had been in no position to arrange a meeting between my father and the two men.

Calum could easily have stayed nearer home, entered the castle secretly, helped himself to a long-barreled muzzle-loader from that gun room over which he gloated so much, lain in wait for my father, whose regular route on Sunday was well known to him, shot him, returned the weapon to its place—and then come back to Faillie several days later, apparently unaware of the tragedy.

What troubled me, as we drove across the causeway, was the feeling that everything was a shade too obvious. I felt intuitively that I had skirted only over the surface of things and that, like the dark and slimy bog surrounding the castle, a great deal more lay hidden, the nature of which I could not even glimpse.

And it was when we drove across the bog that I recalled my experience in the family tomb and my uncanny conviction that Una's body did not lie there . . .

Nineteen

THE FIRST PERSON I met when I walked into the castle was Morag. She was seated by the fire at the far end of the Billeting Room, quietly embroidering. I was arrested by the transformation in her. Gone was the drab gown she had worn every evening since my arrival at Faillie; gone the subdued, mouse-like woman. In her place I saw a figure elegantly gowned in dark blue velvet, with lace at throat and wrists. Her hair was brushed back from her brow, emphasizing the clear-cut features which had been obscured when surrounded by wisps of neglected hair. Now that hair shone silkily, and her skin was enhanced by a discreet application of *papier poudre*. She remarked coolly, "So you are back, Elizabeth.

It would be interesting to know where you have been. I might add that you have had everyone extremely worried, from your silly mother to your empty-headed sister, whose concern, I'm sure, was solely for herself. As for me," she shrugged, "it is of little consequence whether you go or remain, but for Calum's sake I endeavored to trace you. I must say you are an unpredictable creature; diligent in your duties as mistress of Faillie one day, then as the owner of the MacArthur Mills the next, and finally, I suspect, as guardian of your sister's welfare. I can guess what *she* has been up to."

"That," I retorted, "is the longest speech I have ever heard from you. And I would remind you that I can come and go as I wish, without reference to anyone."

"Or consideration?"

"In what way do you merit it? As housekeeper, or as self-appointed Mistress of the Bedchamber, who believes she has the right to ransack my room if she wishes?"

I was satisfied to see the opaque eyes, usually so unrevealing, react with a spark of embarrassment, swiftly replaced by hostility. I felt as if I had sharpened my wits against hers, and won.

"So you have come out into the open, have you, Morag? No more self-effacing housekeeper or poor relation pose? I am glad of that." I untied my bonnet and then my cloak, tossing both aside. "I have had a long journey and would be glad of refreshment. I see wine on the sideboard. Be so good as to pour me a glass."

It was the request of a mistress to a superior employee, and I felt no guilt about uttering it because it was even more necessary now to emphasize the difference in our positions.

The embroidery needle faltered, and I remarked amiably that I had no idea she was such a talented needlewoman. "What other crafts are you mistress of, besides embroidery? Weaving, by any chance?"

"That is your sphere," she retorted.

Still I waited, until at length she was forced to rise and bring the glass of wine to me, but she did so with ill grace.

"I am glad to see you looking so elegant, Morag— pray, do join me in a glass. As I say, I am glad to see you are taking a pride in your appearance again; that velvet gown is too good to hide away upstairs, and your pose of inferior housekeeper, or poor relation, was wearing rather thin, was it not?"

Her nostrils flared, feline and predatory.

"Where have you been?" she demanded sharply.

"On a journey."

"Obviously." She swept back to the sideboard and helped herself to a larger glass of wine than my own. I reflected with satisfaction that evidently she was more in need of it than I. The red liquid was near the rim of the glass when I remarked serenely, "As a matter of fact, I have been to Carrisbrae."

If I had guessed she would be startled, I was disappointed.

"I expected as much."

But the red wine spilled upon the silver salver, like drops of blood.

"In that case, why ask?" I retorted, and sipped the wine negligently.

"What did you think of the place?" she asked, unconcerned.

"Somewhat disappointing, in view of my husband's description."

She laughed, picked up her glass, and returned to her seat on the opposite side of the fireplace. After she had carefully spread her blue velvet skirts she said lightly, "Calum has a tendency to exaggerate. No doubt that is why your sister was deceived by him. You also."

The claws were now unsheathed.

"And you?" I answered sweetly. "Were you deceived by him too?"

"Not as you and Sheena were, but I wasn't brought up in a narrow village household, so my head was unlikely to be turned by the flattery of a handsome and worldly man."

"It would be interesting to know where you were brought up."

"Glasgow," she answered abruptly. "That is why I find country ways intolerably narrow."

"You are at liberty to leave them whenever you wish."

"You would like me to, I know. But I am not ready."

"When will you be?"

"Are you so anxious to be rid of me? Well, I have always known it." She drank deeply, staring at me morosely over the rim of her glass.

"My dear Morag," I answered tiredly, "don't resort to self-martyrdom again. You are drinking very rapidly. Why? What is making you nervous?"

She gave a high, artificial laugh. "I? Nervous? Why should I be?"

"That is what I am wondering. You seemed composed when I arrived. Perhaps my return disconcerted you? It would have disconcerted you even more had I entered my rooms when you were searching for the key to the door of the Keep. And don't deny that you did, please! I realized the other night that for some unknown reason it was essential to Guthrie to keep in touch with you, but I doubted— and still doubt—whether the alliance between the pair of you is amatory. I am not wholly naïve, despite the fact that I am country born."

Her laughter echoed beneath the arched stone ceiling.

"And yet you had no suspicion of Sheena's involvement with your husband! My poor Elizabeth, how you deluded yourself! As soon as that girl walked into the place I knew what would happen. I knew why Calum wanted her to stay and I knew why Sheena accepted so eagerly, just as I knew, on the night you all came to dinner here, that she was enamored of him. So did he. But Sheena was bound to pall. That is why he has gone away. And I knew all this would happen, and that was why I didn't want her here. I didn't want you hurt. Against my will, I liked you, but I couldn't stop the inevitable, and nor could you, despite your beautiful body and striking looks. When Calum has enjoyed one woman, he turns to another."

"And how do you know all this?" My voice was calm, but my fingers clenched the stem of my wine glass.

"Observation."

"Have you known him so long, then?"

"Long enough."

"But you have never been—involved—with him, have you?"

"You mean, have I ever been his mistress? I have not. Nor Guthrie's, in case you are wondering. Nor is there any involvement of any other kind."

I believed her on the first two counts, but not on the third.

"I notice you don't ask if I have brought Calum home with me," I said.

"From Carrisbrae? Of course not. I knew perfectly well he wouldn't be going there, and now you have seen the place, you can surely understand why. A castle in the Highlands is one thing, especially one that is being rapidly improved and offers all the comforts, plus the status of the life of a laird, but can you imagine your luxury-loving husband returning to vegetate in a small country house? If you had only told me where you were setting off to, I could have saved you a wasted journey."

"It was not wholly wasted. I met Grant, for instance."

"Ah, yes, the 'resident factor.' And Mrs. Grant?"

"Dead these ten years, as you surely know."

"How should I know?"

"Because you have visited there several times. You told me so yourself, and Grant confirmed it."

"You questioned a servant about me? What other probing did you indulge in, pray?"

"What other probing could I indulge in?" I parried.

"Having gone so far, curiosity might have persuaded you to question him about your predecessor. I understand the wife of a widower is often jealous of the woman he first married, but after seeing the house on Deeside and comparing it with Faillie as it now is, any jealousy you felt must surely have died. Carrisbrae is a dreary place, don't you think?"

"I have little idea, for I saw only the bedroom and drawing room."

I yawned, remarking that I was more than ready to go to bed, but as I set aside my unfinished wine Morag said at a tangent, "You are wasting your time if you hope to persuade your husband to do his duty by your sister."

I answered swiftly, "And what duty do you imagine he owes her?"

"Oh, come, Elizabeth, I am neither blind nor a fool. I knew as soon as she came to stay that he would be in her bed before long. I am sorry if it hurts, but give me credit for not encouraging her to remain. Calum received a letter delivered by your old family coachman; I saw him arrive. I was in this room, dusting the furniture—a housemaid's task, I might add, but I have suffered many indignities in this household. I saw him from one of the windows, and watched him descend from the box, a missive in his hand. The only letter that could have either summoned Calum away, or driven him away, was the one brought by your mother's coachman. Poor Elizabeth, you've been having a trying time one way and another, haven't you?"

I picked up my cloak and bonnet and headed for the stairs.

Her voice followed me. "By the way, I dismissed those men who came to clear the bog."

For a moment my mind was blank. I had forgotten all about the arrangements I had made for clearing the bog, but now it seemed vitally important. And Morag's assumption of authority angered me.

"*You* dismissed them? On what grounds, pray?"

"That the work was not sanctioned by the laird."

"It was sanctioned by me!"

"But Calum *is* laird. I couldn't risk his displeasure

should he return and find work under way that he had not agreed to."

"And how do you know he had not agreed?"

"Because he wouldn't—" She broke off, and for a fraction of a second I had the triumphant feeling that I had caught her out, but with a certain smugness she finished, "Because he wouldn't consider putting that work in hand until all other improvements had been attended to."

I wanted to retort that he who paid the piper called the tune, but merely shrugged and went on my way. Before going to my room I walked down the short passage to the Keep. There was no key in the lock, and when I lifted the heavy iron latch the door would not yield. It was exactly as I had left it, except that I no longer had the key. That was in the hands of some-one else, and in view of the fact that Morag had been too nonplussed to make any denial when I accused her of searching my room, I had no doubt that it was she.

Walking back along the passage, I glanced down to the inner courtyard. I could see the rooms above the stables, and the windows of the store rooms in the angled wall adjoining, which also linked with the Keep, forming three sides of a square with the fourth comprising the courtyard entrance, and I recalled Hamish looking up at the store room windows, and his remark that Guthrie seemed to ferret wherever he willed.

But perhaps Guthrie had not been ferreting. Perhaps there was a means of access into the Keep from one of those rooms, just as there was a means of access from here. It seemed more than likely that a tower which had once been used to house ammunition and supplies should be linked with other store rooms. During my unpleasant visit to the neglected place I had searched for no other door than the one leading back into the main part of the castle, but in the gloom I could have overlooked one leading from a lower floor into the adjoining wing. It was possible that

Guthrie had needed no ladder to climb up to that high entrance above the inner courtyard.

Before going to bed, I locked the thread-count-sticks in my bureau and put the key in my reticule. As I did so, I thought of Duncan. He had been right in guessing the source of the tartans. In how many other things had he been equally right?

I knew it was essential to carry on as if everything were normal, even to continuing with improvements at the castle, so the next day I called upon the man I had employed to clear the bog, told him to get his crew together again, and to bring them to Faillie at once. I was driven by a feeling of urgency about this project.

I stood on the causeway as the men made a start and, looking up, caught sight of Morag high up on the ramparts, watching the scene. Even from this distance I knew that she was taut with anger.

But on coming face to face with her, I was shocked to see how alarmed she was.

"Calum will be angry," she warned.

But I could be angry too, and had a great deal more to be disturbed about than the mere flouting of orders. I brushed past her, saying that I was going to the mills and had instructed Hamish to see that the men got on with the work without wasting time. In my room I unlocked my bureau and placed the thread-count sticks in my reticule. I was determined not to be parted from them.

When I went outside, my pony trap was waiting and as I picked up the reins I was aware of Morag watching me from the main door of the castle. Something compelled me to look back at her.

"What are you frightened of?" I demanded.

"Frightened? I am not in the least frightened. Why should I be?"

"That is what I am wondering. As for Calum's anger, it will be vented on me, not you—if and when he returns."

"He will return."

Eventually, I thought. When he is ready. When he has invented a ready answer to clear him of guilt where Sheena is concerned. But what about his guilt where other matters were concerned? It would be dangerous to accuse him of things I could not prove.

As I approached the causeway, I felt no envy for the men working in the bog, for the recent heavy rains had swollen it excessively. The inky blackness was deeper and wider than ever before, with all sorts of debris floating on the surface: dead wood, rotten branches, soggy masses of slimy leaves. It must have been years since it resembled anything like a moat. I saw the men wading in, legs encased in thigh-length fishermen's boots.

Then I saw Guthrie striding toward them. I reined sharply, guessing that he was going to interfere. Morag was following, and I knew that she had fetched him. I dropped the reins, sprang down, and marched across to them.

"Get back to your work, Guthrie."

"I take orders from the laird, not from you—Mistress."

"Then get on with the work he ordered you to do."

His dark face became threatening. His sensual lips tightened brutally, but before he had a chance to speak, I rapped out, "I will tolerate no interference. This is work *I* have put in hand."

"The laird put me in charge of all outside work."

"And I have put Hamish in charge of this. He will report to me on the men's progress. I trust him more than I trust a liar."

The man's great fists clenched and unclenched at his sides. I felt a lick of fear in my heart, and forced it down. He could not attack me here, in front of this gang of men, and I was aware of Hamish standing nearby, listening and watching.

Guthrie took a deep breath.

"Somehow I don't think I heard aright—Mistress. It seemed to me that you called me a liar."

"Indeed I did, for that is what you are." Morag

was beside us now, listening to every word. "You also," I said to her. "Guthrie told me he was employed at Carrisbrae before coming to Faillie, and you confirmed it although no one of that name ever worked there. I don't know why such a tale was invented, nor do I know why you are both so anxious that this bog should not be cleared, but it seems to me that it isn't my husband's anger you are afraid of."

I had shot an arrow blindly, but aimed it well. From bullying arrogance, Guthrie's expression changed to shiftiness, and the tone of his voice swung from threat to bluster as he stammered incoherent excuses. As for Morag, the ebb and flow of color in her face betrayed her. She turned on her heel, and I watched her retreating figure with interest. It seemed to me that she was exercising the sternest self-control.

I turned a cool glance upon Guthrie, and without a word, he too walked away. When both were out of sight I said to Hamish, "If anything untoward happens when I am at the mills, fetch Mr. Mackintosh."

That pleased him. He nodded his grizzled old head with satisfaction, and I went on my way feeling easier in my mind, although what I had to fear in Calum's absence I could not really define.

When I returned everything was as usual, and there was no further opposition from Morag. Everything seemed so normal at supper that it was difficult to imagine why I had ever felt suspicious and afraid, but my uneasiness persisted and I knew it would remain with me until Calum returned, or was eventually traced, when every suspicion and doubt in my mind would have to be thrashed out once and for all.

Twenty

A STRANGE THING happened during the night. I wakened abruptly, fully aware that no noise had been responsible. My every sense was alert, as if sharpened by secret warning. I was not alone. I lay quite still, listening for the sound of breathing. There was none, nor was there any movement.

And then it came to me—the scent of the cologne that Calum used. I shivered violently, realizing he had come back and that the moment I dreaded had arrived. But still there was no betraying sound or movement.

In the hint of early dawn seeping through a gap in the curtains I could see the closed door of his dressing room, and as my eyes became accustomed to the dim light I could also see that the bedroom was empty. Had it been a dream then, or had he actually been here, leaning over me, looking down at me in the semi-darkness? And was he now on the other side of that door, quietly undressing?

The idea of him lying beside me was suddenly intolerable. The thought jerked me out of bed, heedless of whether he heard the creaking springs or not. *Get it over—dear God, get this meeting over!* I pulled on a robe, wrapping it around my body as if for protection and, holding it tightly, forced myself to open his dressing room door.

The place was empty. It was exactly as it had been since his departure, except for that scent of cologne.

Slowly, I went back to bed, and lighting my bedside candle I sat with the counterpane huddled around me until at length the candle flickered and died. By that time dawn had mercifully increased, and I flung back the curtains to admit the pale light of day. The rolling hills were shrouded in mist, gray as a pall, and as I stood there it crept, ghostlike, toward my windows, touching the panes. If Calum were indeed back, it seemed appropriate that he should arrive in a sinister atmosphere like this.

The household would not be astir for an hour or more and I decided to go down to the library and get a book. The room struck an immediate chill into me, for no fire had been lit during my husband's absence, and the ancient stone walls and floor did nothing to repel the coldness. I ran my fingers hurriedly along the shelves, seeking something light enough to occupy my mind, finally halting as a projecting volume, half pushed back, made my fingers stumble. It was a slim book, much handled, and fell open automatically at a page where the top right-hand corner had been turned down—an unforgivable habit in my father's eyes, and in mine.

But if this one had not been treated with respect, it had at least been much read, and I guessed by whom, for it was a book on herbs and their uses, and since this page had been particularly marked, I judged it to be of special interest. Therefore I scanned it until my eye was caught by a brief paragraph headed TANSY.

The information about it covered the uses Morag had told me about, but I was unprepared for the rest.

"Safe if used in the right quantities; deadly poisonous if not. Cultivated widely in ancient times, particularly Tudor, when poisoning was used indiscriminately for the disposal of enemies." Then came the derivation: "From Gk *athanasia,* immortality . . . *thanatos,* death."

The book fell to the floor and I left it there as I turned away blindly and fled back to my room.

In the normal light of day I tried to think more

calmly. Who would believe me if I declared that someone was trying to kill me, and that I suspected three people—my husband, who had threatened me in no way; the housekeeper, who had nursed not only me, but other members of the household, with diligence and efficiency; and a man whose only offense was insolence?

Only one person would heed me: Duncan, who had first planted doubt in my mind and told me to watch out for the future. Still, one had to have strong evidence before producing accusations of attempted murder, and I had none. Lies and deceptions proved nothing, fears and fancies even less.

I forced myself to act normally throughout the day. Work helped, but concentration was lacking. At the back of my mind lingered the troublesome recollection of my sudden wakening in the night. I could see no reason why the scent of cologne should come to me unless someone had opened the door of Calum's dressing room and let a drift of it through. Even more disturbing was the book I had stumbled on. If I allowed suspicion to wander unchecked I would be asking myself if, in Calum's absence, Morag had been instructed to get rid of me.

But how would my sudden death be explained, or my body disposed of?

The answer to that was presented to me by Hamish when I returned from the mills. He was waiting for me by the causeway, greatly agitated.

A body had been dragged from the sluggish depths of the mire.

I saw the men grouped about something on the ground. In the center of them a white-haired man stooped over it. Beside him was Duncan, and I recognized the man as the guest I had seen in his coach the other day.

I have no recollection of moving, only of Hamish grasping my arm and his voice saying sharply, "Don't go down there, Mistress!"

I was shaking. Una, I thought. Who else could it be? My conviction that she did not lie in the family tomb had been right. At the back of my stunned mind facts clicked into place. She had not died in childbirth; she had been murdered, as my father had been murdered, and in each case Calum had stood to gain.

First Una, and then me? That had been his plan, and Morag and Guthrie, his two accomplices, knew it. This was the reason for their opposition to clearing the bog. They knew what it concealed, and if Una were found, the second wife would learn the truth; the whole world would learn the truth.

I leaned against Hamish, and his old arm went around me. And then I saw Duncan approaching, and I cried to him, "They are all in it together, all three of them! And the drunken doctor who signed her death certificate—he was killed too, run over, silenced forever . . ."

Morag's face swam into focus.

"Elizabeth is beside herself. She has no idea what she is saying. Come indoors, my dear. I will look after you."

I drew away from her sharply, and she was forced to step aside when Duncan placed himself between us.

He looked at me compassionately and said, "That is not my sister lying there. It is a man."

Twenty-One

AFTER A STUNNED MOMENT I jerked, "*Calum?*"

"Definitely not Calum. This man has been immersed for some weeks, Dr. Cameron says."

"Then he must be unrecognizable, whoever he may be." Morag's voice was high-pitched, sharp, unlike her normally dulcet tones.

"Not necessarily, Mistress." The white-haired man had followed Duncan and now stood beside us, carefully wiping his hands. He turned to me. "I have given orders for the body to be placed in the stables for the time being. I trust you have no objection? The local constable will have to be informed, and an examination can be carried out there more easily than on a marshy bank."

I stammered. "Who is he? Can he be identified?"

"Very possibly. A bog such as this can be a substantial retarding influence, for the thickness of the mire has acted as a protection against the elements. The features, of course, are blurred and swollen, and the hair—what is left of it, for hair drops out rapidly in water—is caked with mud, but there were various articles in his pockets which should prove useful. Mr. Mackintosh has taken charge of them."

The cold, professional detachment with which he spoke had an oddly steadying influence; added to this, there was something about Duncan that made me feel he was ready to take charge of everything. I also felt he was watching everyone on the scene. A meaningful glance passed between him and the doctor, and I said anxiously, "You are not going?"

"Not I, Ealasaid. Dr. Cameron is leaving for a while, but he will return. And now, Mistress Crombie, I think we will all take your advice and go indoors."

"Really, Mr. Mackintosh, there is no need for you to remain . . ."

He interrupted. "There is every need. I understand Mr. Huntly is absent. At a time like this women need a man to take charge."

His voice brooked no argument, and the same note was in it when he commanded Guthrie to come with us. For the first time in my recollection the man seemed unwilling to enter the castle, but he was forced to follow, with Morag at his side and Hamish forming a rear guard. In this order we climbed the spiral steps to the Billeting Room.

I felt Duncan's hand beneath my elbow, and was glad of its support; even more glad of it when I saw Calum at the end of the long room, his back to the fireplace, with General Wade's historic document high on the wall above him. Standing there, he admirably portrayed the Highland laird beside his ancient hearth.

"What the devil's going on outside?" he demanded. "Who are all those men, and what are they doing down by the causeway? I noticed them as I rode across. And if it comes to that, Mackintosh, what are you doing here, also?"

"At the moment, looking after your wife. She has had a shock."

"I'm sorry to hear that. What sort of a shock? And how did you come to know about it?"

"I knew in advance. Hamish fetched me."

"The devil he did! And why did the man go running to you?"

I put in quickly, "Because I asked him to. I told him to go to Duncan if anything untoward happened in my absence. And yours," I added significantly.

I looked at my husband's handsome face and marveled that he could appear so bland and assured.

"Where did you run away to?" I asked.

"I don't know what you mean by 'run away.' I was summoned, as you very well know."

"But not to Carrisbrae. I found it an interesting house, by the way, and particularly what I found in one of the attics." I realized then that I was still clutching my reticule. I opened it, and took out the thread-count sticks. "These, for instance." I handed them to Duncan. "They match the tartans in the paintings, which were also hidden there. Who copied them for you, Calum? Not poor Una, I'm sure. I strongly suspect it was Morag, because I suspect her of many things, including a knowledge, shared by Guthrie, of the identity of the man whose body has just been found."

"What man? What body? Would someone kindly tell me what my wife is prattling about?"

"I think you know already," Duncan stated.

"And ye didna' come riding across the causeway," Hamish growled. "I was there all afternoon, until the body was dragged out, then I rode off to fetch Master Duncan, and told the lodgekeeper not to open those gates to anyone until I got back, or it'd be the worse for him. He slunk back into the lodge and stayed there until I yelled for him to open up again."

"Get out," Calum rapped at him. "Get back to the kitchen or the stables where you belong. Morag, what are you thinking of, letting this old man come up here as if he were one of the family?"

She snapped, "*I* have no authority here, it seems. Your brother-in-law appears to have assumed that, and Hamish seems to be your wife's self-appointed bodyguard!" She moved away briskly. "I am going to my room. I have had as great a shock as Elizabeth, but no one seems to take that into account."

"Not even Guthrie," I commented. "Not that his indifference on that point surprises me, for I suspect his attentions to you have always been based on self-interest of some kind. You have kept in close touch with her, haven't you, Guthrie, ever since I mentioned how she dressed up in secret. That made you suspicious for some reason, and she didn't like it. Was she hiding something from you?"

"Partners in crime are always ready to cheat each other," Duncan put in. "I know Guthrie's record. I investigated it before he came to work for me. In fact, I employed him for that very reason. A man recently out of jail is always glad of money, and you've been glad to take it, haven't you, Guthrie, so long as it didn't risk your neck. It's not so long since you came out of that Glasgow prison where James Crombie still awaits release. How much longer has your husband to serve, Mistress Crombie?"

Morag had already come to a halt. Now her pale

eyes narrowed venomously. I sensed a cold fury in her, but before it could explode, Hamish said, "I daresay the laird knows that just as well as she does. Guthrie's been visiting him daily in that room he's been hiding away in. The housekeeper, too. Reporting everything that's been going on, I daresay, including the mistress' secret journey."

Calum blazed, *"I told you to get out!"*

I cut in firmly, "And I insist that he stay. I want to know how he discovered where you were."

" 'Twere easy enough, Mistress. Those rooms above the stables lead one from the other, all the way to the Keep. But the last one of all has been locked these past days, and I've listened and heard voices talking low. Men's voices and sometimes a woman's. And once I saw Guthrie looking down from the window; that were when we were leaving for Deeside. Guthrie must've heard me getting out the carriage and then, ye recall, he came hurrying down to ask why I hadna' taken it round to the main entrance."

Calum laughed. "I've listened to enough of this nonsense. And if a body has been found, it must be that of a poacher."

"Yet another?" Duncan murmured.

"What made you reappear, Calum? And what brought you to my bedroom about dawn? A change of clothes? Those riding breeches you are wearing now were left in the closet during your absence. You didn't pack them, or that jacket, when you left so hurriedly—but you must always dress the part, mustn't you? The kilted laird, or the traveler returning from a journey—"

"Or a deerstalker?" Duncan interrupted. "Did you dress correctly that day too? But a deerstalker always gets downwind of his prey. And the shot that killed Aindreas MacArthur was fired upwind, so it was no wild aim from a poacher's rifle. I was nearby and noted the direction of the wind, also the direction from which the shot hit him."

"And kept quiet?" Calum scoffed.

"Until I had proof, I had no choice but to remain silent."

My husband said contemptuously, "Nor can you prove it now. I suppose you just happened to be passing when my father-in-law was accidentally killed?"

"No. Wherever Ealasaid has gone, I have endeavored to be near. Unfortunately, I didn't know she had gone to Carrisbrae or I would have followed her there, despite the fact that other things have kept me close to home these past days."

Calum yawned. "I'm not interested in your private affairs, Mackintosh, nor in your ridiculous theories, but for your information I was in Edinburgh, at my father-in-law's behest, at the time he was killed."

I said swiftly, "If you were, it was not to contact the two men from whom you pretended to purchase the tartan designs. They have never met you. Duncan has confirmation of that."

"Damn you, Mackintosh! What right have you to pry into my affairs?"

"Every right, in view of your treatment of my sister."

Footsteps sounded on the spiral stairs behind us. I saw my husband's handsome features glance idly across, then stiffen as Dr. Cameron appeared, with a young woman at his side.

I recognized her at once, from her portrait.

Duncan went to her and drew her gently into the room, and as he did so Dr. Cameron said to him, "That young man you introduced me to the other day, Angus Fraser, has gone to fetch the local constable. No doubt the body will be examined before anyone is questioned, but Una can be spared a great deal of stress if you show her those articles now."

Duncan took a kerchief from his pocket, unfolded it, and laid upon a table a tarnished watch and chain, a man's seal ring, and a small, discolored silver frame containing a blurred miniature. His sister stared at the pathetic objects, then slowly reached out and touched them, one by one. Finally, she picked up the heavy watch and, holding it to her cheek, broke into frantic sobbing.

"Calum! My dear, dear Calum! What has happened to you? Where have you gone?"

Twenty-Two

EVERYTHING happened quickly after that—it is hard to remember the exact sequence. I am not sure even now whether it was Morag or Guthrie who first tried to escape, for my attention was held by Una's tragic face and the bewilderment in her eyes. I remembered them, so vivid and alive in the portrait, but now their expression was blank.

Then she looked up, and I saw a flicker of recognition. She was looking at my husband. I stared at him too, standing rigid beside the great fireplace, and I could see that his arrogance was shaken.

Una took a faltering step toward him.

"Malcolm?" she quavered. "You are Malcolm, are you not? But why are you still at Faillie? And where is Calum? I've waited for him so long. . . ." One hand still clutched the tarnished watch, but the other passed shakily across her eyes. "You said you would bring him to me—here, at Faillie . . ."

Her voice trailed off uncertainly. Duncan put his arm about her shoulders. "Doctor, must she go through this? She is suffering . . ."

"I'm afraid she must. It is the best possible chance of bringing back her memory."

It must have been then that Guthrie tried to get away, and the sound startled Una so much that she jerked around. And screamed. And screamed again.

The sound echoed piercingly beneath the length and breadth of the arched ceiling.

"It was he—*he* who drove me to that place the night Calum was shot! And *she* who took me there!"

Quick as a flash Morag made for the stairs, but I was there before her. Duncan seized Guthrie as the doctor put his arm around Una. Now her sobs came violently as memory erupted from the dark vale into which it had retreated.

I heard Guthrie protesting loudly, "But I didn't do the shooting! *He* did that—his own brother!"

"His half-brother," Morag said. "Let us be precise on every point. And you should thank me, Duncan Mackintosh, for taking care of your sister. Yes, I took her to 'that place,' as she calls it. There's ingratitude indeed! If I had not formerly been employed there, teaching the wretched inmates how to weave so that they could earn their support, she would never have been so fortunate as to be admitted. And we even sent money, didn't we, Malcolm, so that she wouldn't be housed with the common herd, or sew harsh pillow cases, or scrub floors with the rest. She has been well looked after, with her own room . . ."

"A wretched cell," Dr. Cameron interrupted, "in one of the worst institutions in Scotland. If I had not been appointed to the Board of Investigation recently set up to improve our asylums, I would never have come across her tragic case, or have been in a position to restore her to her brother."

"Nor would her brother have traced her whereabouts if I hadn't listened to my conscience and given him the address," Guthrie whined, no longer insolent, but craven.

"I paid you well," Duncan reminded him curtly. "And now, Cameron, I would like my sister to go home. She has endured enough."

I heard the main door of the castle open and shut with a crash, and a man came leaping up the stairs. It was Angus, and I saw at once that he was in a dangerous mood.

"I came back with the constable. We rode hard. He

222

has gone straight to the stables and I've come straight here to see Huntly. Alone."

Morag cried furiously, "It's that girl, Sheena MacArthur! I knew she would be our undoing! Damn you, Malcolm, for your lust and vanity! If you had kept your hands off her you would never have had to run off and Elizabeth would never have gone to Deeside. But for that, you could have stayed in the open without arousing any suspicion until everything was accomplished . . ."

"Meaning my death? By accident of some kind, or by poison?" I demanded.

Morag didn't even hear me. Beside herself, she stormed on. "I threw in my lot with yours for Jamie's sake, so that when he came out we'd have plenty of money for a fresh start, but I'm ready to tell everything now. What else can I do? What is there left for any of us? But *you* will hang for the murder of Calum Huntly, and your hired assassin for the murder of Andrew MacArthur. You should have tutored Guthrie better in the art of deerstalking."

The man I had married came to life abruptly. All this time I had been watching his defenses crumble; Malcolm Huntly, half-brother of the man I believed to be my husband. A liar. A schemer. A murderer. But still my husband. Or was he, since he had assumed his half-brother's name? The question darted through my mind and away again as he raced up the spiral steps to the floor above. I heard the thunder of his feet in their heavy riding boots, and those of Angus in pursuit. They raced overhead across the floor of the Banqueting Hall and out the door leading onto the ramparts. The door closed with a bang.

Silence. We were six figures, waiting in an expectant tableau. Then out of the silence came a distant and horrifying scream, rising on a crescendo of terror and dying into emptiness and space.

Angus returned slowly.

"He fell from the battlements. I didn't even have a chance to strike him. He backed away, and lost his balance. I saw him crash on the stones below. . . ."

223

Twenty-Three

"JAMES CROMBIE was arrested in Glasgow two years ago on a robbery charge," Duncan said. "Guthrie was involved, but received a lighter sentence. Some of the stolen jewelry was recovered, but not all. We know now who kept it."

"And why," I answered. "Morag really loves her husband; she must have been keeping the jewels to use when he was released."

Duncan nodded.

"With those, and the payment she expected to receive from Huntly when he inherited the mills, they could have shipped out of Glasgow to a new life overseas."

I felt that Duncan wanted to reach out and touch me, but this was not the moment. Nor was it the moment for me to confess my shame for ever doubting him, so I went on to relate how Guthrie had discovered her possession of the jewels. "I was responsible for that, quite accidentally. I understand now why he would scarcely let her out of his sight afterward, and why she was forced to maintain a friendship with him. He could have revealed too much about her."

"They could have revealed too much about each other, as they now have."

We were sitting in my small sitting room: Dr. Cameron, Duncan, Angus, and myself. The doctor had attended to Una, now asleep in the bedroom that had once been her own, and which I would never occupy again. Morag had been taken away, Guthrie also, and the body of Malcolm Huntly had left Castle

Faillie in ignominious death. But Calum, beloved husband of the Heretrix, would be interred with the reverence she desired.

In time, Una would be herself again. Meanwhile, much of her story had been gleaned from a craven Guthrie, only too anxious to exonerate himself as much as possible, and from Morag for the same reason. Malcolm Huntly had offered Guthrie a job when he emerged from jail, the perfectly respectable job of coachman. "It was a chance to go straight, and I was glad of it." But his desire for respectability had not prevented Guthrie from contacting the wife of his partner, James Crombie, compelled by a greed for the untraced jewels, and knowing full well that if anyone had a knowledge of their whereabouts, it would be Crombie's wife. But Morag had professed to know nothing.

Nevertheless, she too proved useful to Malcolm Huntly, who knew of the valuable paintings at Faillie, and was anxious to lay his hands on them, but there had never been any close association between the two half-brothers, and he needed some ploy to get into the household on Deeside. A casual call would not be enough, but the introduction of a widowed relative in need insured it. Morag was promised substantial reward for posing as a distant relation and, obeying the dictates of Scottish hospitality, Calum and Una welcomed her into their home. Encouraged by the woman's interest, Una talked of Faillie, and of her ambition to restore it, but when Malcolm suggested that she should let him sell the Mackintosh collection of paintings she adamantly refused.

"Then, according to Guthrie, and I imagine it is true, Malcolm tried to bring pressure on Calum when my sister was staying at Faillie. But Calum was a very different type of man from his half-brother. Home-loving, retiring, understanding his wife's pride in her inheritance, but preferring the simplicity of life in a modest country house. I never met him, for as you know they married after I left for New Zealand, but her letters were always full of him. Obviously, theirs was the attraction of opposites, but it endured. And I knew exactly what he was like and how he looked —an unassuming fair-haired man."

"So you knew, as soon as you met Malcolm Huntly, that he was not your sister's husband?" Cameron asked.

"I was suspicious, but it had to be proved. The term 'fair' can apply to hair as light as Malcolm Huntly's, or to hair less blond. That detail didn't make me so uneasy as the man's sophistication, a quality the real Calum lacked. 'In some ways,' Una wrote, 'my dear Calum is as naïve as a child. He trusts everyone, because he can never imagine that people can be untrustworthy.' So when Una was visiting Faillie and Malcolm came to him saying that she had been taken ill and needed him, Calum left for Faillie at once. Guthrie drove them."

"So Grant spoke the truth. Guthrie never worked for his real master."

Duncan nodded. "Grant may have seen him, driving Malcolm to and from Calum's house, but that is all, and when you questioned him, he obviously didn't associate the name with Malcolm Huntly's coachman. Guthrie, by the way, denies driving the coach that killed Craig. Malcolm could have done that, but we shall never know. All we do know is that the doctor signed a death certificate testifying that my sister died in childbirth—and then needed to be silenced because he was a risk."

"And Una wasn't ill at all."

"Not in the least, but she was certainly under pressure from Malcolm, who had followed her to Faillie, with the intention of forcing her to hand over the paintings. Her stubbornness must have astonished him, since he seized on the idea of fetching her husband to add his persuasion. That, he thought, couldn't fail, because Calum was seemingly weak, and Una was so much in love with him that she would yield. But once at Faillie, even the trusting Calum realized he had been tricked and not only opposed his half-brother but threatened to expose him. Morag was present, and so was Guthrie. Both have independently confirmed that it was then that Malcolm resorted to violence.

"Una saw her husband shot in front of her—and you know what happened to her as a result. Her derangement probably saved her life, for all that was necessary then was to put her safely out of the way, and here the alcoholic doctor came in useful again. It is likely that the man was too drunk at the time to realize that he was certifying her. And, of course, if Una's memory ever returned, who would believe the ramblings of a mental patient?"

"Not in this day and age," Cameron agreed, "but the time will come when people suffering from mental afflictions will no longer be regarded as lunatics."

Duncan said quietly, "We also know the truth about your father's death, Ealasaid. Guthrie's denials won't acquit him. Morag Crombie's evidence has taken care of that."

I turned away from the compassion in Duncan's eyes because sympathy, at this moment, threatened to be my undoing.

I let my head fall against the high back of my chair. My personal nightmare was over, but Una must still recover from hers. I would remain here until she did so, and then leave Faillie once and for all.

I realized that Angus was looking at me intently, and that he wanted to talk to me alone. Reluctantly, I rose and left the room with him. If he was going to ask me to break Sheena's unhappy news to my mother, I would have to refuse for the time being. One thing at a time. One problem at a time. One person at a time. And then, perhaps, time to think of myself.

But as soon as Angus spoke I knew my conclusion was wrong.

"She went riding on the moors. She's no horse-woman and she rode recklessly. Deliberately. And she fell, which was what she wanted. And it achieved what she wanted."

"She's all right?" I asked swiftly.

"Injured, of course, and badly shaken, but yes, she'll

be all right. The local midwife called a doctor, so your mother knows the truth. I came to tell Huntly; I wanted to thrash the life out of him. She'll be needing you, Elizabeth, and so will your mother."

"Poor Mother. I will visit her as soon as I can, and Sheena too, but my sister must get over things without anyone's help, including yours. Don't indulge her, Angus. She must learn to be a woman, and she will never be that if you are ready to fight her battles for her, or take her by the hand."

He was silent for a moment, then nodded. "Aye, you are right, Elizabeth. You were always the wise one."

Wise—I, who could be deceived so easily, and possessed neither wisdom nor foresight in regard to myself?

I climbed the slope to the watchman's stone. Below, the waters of the Beauly Firth wound like a silver ribbon. No whisper came from Drummossie Moor; the ghosts of Culloden were silent. I was alone in this isolated spot, and no message came to me from the past, nor any premonition about the future. The sight, when I needed it most, had deserted me.

Perhaps my future held no more than lifelong service to the mills, and perhaps with that I should be content, but passive acceptance was not for me. Life had to go forward and it was not in my nature to drift in its wake. Since I last sat here I had become a woman; I had known passion, and terror, and disillusion, but when I tried to conjure up the features of the man who had led me through such quicksands, I found them elusive. Another face remained imprinted on my mind.

I gathered my cloak around me, the same cloak I had worn when he first walked into my life. I had taken it from its peg in the hall of my mother's house and flung it carelessly about my shoulders, anxious to escape from the restrictions of a life to which I could never again belong. After leaving Faillie I had returned to the home I had left so eagerly, only to find I had outgrown it. That was the difference between Una and me; she had never completely uprooted herself, and now that she was reinstated as Heretrix of Castle Faillie, her brother's fortune completing its restoration and with Hamish and Grant devotedly serving her, it had become the center of her life.

Among the Mackintosh collection of portraits is one of the legendary Colonel Anne, wearing a man's blue bonnet and the white cockade of the Jacobites, and in her face I see a reflection of Una, just as I see a reflection of Duncan in the portrait of Colonel Anne's Royalist husband—both typifying this temperamental and divided clan, both to be loved and respected.

But the void in my own life could not be so easily filled as the void in Una's. The mills were my pride, but not the core of my existence. There was loneliness in my heart.

The sound came to me only because I associated it with this place: the snapping of twigs, a heavy footfall. It was conjured up by my own desire, and so was he, coming toward me through rock and scrub. By some trick of fantasy I had stepped back to the moment of our first meeting, and I could hear the echo of his voice saying, "He isn't the only man who could match the passion in you . . . you are hot-blooded and hot-headed, the same as I . . ." But with him there would be no quick death to our desires, no terror, no disillusion.

And then he was before me, and it was no mere echo of his voice that said, "Ealasaid, my witch, why didn't you come to me when you were ready to leave Faillie? I told you I would be waiting."

Acknowledgments

The Scottish Tartans Society, Broughty Castle Museum, Dundee.

The Curator of Historical Records, Scottish Record Office, Edinburgh.

The National Library of Scotland, Edinburgh.

The Scottish Room of the Central Public Library, Edinburgh.

The National Association of Scottish Woolen Manufacturers, Edinburgh.

The Scottish Woolen Publicity Council, London,
and
my thanks to my friend, the Scottish journalist, television writer and interviewer, Ruby Turberville, wife of Superintendent Leslie Turberville of Aberdeen Police, for verifying the ranking of Constables in Invernessshire in the year 1822, and other details of Scottish customs.

Bestsellers from BALLANTINE